The Haunted Purse

by
Kimberly Baer

The Haunted Purse

Contact information: authorkimberlybaer@gmail.com

Publishing History

First edition: 2020

Second edition: 2025

ISBN: 979-8-218-75341-2 (paperback)

ISBN: 979-8-218-75342-9 (ebook)

Published in the United States of America

"Do you think we should tell my mom about the purse?"

"No." I wasn't ready to trust an adult. Not even Toni's mom, nice as she was. "Your mom is like you," I said. "Practical. It would take a long time to convince her there's something supernatural going on."

We went back to watching the purse. There was a moment when I thought I saw it twitch, but that might have been my imagination.

"You could always get rid of it," Toni said. "You know, donate it back to the thrift store."

I considered that. "I could. But I don't want to. Not yet, anyway. This purse is the coolest thing I've ever owned. I want to find out more about it. I want to see what it does next."

She moved her eyes away from the purse long enough to glance at me. "Aren't you afraid it'll crawl into your bed some night and strangle you with its straps?"

"No. I think it's trying to get my attention. It's trying to tell me something."

"Like what?"

I didn't have a clue.

Praise for Kimberly Baer

The Haunted Purse

"A beautiful standalone story that teens and adults alike will enjoy. Recommended!" – *Dr. Who Online*

Would You Rather...

"A thrilling, edge of your seat read. Very highly recommended." – *Reader's Favorite*

Out of Body

"A captivating and relatable read." – *Literary Titan*

Mall Girl Meets the Shadow Vandal

"A lively, jaunty mystery with a terrific cast of characters." – *Kirkus Reviews*

For anyone who has ever lost something in their purse, only to have it turn up later...*in their purse.*

Chapter 1

"Your purse ate your homework. Is that what you're telling me, Libby? I must say, that's a new one."

I was standing at Ms. Eckhart's desk, close enough that a hushed, private conversation should have been possible. Yet the conversation we were having was anything but hushed, at least Ms. Eckhart's end of it. Of course, that was Ms. Eckhart—show-offy, look-at-me-ish. She wanted the class to hear when she said something clever or sarcastic, even if it was at the expense of a student.

World history class hadn't officially started, but my classmates were facing forward in their seats, unabashedly eavesdropping. Amelia Drake, cool girl supreme, snickered at Ms. Eckhart's comment.

I pivoted slightly, turning my back on all those staring eyes. "I don't know what happened to it. This morning, after breakfast, I zipped it in here"—I yanked open a side pocket of my big denim purse—"and I didn't unzip till I got to class. My report just—*disappeared*."

"Disappeared!" Ms. Eckhart echoed theatrically. "My, my. That *is* unfortunate."

Our eyes met, hers impassive, mine desperate.

"Maybe I dropped it in the hall," I said, though I knew I hadn't. "I'll check the lost and found box in the school office. If I can't find it, I'll reprint it and get it to you by the end of the day. I have computer lab sixth period."

Connor Tipton, blond god of the sophomore class, sauntered into the room, almost late but not quite. His sultry gaze skimmed down the length of me as he dropped his report on Ms. Eckhart's desk. He ambled to his seat in the back of the room, high-fiving several buddies along the way. I wasn't watching, but I heard the telltale slap of hands.

Ms. Eckhart picked up the stack of reports, tapped them on her desk to align the edges, and set them down again. "Fine, turn it in later. But I'm going to have to dock you one letter grade."

"What? That's not fair!"

"Homework assignments are due at the beginning of class. You know that."

"But this is the first time I've ever been late. Can't you cut me some slack?"

"If I cut you some slack, I'd have to do the same for everybody."

"So do the same for everybody."

I said it lightly, but I was only half-joking.

"Don't be ridiculous," she snapped. "That's not how I run my classroom."

A hot flush spread over me. I'd never been on the receiving end of that scowl before. "Let me look again," I said. "It's got to be here."

I upended my purse, and a mini avalanche cascaded onto Ms. Eckhart's desk—wallet, calculator, mini flashlight, hairbrush, three pens, two pencils, a notepad, my most recent grocery list, the key to my apartment, and a scattered rainbow of hair scrunchies.

Everything but my history report.

THE HAUNTED PURSE

Ms. Eckhart stared in mild disgust at the pile of purse-debris cluttering her desk. "Libby, please gather up your belongings and take your seat."

"But—"

"Now," she said crisply, handing me my wallet. "We have a lot to cover today."

I herded my possessions into my purse and slunk to my desk, careful to avoid eye contact with my classmates.

I didn't hear one word of the history lecture. It wasn't because I was thinking about the missing homework, though there was plenty to think about there. No, I was thinking about Ms. Eckhart and what had just happened between us. I knew I shouldn't let it bother me, but it did.

Ms. Eckhart was a newish teacher, just a few years out of college. Tall and big-boned, a sturdy oak tree of a woman. Though not conventionally pretty, she had a polished look that almost passed for beauty. Her raspberry-red hair was always stylishly tousled, her face glowed beneath photo-shoot-perfect makeup, and she dressed like a slightly more sophisticated version of the most popular tenth-grade girls.

Which was probably why she fit in so well with them.

I didn't know much about Ms. Eckhart's past, but my guess was that she'd been less than popular in high school and was trying to make up for that now by hanging with the cool kids. The weird thing was, she was a decade older than today's cool kids! But no one seemed to mind. The popular people clustered around her desk every morning, chatting and laughing like she was one of them.

There was a social hierarchy in Ms. Eckhart's classroom, and every student knew their place. I wasn't part of the cool crowd, but I'd always been on Ms. Eckhart's favored list as one of the top students. As a teacher, she probably felt she had to acknowledge academic ability. But generally, she looked down on the not-so-popular kids. The meek, quiet kids. The poor kids, like me.

She was fickle, too. If you weren't one of her tippy-top favorites, like Amelia Drake, Jade Beasley, and Connor Tipton, one little screw-up could send you plummeting from grace.

That had happened to Nathan Ferguson, our self-appointed class clown. One morning last December, Ms. Eckhart had popped into the classroom early and caught Nathan at the dry erase board drawing a picture of a naked lady with humongous boobs. You could tell by the hairstyle that the lady was supposed to be Ms. Eckhart.

She'd given Nathan detention, but that wasn't the worst of it. She'd started bullying him. Calling on him when she knew he didn't know the answer, badgering him till he turned red and started stammering. Totally ignoring him the rest of the time, even when he raised his hand. It was now April, and she was still doing it. Nathan no longer acted clownish in her class. In fact, he'd gotten so subdued, he was practically invisible.

I was pretty sure I'd just lost my spot on the favorites list, too. All I'd ever had going for me was my status as a first-rate student, someone who aced every test and delivered every homework assignment on time. I'd just blown it by acting scatterbrained.

THE HAUNTED PURSE

A brick of despair settled in my chest. There would be no more cheery greetings: "Hey, Libby! How was your weekend?" No more cross-eyed smiley faces on my A-plus tests. No more getting to wear Ms. Eckhart's very own cardigan sweater when she saw me shivering in a threadbare tee shirt on a forty-degree morning.

The bell rang, signaling the end of class.

"Remember, test on Friday," Ms. Eckhart said as people slid out of their seats and headed for the door. I could only hope that whatever she'd talked about today wouldn't be on the test.

I shoved my history book into the middle compartment of my purse. There was a crunch as it hit something papery. Baffled, I withdrew the book and peered into the gaping mouth of my purse. There was my history report. Two pages folded in half, slightly crumpled from the assault by my history book.

The classroom emptied out around me. I caught Ms. Eckhart peeking at me, but she quickly went back to typing on her laptop. I knew she was hoping I'd leave without speaking to her.

I approached her desk. She didn't look up till I cleared my throat.

"Oh. Liberty."

The fact that she didn't call me Libby said a lot.

I thrust my report at her. "I found it. My homework. It was in my purse after all."

She took the report from me. Her eyes roved back and forth like she was reading it, but she was probably just trying to decide what to do.

"Technically, it's still late," she said.

"Just barely."

"Why couldn't you find it earlier?" she asked, as though this mattered.

I shrugged, my lips pressed tight. She moved her eyes back to the report like she couldn't stand the sight of me. "Fine," she said. "I won't lower your grade this time."

"Thank you."

"But this can't happen again."

I needed to get to physics class, but I stayed where I was. Ms. Eckhart shifted in her chair and said, "Was there something else?"

Yes, I wanted to say. *Something weird is going on with my purse. Something supernatural, and I don't know what to do about it. Can you tell me what to do?*

But because we weren't friends anymore, I said, "No. There's nothing else."

Chapter 2

I'd bought the purse ten days earlier at Second Life, the downtown thrift store.

My best friend, Toni Moore, was shopping for a gift for her mom, who was about to graduate from college. I'd been shuffling along behind her for ten minutes, listening to her running commentary as she flipped through crowded racks of ladies' tops.

"No. No. Ew. Ew. Too long. Too short. Too full of itself. Too shear."

"How can a shirt be too full of itself?" I asked. "What does that even mean?"

She didn't answer. Instead, she let out a cluck of joy as she pulled a satiny pale-pink blouse from the rack.

"Now, *this*. Shit, yeah. This could work."

"Okay," I said tentatively. The blouse provided a striking contrast to Toni's light African American coloring, and that meant it would look good on her mom, too. But it wasn't exactly Mrs. Moore's style. "How much is it?"

She flipped over the hand-scrawled price tag dangling from a sleeve. "Ten bucks."

I winced. "Ouch. That's a lot for the thrift store."

"Eh. I can afford it." She squinted at the faded label inside the back collar. "It's my exact size! Talk about meant-to-be."

"*Your* size? I thought you were shopping for your mom."

"I am." She shot me a coy sidelong look. "This is a little something for me."

"But…" I wrinkled my nose. I would never get used to the smell in here, the peculiar odor of other people's things, all jumbled together. "Where would you even wear something like that? It's too dressy for school. You don't go to church. What are you going to do—wait for somebody to die so you can wear it to the funeral?"

Toni draped the blouse carefully over her arm. "It's for the sophomore dance."

I blinked at her. "But we're not going to the dance. Remember? We agreed—"

"We never agreed to anything. I said I wanted to go. You said you didn't."

"And I still don't!" I'd thought we were done talking about the dance, but I should have known better. Toni wasn't someone who gave up easily.

"Come on, Libby. We haven't been to a school dance since eighth grade."

"For a good reason! Dances aren't for people like us. If we show up in our pathetic little thrift store outfits, Amelia Drake and her gang will laugh us right out of the gym."

"But this blouse doesn't look like it came from the thrift store. Amelia will think I got it at one of those fancy stores at the mall. It'll drive her crazy. She'll wish she had one like it."

I stared at the floor so she wouldn't see the pity in my eyes. Toni was smart about a lot of things, but fashion wasn't one of them. Amelia was never going to envy the likes of us, and certainly not over some thrift-store find. The pink blouse was pretty, but it was a good fifteen years out of style. The cool girls would see that instantly, and it would give them yet another reason to ridicule Toni.

"Okay, then," Toni said, taking my silence for surrender. "How about we find something for you to wear?"

"I am not going to that dance," I said through clenched teeth.

"We'll see," she chirped, whirling on her heel.

I followed her to the jewelry table, where she spent maybe twenty seconds picking out a three-dollar bracelet for her mom. She'd planned on spending more, but since she'd just blown her budget on the blouse, that was no longer possible. My heart panged for Mrs. Moore, who did so much for Toni but got so little in return.

Three customers stood ahead of us in the checkout line. As we waited, I glanced around the store, a familiar melancholy settling over me as I took in the shabby merchandise, the shabbier customers. Not that I was judging. I was as shabby as anyone here.

My gaze drifted to a cardboard box sitting on the deserted check-out counter to our right. It was filled with somebody's cast-off goods—a stack of neatly folded clothing, a couple of empty picture frames, a dusty vase.

A triangular swatch of denim was poking up from behind the picture frames as if trying to climb out of the box. I reached over and pulled it out, expecting jeans. Instead, I found myself holding a purse.

I didn't know it at the time, but that was the moment when my life changed. Big time.

Chapter 3

I sucked in my breath. The purse was a retro beauty, its faded blue the exact shade of my favorite jeans. Big enough to qualify as a tote bag, it was decorated with studs and rhinestones and three embroidered hearts on the front. The twin straps were frayed where they had repeatedly rubbed the shoulder of some previous owner.

"Hey." I tugged on Toni's cornrows. "Check this out."

She turned around to take a look. "Cute. I like the jewels and stuff."

"There's no price tag. I wonder how much it is."

"What, you want to buy it?"

"I don't know. Maybe." I gave the black, battle-worn bag dangling at my hip a little swat. "I've had this thing since I was ten. It's held together with safety pins."

"Hey, you don't have to convince *me*."

When it was Toni's turn at the checkout, Selena's eyes fell upon her and immediately moved to me like she knew I'd be there. Because right behind Toni was where I usually was. "Hey. Toni and Libby, my two best customers."

All the cashiers at Second Life knew us by name. Selena was my favorite. She was more than a cashier, though. She and her husband owned the place. She was in her forties, a chunky, perpetually cheerful woman with short brown hair and bright brown eyes. Toni liked her because she was motherly. I couldn't say whether I agreed. I hadn't had much experience with *motherly*.

"Libby has a question about a purse," Toni told Selena.

Selena cocked an eyebrow in my direction. "Oh?"

I lifted the denim purse by one of its frayed straps. "It was in that box..." I jerked my head toward the vacant counter. "I hope it's okay that I took it out. I was just wondering..."

"Yeah, someone dropped that stuff off this morning." Selena peered at the price tag on the pink blouse and poked some keys on the cash register. "I've been meaning to go through it between customers, but we've been so busy, I haven't had a chance. I should be able to get everything priced and out on the floor later today."

I ran my forefinger over a ruby-like rhinestone. It wasn't like I was in some discount department store and ten purses exactly like this one were lined up on a shelf. This was a one-of-a-kind item, a treasure from the past. Once it hit the sales floor, it wouldn't last an hour. Customers would be fist-fighting over it, and somebody else, not me, would end up taking it home.

"Is there any possible way," I said, "that I could buy it now?"

Selena's gaze settled on my face as she pondered that. "I don't see why not, hon. Here, let me take a look."

She turned the purse from front to back, appraising the riot of doodads that adorned the fabric. She unzipped all the zippers, unsnapped all the snaps. She stuck her whole arm inside, like a country veterinarian birthing a calf. She turned the purse upside down and shook it, trying to dislodge any hidden contents. Nothing fell out.

"I'd feel comfortable calling this a five-dollar purse," she said, handing it back with a wink. "That sound about right?"

"Sure!" I said. I was pretty savvy about the value of thrift-store wares. Selena was giving me a nice price break.

The denim purse was probably older than my current purse, but it was in better shape—not a safety pin in sight. I studied it reverently. On the back were two big patch pockets, which made it look like the butt-part of a pair of jeans. Very cute, I thought. The inside consisted of compartments within compartments, too many to count, like different rooms in a mansion. The purse was so big, I figured it could double as a book bag and triple as a beach bag, assuming I actually made it to a beach someday.

I held it to my face and sniffed. There was a stale smell that suggested it had been boxed up in somebody's attic for a couple of decades. But beneath the mustiness was another, fainter smell—a sweet, perfumy scent.

As I moved the purse away from my face, something shifted inside. It was such a delicate and fleeting movement that I thought I'd imagined it. But when I looked inside, I saw something. There at the bottom of the biggest compartment was a glass bottle about three inches long, faceted like a prism, with a pinkish liquid inside. The bottle was half-empty—or half-full, as the optimists would argue. I took it out of the purse and gave Toni's cornrows another tug.

"Look what I found."

"Perfume! It looks expensive. What kind is it?"

"I don't know." The label had worn off, so there was no way to tell what the stuff was. I sprayed some on my wrist and sniffed. It smelled like the purse, only stronger, a pleasing bouquet of aromatic wood and exotic spices.

"Mmm," I said, offering my wrist to Toni, who took a whiff, squinted intelligently, like a forty-year-old tasting wine, and offered an "Mmm!" of her own.

THE HAUNTED PURSE

Selena glanced up from the cash register. "Was that in the purse? How'd I miss it?"

"Is it for sale?" I asked.

Selena pinged open the cash drawer and scooped out a couple of bills for Toni's change. "A half-empty bottle of perfume from God knows how long ago? Just keep it, hon."

"Really? Thanks!"

I zipped the bottle into one of the smaller compartments.

Behind me, somebody cleared their throat. I turned to see Brandon Briggs, a sixteen-year-old who lived on my street. "Since you're giving away freebies," he said to Selena in a gruff, sullen voice, "how about I don't pay for this."

He held up a dog-eared computer-game guide priced at seventy-five cents.

Selena met his malevolent stare head on. "Nice try, Brandon. Tell you what—if you find a half-empty bottle of perfume in that book, go ahead and keep it."

Brandon scowled at me like it was my fault Selena wouldn't give him free merchandise. I edged closer to Toni.

After I paid for my purchase, Toni and I scurried out of the thrift store and dashed across the street. We didn't want to tangle with Brandon Briggs. He was the kind of kid who was always bent on revenge, even if the people he got back at weren't responsible for whatever wrong had been done him. I'd once seen him knock an ice cream cone out of another kid's hand just because he'd dropped his own.

Tim Tuttle of Tim Tuttle Photography was standing on the sidewalk in front of his studio, talking to Jon Abrams from Apex Insurance.

Our school district had a contract with Tuttle Photography, which meant that Tim or one of his employees took our school pictures every year. Everybody wanted Tim, but we didn't always get him. As the best photographer in the county, he was in great demand.

He was probably in his fifties, a compact man with luminous gray eyes. Some of the girls at school had crushes on him. They thought he was cute, with his longish, wavy dark hair splotched with gray at the temples. And they bloomed under the attention he paid them. Tim had a knack for teasing out the beauty in his subjects. He knew the right things to say to make you feel special and worthy and uniquely attractive, and that feeling shone from your face when he snapped the picture. When Tim Tuttle was behind the camera, even the homeliest of students could count on looking good.

"Let's go down the alley," said Toni. "I don't want to walk past those guys. I'm still mad at Tuttle for making me smile."

I looked at her blankly.

"For my school picture last fall? I wanted to be, like, all broody and mysterious, but right before he snapped the picture he said something funny, and I grinned this big, goofy grin."

In my opinion, Toni had taken her best school picture ever this year. But I wasn't about to tell her that. Contradicting Toni usually led to an argument, and I wasn't in the mood.

"And I definitely don't want to talk to Mr. Abrams," she went on. "He's my dad's insurance agent. God, I hate running into that wide-assed jerk. He never shuts up!"

"Hmm," I murmured, carefully noncommittal. It was true that Mr. Abrams had a wide ass. It was also true that he loved to gab. If you stopped to say hello, you could count on being held up for at least twenty minutes. But I didn't consider that a bad thing. Mr. Abrams told interesting stories, and I enjoyed listening to them. I didn't have any uncles or grandpas or even a dad to tell me stories, so maybe Mr. Abrams filled a need in me.

"And," Toni said, gathering steam, "the first thing out of his mouth is always, 'How are your *adorable* little twin brother and sister?'" She blew out a furious breath. "They're not my brother and sister, you fat jerk—they're my *half* brother and sister. And how would I know how they're doing? It's not like I get to see them—*or my dad*—on a regular basis."

"Okay," I said lightly. Mr. Abrams had spotted us. He raised his hand in greeting, hobbling toward us like he had no qualms about ditching Mr. Tuttle for a chance to chat up two fifteen-year-olds. Toni grabbed my arm and hustled me into the alley between Apex Insurance and Wittmeyer's Auto Sales.

We were halfway down the alley when a horn honked behind us. Toni yanked me to the edge of the alley, and we stayed put while a big black car with shaded windows cruised past. The license plate read CAR KING.

"That's Peter Wittmeyer—the guy who owns Wittmeyer's Auto Sales," Toni said. She snorted. "'Car King.' Can you believe the arrogance? Who does he think he is, the ruler of some country?"

I made a noise that was half laugh, half exasperated sigh. "God, Toni. Do you like *anybody* on this street?"

She shrugged. "Selena's okay."

Downtown Ashton was laid out like a spider web, though any self-respecting spider would have scorned the imperfect symmetry. The avenues angled inward, converging at the block where City Hall, the library, the state unemployment office, and First National Bank resided. The streets chain-stitched the avenues together, and those streets got progressively shorter as you neared the center of the web.

We zigzagged our way to the bank and sat on a bench in the little brick courtyard to admire our purchases. Toni pulled her shiny new blouse out of the bag. I watched her mood lighten as she held it up.

"This blouse is amazing. It'll go great with my denim skirt, the one with the pink lace trim. I can't wait till the dance!"

I had to admit the blouse was very pretty, in a retro kind of way. I supposed it would work for the dance if she went retro all the way—clothes, hair, jewelry, shoes. The key was to make retro look intentional.

While Toni prattled on about the dance, I transferred my possessions from my old purse to the new one. They barely covered the bottom of one of the medium-sized compartments. I felt a flicker of buyer's remorse. This had to be the most impractical purchase I'd ever made. For five bucks I could have bought enough boxed mac and cheese dinners to feed myself for a week.

Then my eyes fell on the whimsically embroidered hearts, and my doubts evaporated. This purse was a denim rectangle of splendidness. It was probably the best thing I'd ever owned.

"Hey, can I have a spritz of that perfume?" asked Toni, slipping her blouse back into its bag.

"Sure." I unzipped the compartment where I'd stashed the little bottle. It was empty. I checked a similar pocket on the other side of the purse. Also empty.

"Hang on," I said. "I guess I forgot where I put it."

THE HAUNTED PURSE

I proceeded to unzip zippers. I unsnapped snaps. I checked each and every pocket—three times. And came away empty-handed.

"That's so weird," I said, slumping against the back of the bench. "It's like it disappeared into thin air."

"Let me see." Toni snatched the denim purse from me and pawed through it with the grace of a grizzly bear, no doubt crumpling my grocery list and scattering my hair scrunchies. Abruptly, her hands stilled. "Whoa. What's this?"

I scooched closer as she pulled out a photograph. An old one, judging by the faded colors. She turned it over. Scrawled on the back was a date from twenty years ago.

The picture showed a teenage girl standing outside on a sunny day. She was posing like a model—good posture, big smile, one hip jutting out slightly—in front of a two-story white house that would have been ordinary-looking if not for the rounded turret that rose up on one side like Rapunzel's tower.

The girl was pretty. I could see that even with the sun-cast shadows hollowing her eye sockets and underscoring her cheekbones. Her shining brown hair was tucked behind her ears, so I couldn't tell how long it was. She wore jeans and a short-sleeved white shirt. Slung over her shoulder was—

"That's your new purse!" Toni said with a gasp.

I took the photo from her. "Where'd you find this?"

"Behind your wallet."

"That's—that's impossible. It wasn't there a minute ago."

"Sure it was. It had to have been. You just didn't see it. Anyway, that sucks about the perfume."

"Yeah," I said morosely, slipping the photo back into the purse.

It sucked, and yet it made sense. I wasn't the kind of person who got breaks. The free perfume had been a nice surprise. I wondered if I'd somehow lost the bottle on purpose, in a subconscious act of self-sabotage.

But that wasn't it at all. Something was starting, something so freaky that I couldn't wrap my head around it.

Later, when I decided to take another look at the photo, I couldn't find it. I searched every corner of the purse. I even dumped everything out. The photo was gone—just like the perfume.

Chapter 4

A few days after I bought the purse, my mother showed up at the apartment, her first visit in weeks. She was there when I got home from school, her cigarette smoke wafting through the apartment like poison fog.

I found her in her tiny bedroom, puffing away as she flipped through the handful of dresses that still hung in her closet. She'd taken most of her clothes with her when she'd moved in with her boyfriend, Arthur, more than a year ago.

According to my mother, Arthur was in his late forties and owned three apartment complexes. I had him pegged as a slum lord, because that was the kind of guy my mother usually hooked up with—someone a little sleazy, a little shady. Arthur allegedly owned a big, beautiful house with five bedrooms and a four-car garage and gorgeous professional landscaping and a swimming pool.

The reason I wasn't living at Arthur's house was that Arthur didn't like kids. It was a touchy situation, said my mother. Arthur didn't know she had a daughter. She was working up to telling him, though. Once he got used to the idea, she would come back for me. In the meantime, I was supposed to think about which bedroom I wanted—the one in back with a balcony overlooking the pool, or the one in front, which had its own bathroom and was bigger than our entire apartment.

I played along. I said the one with the bathroom sounded good. But I knew I wouldn't be moving to Arthur's house. If Arthur hated kids, he was never going to come around, and my mother wasn't about to risk losing him over some kid she'd never wanted in the first place.

"Oh, hey," my mother said when she spotted me in the doorway of her bedroom.

"Hey," I said, stepping into the room. "What are you doing here?"

"Looking for something to wear." She took a long drag on her cigarette and blew out a ghostly puff of smoke. "Something, like, mature and classy and not too sexy." She pulled a low-cut jade-green dress out of her closet, gave it the once-over, and put it back. "Arthur's son is coming for a visit tomorrow, and the three of us are going out to dinner. I want to look, you know. Respectable."

I frowned. "Arthur has a son?"

"And a daughter. But just the son is coming."

"So Arthur has kids." I paused to let the words sink into my brain. Then, trying to keep my tone neutral, I added, "I thought you said Arthur doesn't like kids."

She wrinkled her nose as she fingered the skirt of a cherry-red sequined thing. "They're not kids. They're in their twenties."

"But they started out as kids, right?"

She threw me a sharp look. "What are you getting at?"

"You said I can't live with you because Arthur doesn't like kids. I figured he didn't have any of his own."

She took another drag on her cigarette, this one quick and huffy. "Just because somebody has kids doesn't mean they like them. Arthur's kids caused him a ton of grief growing up."

She pulled a modest black sheath out of her closet. It was so unlike her usual tight, flamboyant, skin-baring style that I wondered how it had ended up in her closet in the first place.

"That one's good," I said.

"Yeah, maybe." She made a face. "I'll look like an old grandma."

"No," I said. "You definitely will not look like an old grandma."

My mother was a natural beauty. She had long, glossy blonde hair—though its natural color was light brown, like mine—a Miss Universe face, and a figure that turned heads no matter what she wore. People who knew the two of us said I looked like her, an observation that both pleased and dismayed me.

"Your mother's too pretty for her own good," old Mrs. Manning from downstairs often told me, frowning sternly as if to discourage my own prettiness. I supposed she was right. It was probably my mother's good looks that had led to her getting pregnant at fourteen. She never talked about my father, and I wondered if she even knew who he was.

In my mind he was someone brilliant, someone who'd made just the one mistake in hooking up with my mother and then gone on to become a doctor or a nuclear scientist or a professor of philosophy at some Ivy League college. That scenario at least explained my own braininess.

My mother went through boyfriends the way other women went through disposable razors. Men lusted after her, and she was always willing to drop her current boyfriend for one she thought might be better in some way. Her one great talent was using her looks to manipulate men.

Most of her relationships fizzled out around the three-month mark, which was why it was such a big deal that she'd been with Arthur for a year and a half. But I knew what she was up to. She was looking for security, money, someone who could take care of her. She'd been a server since her teens, first at a diner and later at the swanky nightclub where she'd met Arthur. She was tired of working, tired of struggling to make ends meet.

My mother tossed the black dress on the bare, stained mattress of her bed. Her eyes landed on me and widened briefly, as if she'd just now registered my presence. "Well, look at my Liberty—so pretty, so grown up. Seems like yesterday you were just a baby." She sighed in a wistful way I knew was just pretend. "Soon you'll be having babies of your own."

"Babies!" I exclaimed. "I'm only fifteen."

"So? I was fourteen when I got knocked up. My mama was sixteen when she had me. You remember your grandma, right?"

"Yes," I said, gritting my teeth. "I remember."

I hadn't seen my grandmother for nearly ten years. We'd lived with her out of necessity while my mother was in high school, and for a few years afterward. We'd moved out after the two of them had a fight over money, and we hadn't been back since.

I would never forget my grandmother. And I didn't mean that in a good way.

THE HAUNTED PURSE

She was skinny, too skinny; the bones in her face were sharp, like broken rocks. The smoke from her cigarettes made me cough. She yelled a lot, and when I did something she didn't like, she'd pinch my arm till I cried.

Although she was my mother's mother, she was no grandma. I knew what a grandma was supposed to be from the TV shows I watched. Grandmas had soft white hair and pillowy bosoms. They hugged you and read you stories and gave you presents even when it wasn't your birthday. They baked cookies for you. And they never, ever pinched you.

"You're not pregnant now, are you?"

I blinked, momentarily disoriented. My mother was eying my stomach speculatively, almost hopefully, like she *wanted* me to screw up my life the same way she'd screwed up hers.

"What? No!" I said, folding my arms across my belly. "And you're wrong. I am not going to have babies anytime soon."

"So you're on birth control."

"No! I'm still—I don't—I'm not having sex." I felt my face go red.

"Well, you soon will be. Hell, I started at twelve. If you don't want to get knocked up, you better get yourself on the pill."

"I need money," I said, staring at a stain on the carpet that looked like a fish with a serious underbite. Piranhas looked like that, I thought. "I'm just about out of groceries. Could you leave some blank checks, too? The rent's due next week, and the electric bill just came in the mail."

"Yeah, sure." She pulled her wallet out of her purse and thumbed through a wad of bills. Now that she was with Arthur, she always seemed to have money, though she didn't throw much my way. Just enough to pay the bills and keep me from starving to death.

"Oh, hey." She pulled out a rectangular slip of paper and handed it to me. "Could you run down to the drugstore and get this prescription filled?"

I glanced at the paper. "Misty Dawson," it said. "Alprazolam," it said.

"I could make us something to eat while you're gone," she went on, tilting her head in a charming way she usually reserved for others, mainly men. "If you want."

"Yeah, sure," I said, even though it was only four o'clock and I wasn't hungry. But I wasn't about to say no. My mother actually wanted to have dinner with me! I couldn't remember the last time we'd eaten together.

Chapter 5

I slipped the prescription into one of the butt pockets of the denim purse and hurried outside. The day was unseasonably warm, more like June than April. I crossed to the shady side of the street and headed for the center of town.

Riverview Lane was a far too scenic name for my street, though it was technically accurate, there being a river and all. I wanted to believe there was another Riverview Lane somewhere, this one named for a clear, cool stream that meandered through a land of rolling lawns, stately trees, and crisp white picket fences.

There was nothing stately or crisp white about my neighborhood. Riverview Lane was a one-way street at the eastern edge of downtown Ashton, as narrow as a ravine at the bottom of a canyon. If you were nearsighted and didn't know this was eastern Ohio, you might think you were in some stony, desolate place out west.

Mine was a concrete neighborhood, a place where crumbling apartment buildings and shabby shops crowded the cityscape like bleak, gray rock formations. There was no greenery, unless you counted the weeds that sprang defiantly from the sidewalk cracks.

The river itself, the Arihanna, was a vile, polluted thing that flowed directly behind my apartment building. Concrete walls covered in decades of spray-painted graffiti sloped down to the water a good thirty feet below. The fish population had died off decades ago, done in by toxic runoff from the mines upstream. The river often gave off a sour smell that wafted through the doors and windows, even when they were closed.

On the stinkiest days, Mrs. Manning would say, "Smells like God's boiling cabbage again."

There were no other customers at the drugstore's prescription counter, so I marched right on up. The lady behind the counter eyed me guardedly. She had dark hair pulled into a tight bun and eyebrows steep as ski slopes. I felt her judgment wash over me like dye: I was a teenager and therefore must be up to no good.

"Hi, I have a prescription for my mom," I said, dragging out the final *m* in *mom* because I didn't get to say that word very often. I slipped my fingers into the left butt pocket of my purse. The prescription wasn't there. I checked the right butt pocket. Empty.

How could that be? I was sure I'd slipped it into one of those pockets.

I set my purse on the counter and rummaged through the smaller zippered compartments. No prescription.

"Sorry," I said with a glance at the pharmacy lady's stony face. "I know it's in here somewhere."

She let out a long, quiet breath. It wasn't quite a sigh, but it conveyed a clear message. *Kids today. So irresponsible.*

I unzipped the middle compartment and pulled the sides apart. The cavity gaped at me like a large, toothless mouth.

I heard the rustle of clothing behind me as another customer stepped into line.

THE HAUNTED PURSE

A pounding started in my head, a steady drumbeat of doom. I had to find that prescription. I began pawing through the other compartments. I looked everywhere—big compartments, little compartments, medium-sized compartments. I unzipped all the zippers, unsnapped all the snaps. I checked the butt pockets three times. I groped beneath things. I took stuff out. The prescription wasn't there.

"Well?" The pharmacy lady's voice cracked like a whip, making me jump. "Do you have it or not? Other people are waiting."

I turned around. There were now three people in line behind me, including Mrs. Manning, who caught my eye and quickly looked away.

"I don't know what could have happened to it," I said, stepping aside. "I'm sure I put it in my purse, but..."

She wasn't listening. She'd already moved on to the next customer.

I scanned the ground as I walked home, though I really didn't think the prescription had fallen out of my purse. I thought of the perfume and the photograph, which had vanished in a similar fashion. What was wrong with me? Why was I suddenly losing things?

And why did this have to happen today, when my mother wanted to spend time with me?

Back home, I lingered outside my apartment door, chewing the inside of my cheek as I tried to think of a good way to tell my mother what had happened. I finally realized there wasn't one. I squared my shoulders and pushed open the door.

She was standing at the kitchen counter, cranking a manual can opener around the top of a can of peaches. A pot of water churned on the stove.

"We're having spaghetti," she said. "It was either that or canned soup. You're right—you need groceries."

I drew in a breath of smoky air and blurted out the awful truth. "I can't find your prescription. It's not in my purse. I was thinking maybe I accidentally left it here."

She plunked the can of peaches down on the counter so hard that some of the liquid sloshed out. "You lost my prescription?"

"No! I mean, I definitely put it in my purse, but when I got to the drugstore—"

"Oh, Christ. I should have known you'd screw this up." She stormed down the short hall to the bedrooms, presumably to conduct a search. Meanwhile, I checked all the horizontal surfaces in the main living area—kitchen table, kitchen counter, couch, chair, coffee table. I even looked under the furniture.

She came back into the living room as I was searching my purse again. "You find it?"

"No."

"Christ." She dropped into the couch, rubbing her temples. "That prescription is for my anxiety medicine. I need it filled *today*."

"I'm sorry," I said, planting myself in front of her. "I don't know what happened to it. You saw me put it in my purse, right? But when I got to the drugstore, it wasn't there."

THE HAUNTED PURSE

She stared up at me, her eyes slitted in fury. She looked like a venomous snake about to strike. I stared back, and I'm ashamed to say I tried to use my beauty against her. I made my eyes big and trembled my lower lip. I searched my mother's eyes for a trace of love, or even compassion. I would have settled for compassion. But I saw nothing but anger and loathing and bitterness over how very hard I was making her life.

"Give me that purse," she snarled. She yanked it off my arm so roughly that I staggered. She turned it upside down and shook it. The contents tumbled onto the coffee table. The last item to flutter out, like a dizzy butterfly, was a rectangular piece of paper. I saw it slip from one of the butt pockets.

"Well, hey. What have we here?" she said sardonically, snatching up the prescription. She glared at me. "God, you're useless. I can't count on you for anything."

I couldn't take my eyes off the prescription. "That's...impossible. It wasn't there before, I swear. I looked everywhere."

"Sure you did."

I lowered my eyes. "I'm really sorry. I'll be more careful this time. The drugstore is closing soon, but if I hurry—"

She held the prescription out of my reach. "You think I'm going to trust you after this? Hell, no. I'll go myself."

She strode into the bedroom and came out with the black dress slung over one arm, her purse swinging from the other.

"Are you coming back to eat?" I asked.

She didn't answer. She left the apartment without so much as a goodbye, slamming the door behind her.

I finished cooking the spaghetti and kept it warm for nearly an hour, but she never came back.

She'd left a couple of twenty-dollar bills and some blank checks on the kitchen table before she got mad at me. I supposed that was all that really mattered.

Chapter 6

The next day after school, Toni asked me to come home with her. She said she had something to show me.

Mrs. Moore was in the kitchen chopping carrots, her eyes glued to the screen of her laptop. She multitasked like that all the time, and I found it miraculous that she'd never chopped off a finger. She shot us a harried smile and asked if I'd like to stay for dinner.

"Better find out what we're having first," Toni muttered to me.

"I heard that," said Mrs. Moore, pretending to take umbrage. "We're having chicken pot pie."

"Again?" Toni made a face. "We have that, like, four times a week."

"We do not have chicken pot pie four times a week. I make it maybe once a month."

"You make it every week," Toni spat, "and then we have to eat leftovers for the next three days. And the stuff gets soggier and more disgusting every day."

"It wouldn't get soggy," said Mrs. Moore, "if you'd heat it up in the oven instead of the microwave."

"The oven takes forever. Plus, there's never enough chicken."

Mrs. Moore looked wounded. "I use what the recipe calls for."

"Of course you do," Toni said contemptuously. "You always have to follow the recipe. Seriously, Mother. Can't you think outside the box? Be at least a little creative?"

The two of them locked eyes in a silent, ferocious battle. Mrs. Moore was the first to look away. That disappointed me. Most of the time I was secretly rooting for her.

Once, a couple of months ago, after Toni had slammed herself in the bathroom following a mother-daughter spat, Mrs. Moore whispered to me, "I wish Toni was mature like you."

No, you don't, I almost said. I was mature because I had to be, because I was my own parent. But it wasn't a good thing. I'd been cheated out of a whole phase of growing up, and I often wondered how screwed up I was because of it. I wasn't the normal teenager. Toni was.

Still. I wished Toni would be nicer to her mom. I wished she would realize how lucky she was to have such a good one.

"Anyway," Mrs. Moore said with a beleaguered sigh, "Libby, if you're not too repulsed by my cooking, you're welcome to stay for dinner."

"Thanks, Mrs. Moore. I'd love to stay."

She told me to call my mom to make sure it was okay.

"Tell her I've been meaning to invite her over for coffee," she said, as Toni and I headed into the living room. "I feel terrible that we've lived here for four years and I've never even met her. We're just so busy with our jobs, not to mention all the things we have to do in our personal lives. Being a single mom, it isn't easy."

"Oh, here we go again," said Toni, loudly enough for her mother to hear. "Everybody, let's take a moment to pray for those *poor single moms.*"

A hurt silence emanated from the kitchen.

THE HAUNTED PURSE

While Toni flicked apathetically through TV channels, I called home and had a pretend conversation with my mother.

"Just dinner and then, you know, hanging out for a bit... I don't know, like an hour or two? ...Yeah, I know. I'll be careful... Mom, please. I'm three blocks away. Love you, too. See you later."

Even though Toni was my best friend, I couldn't risk having her find out about my absentee-mom situation. My living arrangement suited me just fine, but if Child Protective Services ever got wind of it, I would be yanked out of my apartment and thrown into foster care. And I couldn't imagine a worse fate than being forced to live with strangers.

"So it's all good?" Toni asked after I ended the call.

"Yeah, I won't be missing much. She's heating up leftover meatloaf and rice for dinner and then watching some sappy movie on TV." Damn, I'd gotten good at lying. I didn't know whether to feel ashamed or proud.

"Your mom is so cool. Like, does she ever tell you no?"

"Oh. You know. Sometimes."

Toni had met my mother just once, two and a half years ago, when she'd come home with me after school. I hadn't expected my mother to be there, but she was. She was on her way out, and because it was November, her short skirt and low-cut top were concealed beneath a coat. She made a few jokes, gushed over Toni's cornrows, and even uttered some mom-isms I'd never heard from her before. "Don't forget to do your homework." "Make sure you lock the door behind me." "Have fun, girls!"

It was funny. The woman was a complete failure at mothering, yet somehow she knew how mothers were supposed to act. She'd made a good impression on Toni, an impression that had never been superseded, because I'd made sure their paths never crossed again. Toni thought my mother was A-OK, a fun, gorgeous, sit-com kind of mom.

"Mason," Mrs. Moore called from the kitchen. "Come set the table."

Somewhere a door clicked open. A boy zoomed into the living room—Toni's ten-year-old brother. He wore blue plaid boxer shorts over gray long johns, along with chunky winter boots and a red checkered cape.

"Liberty Bell! Toenail! Greetings!" he shouted.

"Don't call me that," Toni said irritably.

Mason galloped in circles, stirring up the pot-pie-scented air. His cape rippled behind him. It had a ruffle down one side that suggested it had once been a kitchen curtain. "Toni Toenail, Toni Toenail," he chanted.

"Shut up, Mason!"

"Who is this Mason you speak of? I am Astound-o Man." Mason veered into the kitchen. "See you, Liberty Bell! See you, Toenail!"

"Stop calling me Toenail!"

"He only does that because it bugs you," I said. "Why don't you tease him back? Like, make fun of him for running around the house in curtains and underwear."

"I've tried that. It doesn't faze him. Mainly because my mother thinks it's totally fine for a ten-year-old to play superhero."

In fact, Mrs. Moore had consulted a psychologist, who said the superhero thing was a phase, a response to her divorce from Toni and Mason's dad. Mason was trying to assume the role of Man of the House. He would eventually outgrow the behavior. In the meantime, Mrs. Moore was encouraged to let her son play superhero to his heart's content.

That explanation made sense, but I wasn't sure it was the right one. Maybe Mason was just looking for attention. For four years Mrs. Moore had been a full-time college student with a part-time job. She was due to graduate in a few weeks and was currently working odd shifts as a salesclerk at a ladies' clothing store while trying to find a permanent job as an accountant. She was rarely home, and when she *was* there, she was usually shut in her bedroom, doing homework or scrolling through job sites on her laptop.

Mr. Moore wasn't any better. He had a full-time job as a supermarket produce manager, and he drove for a ride-sharing service on the weekends. Plus, he was preoccupied with a new family that included three-year-old twins.

Poor Mason. I might have donned a cape and boots at his age, too, if I'd thought it would get me some parental attention.

"Toenail," Toni lamented. "Why do I have to have such a crappy name?"

"Dude. Your name is not Toenail."

"It might as well be. If Mason keeps calling me that, pretty soon everybody will be doing it."

"You want to talk about crappy names?" I said. "How would you like to be called Liberty?"

"At least you got a good nickname out of it."

"Yeah, there's that." I supposed even Liberty wasn't so bad when you considered that my mother had almost named me Pizzazz.

"So what is it you wanted to show me?" I asked.

She flashed a mysterious smile. "Come with me. What you're about to see could change your life."

Chapter 7

I followed Toni to her bedroom and sat on the bed while she opened her closet door.

She pulled out a dress. "What do you think?"

The dress was navy blue and sleeveless, with a lacy bodice and a tie belt. A layer of chiffon skimmed over the A-line skirt, and a cascade of ruffles flowed down one side. The style was in vogue, though I'd seen it mostly on ladies and older girls.

"It's pretty," I said.

Toni was watching me closely. "You like it? It's my mom's. She got it for her college graduation. She said I can borrow it anytime I want."

"Cool."

"She also said *you* can borrow it."

"Me?" I goggled at her. "Why would I want to borrow your mom's dress?"

"So you have something nice to wear to the dance."

I felt my jaw clench up. "Toni, I told you—"

"I know what you told me. Just listen."

I groaned and flopped back on the bed.

She flung the dress over her desk chair and centered herself at the bottom of the bed. She looked like an orator about to make an important speech.

"This dance, it's a once-in-a-lifetime thing, like Mars aligning with Jupiter or something."

I raised my head to scowl at her. "What are you talking about? The school has dances all the time."

"Not like this. It's our *sophomore dance*, Libby. Our first semi-formal. Do you really want to miss it?"

"I really do."

"Well, I don't!" She stamped her foot so hard, the jarred candles on her dresser clattered.

"Then go." I made a sweeping gesture with my arm. "Go to the stupid dance. You don't need me there. You can hang with other people. Louie, Charlie—"

"I want to go with my best friend."

"Well, your best friend isn't going."

She paced to the window and back again, a round trip of maybe six feet. "Think of it this way—the dance is from six to nine. That's three hours out of your whole life. You can stand three hours in the school gym, can't you? And if we're not having a good time, we'll leave early, I promise."

"Not interested."

"I'll owe you. I'll pay you back. Best friends do favors for each other, right? If things were the other way around, if you wanted to do something and I didn't, I would do it anyway."

I eyed her skeptically. "So if I said, 'I have free tickets to go bungee jumping next weekend, and I want you to come with me,' you would come?"

"Totally."

"Even though you're scared of heights."

"If it was something you really wanted to do, I would do it. And, yeah, it would be hard for me because I'm scared of heights, but you're my best friend, and that's what best friends do. They make sacrifices for each other."

She gazed at me triumphantly, her feet splayed, her shoulders squared, like a combat soldier. I could picture a helmet on her head, an assault rifle in her hands.

I seriously doubted that she—or anybody—could conquer a phobia just to indulge a friend's whim. But there was no way I could call her bluff, because I wasn't going to get free bungee-jumping tickets anytime soon.

Stupid me. I'd just argued myself into a corner.

"Fine! All right! I'll go to the stupid dance with you," I said crossly. I sat up, though what I really felt like doing was rolling over and going to sleep. Dueling with Toni always wore me out.

She let out a victory whoop and rushed over to hug me. "Thank you! You won't be sorry. The dance is going to be fantastic. Now try on the dress."

"Wait, why don't you wear it? I mean, it's *your mom's*."

"I already have something to wear, remember? Anyway, the dress is too long on me. You're a little bit taller than my mom, so it should be just the right length. Sure, you're skinnier than her, but once you tie the belt, the dress will fit fine. And the color's going to be gorgeous on you."

I lobbed a dubious glance toward the dress, which was still hanging over the desk chair, its chiffon skirt fluttering in the breeze from the forced-air heating. "I don't know, Toni. I've never worn anything that nice before. What if I spill something on it?"

"You won't. Anyway, it's not like Mom paid full price. She gets a really good employee discount. Come on, try it on."

A few minutes later I was standing in front of the slightly warped full-length mirror mounted on Toni's bedroom door, staring in delight. It was amazing how different a person could look when she traded her jeans for a stylish dress. This new version of me looked older, confident. Cool, even.

Maybe Toni was right. Maybe this dress *would* change my life.

After dinner, Mason hauled a battered board game out from under the living room couch. Toni and I agreed to play, even though we knew he would win. Board games came naturally to Mason like math or art did to some people. Tonight, though, his game seemed off, and for a while it looked like Toni or I might actually beat him. But in the end, he rallied and defeated us both. I had a feeling he'd been holding back so the game wouldn't end too quickly.

By that time, darkness was descending beyond the windows, as silent and heavy as snowfall. Mrs. Moore poked her head out of her bedroom and asked if I wanted her to walk me home. I knew she was busy, so I said that wouldn't be necessary. I made a pretend phone call home, and my imaginary mother insisted on meeting me halfway.

Riverview Lane wasn't exactly wholesome in the light of day. At dusk it became downright sinister. Every shadowy doorway was a hiding place for vampires, werewolves, and demons. The darkened alleys were full of huge, fanged night-monsters that slithered up out of the polluted river to hunt for human flesh. That was what I'd believed when I was little, anyway. Brandon Briggs had told me so.

THE HAUNTED PURSE

Nowadays I knew better. The real monsters of Riverview Lane were robbers, rapists, and drug dealers. And in their own way, they were just as scary as river monsters.

I sprinted the whole way home.

"Well," said a raspy voice in the gathering darkness. "If it ain't the girl who raised herself."

"Hi, Mr. Owens. What's new?" I stopped to catch my breath, peering down at a scruffy man in a wheelchair who was blocking the sidewalk leading to my apartment building.

"New York, New Jersey, New Guinea." He ticked them off on his fingers.

"You forgot New Zealand," I said. "And New Delhi."

"Most of 'em ain't so new anymore. Should start calling them Old."

"Old York? I don't think that would catch on."

He grunted and wheeled himself to the edge of the sidewalk, allowing me passage.

Mr. Owens had fought in the Persian Gulf War, but only for two weeks. He got injured in an explosion and came home paralyzed from the waist down. He'd been in a wheelchair ever since. For nearly three decades he'd lived alone in an apartment on the first floor of my building. He spent a lot of time outside, watching people pass by.

"Lock your door when you get inside," Mr. Owens called gruffly. "There's some shady characters around these parts. Drug dealers and such."

"I will," I said, throwing my weight against the door to the apartment building. It tended to swell against the door jamb, especially in humid weather.

There was a familiar odor in the building—God boiling cabbage. I tromped up the creaky staircase to the second floor, wondering why Mr. Owens always called me the girl who raised herself, as if the raising was done.

Mr. Owens was the only person who knew I lived alone, and that was only because he was so attuned to the comings and goings of the apartment residents. He'd noticed my mother's perpetual absence, but he wasn't the type to get involved in other people's affairs. My secret was safe with him.

Chapter 8

A vanished perfume bottle.

A missing photograph.

A disappearing/reappearing prescription.

At first I chalked those incidents up to my own carelessness, but when my history report went missing, I could no longer deny the truth. Something weird was going on with my purse. Something other-worldly. I decided to tell Toni about it. After school we sat on a bench outside the thrift store, sharing a mini pack of chocolate chip cookies while we watched Tim Tuttle sweep his sidewalk.

When the last of the cookies was gone, Toni brushed crumbs off her lap and said, "So what's the weird thing you wanted to tell me about?"

"Oh. Well..." Now that the time had come, I was losing my nerve. Toni tended to be a contrarian, and what I needed was a sympathetic listener. Plus, she didn't believe in the kind of weirdness I was about to describe. Still. I was desperate to talk to somebody, and Toni was really all I had.

So I told her about the denim purse, how things kept disappearing and, in some cases, reappearing. As I talked, she picked at her flaking fingernail polish, looking up now and then with an air of polite attentiveness. When I'd finished my story, she said, "It's a big purse, with lots of compartments. I'd probably lose stuff in there, too."

I fought back a wave of irritation. "I'm not losing stuff. Today in history class I dumped my purse out on Ms. Eckhart's desk. The report wasn't there. But a little while later it was back."

"So it was there all along. It had to be. Maybe it was stuck inside one of those zippered pockets."

"It wasn't. I checked everywhere. This same thing has happened four times now."

"You know what you should do? Keep all your stuff in one compartment. Don't even use the other ones. That way you'll always know where things are."

"Toni! Are you even listening to me? This isn't about me forgetting where I put stuff. Something's going on with that purse. I think it has...supernatural powers."

She snickered. "Supernatural powers? Oh yeah. That's gotta be it."

I stared at her gravely.

"Wait. You're serious?" She stood up, shaking her head. "You know I don't believe in that woo-woo crap. Ghosts, witchcraft, demon possession—"

"I know."

"—vampires, Bigfoot, telekinesis."

"I told you it was weird."

"No. Peanut butter and tuna sandwiches are weird. What you're talking about is—*impossible*."

"All I'm asking is that you keep an open mind. Can you do that for me? I mean, considering how best friends are supposed to make sacrifices for each other and all?"

She glowered at me. Toni hated it when I used her arguments against her. "Fine. I'll keep an open mind, on one condition."

I waited.

"Let me borrow that supernatural purse of yours for the dance. It'll go great with my retro outfit."

Chapter 9

Toni's birthday was a week later, and the two of us celebrated with a Friday night sleepover at her apartment. Mrs. Moore made Toni's favorite meal: lasagna, salad, and garlic bread. After dinner, she scurried to the kitchen and came back with a slightly lopsided homemade cake ablaze with sixteen candles. "Happy Birthday Toni" was spelled out in candy letters from the grocery store. We sang "Happy Birthday to You" (though Mason loudly replaced the last two lines with "You look like a monkey and you smell like one, too!"). Toni blew out the candles, squeezing her eyes shut as she made her secret wish.

Toni's grandparents had sent a check for her birthday, and she'd also gotten money from her dad. She decided to use some of her newfound wealth to take the two of us to the movies.

"Toni, no. Don't waste your birthday money on me," I protested. "I can pay for myself."

That wasn't true. Going to a movie was a luxury I couldn't afford. If I paid for a movie tonight, I would deplete my grocery fund and would have to live on whatever canned goods inhabited my pantry, at least until my mother tossed another wad of cash my way.

"Seriously, I want to do this," said Toni. "Please, just let me."

I made some perfunctory tortured noises and hung my head, trying to project injured pride tempered by humble gratitude. "Okay, okay. Thanks, Toni. This is really nice of you."

THE HAUNTED PURSE

The movie theater was in a strip mall a few miles from the downtown area. Mrs. Moore dropped us off early, so we had time to do some window shopping. Raindrops pattered noisily on the aluminum roof over the sidewalk.

We ducked into a clothing shop, where Toni spent some of her birthday money on a new pair of jeans. The bag was too big to fit in her purse, so she asked if I'd put it in mine.

I hesitated. I almost said, "Are you sure you want to do that?"

But I didn't. I just said, "Sure." I stuffed the bag into the roomiest compartment of my purse and zipped it shut. I stood squarely in front of Toni as I did it to make sure she saw. And then I wished a terrible wish. I wished that the bag containing my best friend's new jeans would disappear. Because that was the only way Toni was going to believe that my purse had supernatural powers.

Lucky me. I got my wish.

Chapter 10

"I'll take my bag back now," Toni said. We were standing on the sidewalk outside the movie theater, waiting for Mrs. Moore to pick us up. My heart lurched hopefully as I slid my purse off my shoulder. Was it my imagination, or was the purse less bulky than it had been earlier? I unzipped the main compartment and peered inside. And though I wasn't totally surprised, I gasped.

"Oh crap. Toni! Your bag isn't here."

She whirled to face me, her mouth dropping open in dismay. "What do you mean it isn't there?"

Wordlessly, I handed over the purse and let her rummage through it.

"What happened to it?" She glanced wildly behind us, retracing our footsteps with her eyes. She turned in a circle, her gaze roving everywhere, like a frantic mother searching for her lost toddler.

I said coolly, "I think we both know what happened to it."

She wasn't listening. "I can't believe you lost my new jeans! Do you know how often I get brand-new jeans? Like, never! We have to go back to the theater; we have to search—"

"Toni! I did not lose your jeans. You watched me put the bag in my purse. You saw me zip the zipper. It's like all the other times, the other things that disappeared. You said you'd keep an open mind, remember?"

She flung the purse at me, her eyes narrowed in sudden understanding. "Oh, okay. Now I get it. You did this on purpose. To make me believe your crazy story. Where's my bag, Libby? What'd you do with it? Stuff it under your seat in the theater?"

I stamped my foot on the hard concrete, jarring my shinbone. But I barely noticed the pain. "Do you honestly think I'd do something like that? God, you're my best friend. Think about it—I haven't opened my purse since I put your bag inside. We've been together every second. We didn't even go to the restroom. When could I have taken your bag out of my purse without you seeing?"

But she was already flouncing back to the movie theater. "I'm going to check inside. Wait here in case Mom comes."

I paced in a tight circle the whole time she was gone. Why had I wished for this? Hadn't I had enough ugly scenes over my purse's tendency to swallow things whole?

Toni came back, empty-handed and tight-lipped, as her mom pulled up to the curb.

"So how was the movie?" Mrs. Moore asked as we climbed into the back seat.

"Good," I mumbled.

"Can you please just leave us alone?" said Toni.

Mrs. Moore sighed.

We rode home in silence, Toni and I staring moodily into the darkness beyond the car windows. The earlier rain had intensified into a storm. Lightning flashed sporadically across the sky. Rain pelted the car.

Every few minutes I patted my purse, performing a kind of manual pregnancy test to see whether it had gained any bulk. It remained slim and trim, inhabited only by my meager possessions.

Back at the Moores' apartment, we went straight to Toni's room. We didn't look at each other. We didn't speak. I heard the squeak of springs as Toni plopped down on her bed. I dragged the desk chair to the window and sat down, keeping my back to Toni. I watched the lightning flashes grow weaker and less frequent as the storm edged away beyond the hills.

Toni was restless. I heard her rustling around on her bed. Every few minutes she sighed in torment. Finally, in a small, resigned voice, she asked, "So, how long does it take for stuff to come back?"

I swiveled my chair around, eying her warily. "I don't know. Maybe an hour or so? It's only happened a few times, so I can't be sure."

She nodded solemnly. When she looked at me, I saw remorse in her eyes. "I'm sorry, Libby. I didn't mean what I said. I know you didn't lose my jeans on purpose."

"It's okay."

"Do you seriously think they'll come back?"

"I seriously do."

Her gaze wandered to my purse, which I'd tossed onto the desk. "Have you checked lately?"

"Not since we got back." I wheeled myself over to the desk. Gingerly I opened the purse and peered inside. I couldn't suppress a grin as I pulled out the jeans bag.

THE HAUNTED PURSE

Toni let out a shriek and leapt off the bed. She snatched the bag from me, hugging it to her chest like a pet kitten. Then she slipped the jeans out of the bag, letting gravity unfold them. "I can't believe they're back! But, oh my God, it's true." She stared at me. "Your purse has powers."

I nodded happily. "My purse has powers."

Chapter 11

Toni and I sat on the bedroom floor, the purse centered between us. We eyed it uneasily, as if it were a wild animal that might suddenly rear up and bite us.

"It's obviously enchanted," Toni said, in a tone of wonder. "Your purse is literally a magical object, like Harry Potter's invisibility cloak."

I started to nod but stopped as her words took root in my brain. "Wait, how do you know about Harry Potter's invisibility cloak?"

She'd made fun of me when I was reading the Harry Potter books. She'd cut me off every time I tried to tell her how good they were. And she swore she would never, ever read them, or even watch the movies, because they were stupid made-up stories about wizards and dragons and other things that didn't exist. Toni preferred realistic fiction.

She clapped a hand over her mouth. "Oops."

I stared at her. "You've read Harry Potter?"

"Yes, I've read Harry Potter!" She had the look of a kid who's been caught sneaking into her parents' liquor cabinet—defiant, defensive, humiliated. "Mason got the books at the library last summer. I picked up the first one and couldn't put it down. I went through the whole series in, like, six weeks."

I shook my head, dazed by this confession. "Why didn't you tell me?"

THE HAUNTED PURSE

"I don't know." Her gaze bounced around the room, landing everywhere but on me. "I guess because I always made such a fuss when you talked about Harry Potter. But you were right. Those books are amazing."

I just looked at her. Sometimes I wondered if our friendship was as solid as we pretended it was. Friends told each other things. They shared the details of their lives—the places they went, the things they did, the books they read.

Of course, I wasn't exactly keeping my end of that bargain. Toni had no idea I lived alone, and I wasn't planning to come clean anytime soon.

"Well. I'm glad you liked the books," I said, with more grace than I was feeling.

"Me too." She flashed a conciliatory grin. "Anyway. Do you think we should tell my mom about the purse?"

"No." I wasn't ready to trust an adult. Not even Toni's mom, nice as she was. "Your mom is like you," I said. "Practical. It would take a long time to convince her there's something supernatural going on."

We went back to watching the purse. There was a moment when I thought I saw it twitch, but that might have been my imagination.

"You could always get rid of it," Toni said. "You know, donate it back to the thrift store."

I considered that. "I could. But I don't want to. Not yet, anyway. This purse is the coolest thing I've ever owned. I want to find out more about it. I want to see what it does next."

She moved her eyes away from the purse long enough to glance at me. "Aren't you afraid it'll crawl into your bed some night and strangle you with its straps?"

"No. I think it's trying to get my attention. It's trying to tell me something."

"Like what?"

I didn't have a clue.

"Did the perfume ever come back?"

"No."

"Maybe it came back with the jeans. We should check."

So I upended the purse, shaking its contents onto the floor. The little bottle of perfume wasn't there. But something else was—the photo of the brown-haired girl, the one that had appeared in the purse the day I'd bought it and then promptly disappeared.

I picked up the picture and studied the girl, who had my very own purse clutched against her hip. An odd tingle went through me. I'd gotten so used to the purse being mine, I sometimes forgot it had a history I hadn't been a part of.

I flipped the photo over, noting again the twenty-year-old date scrawled there. Then I flipped it back. "I wonder if the purse made stuff disappear when it belonged to her. And I wonder where it came from. Like, did somebody give it to her as a gift? Did she buy it new at the mall? Did she get it at a thrift store like I did?"

"Good questions. Let's track her down and get some answers."

I shook my head, not in refusal but in doubt. "How? We don't know her name. We don't know anything about her."

"Except—maybe we do." She snatched the photo out of my hand and tilted it to catch the light from her desk lamp. "I know this house! It's in Rosedale. We pass it sometimes on the way to my dad's place. Mason calls it the castle house."

"Are you sure it's the same place?"

"Pretty sure. It's a different color now, and the trees are taller, but it has that same tower thingy out front." She handed the photo back to me. "We have to go there."

"But we don't even know if that's where she lived. Maybe it's just some random house that happened to be in the background when she got her picture taken. And even if she did live there, she probably doesn't anymore. This picture was taken twenty years ago."

"Her parents might still be there. And if they aren't, maybe whoever's living there now can tell us their name."

Studying Toni's determined face, I had to bite back a smile. I couldn't believe how quickly she'd gone from scoffing at the notion that my purse had supernatural powers to embracing the fact that it did. Now she wanted to solve the mystery as much as I did.

Chapter 12

Toni and I planned our trip to the castle house for a Saturday morning in early May. Toni's mom was working the day shift, and Mason was visiting a science museum with his friend Albert's family. I said my mom would be gone all day, too, which wasn't a lie.

We walked to the bus stop around ten a.m. and boarded the bus for Rosedale. We'd each packed a lunch, because we weren't sure how long we'd be gone. As we slid into an empty seat, we grinned at each other with the festive air of travelers on an exotic vacation.

The castle house was less than seven miles away, but the bus ride took forty minutes because of all the stops. People got on, people got off, yet the bus was never more than two-thirds full. Toni and I took turns playing a hand-held video game she'd swiped from Mason's room. Then we studied the photo of the girl.

"So if she was our age twenty years ago," Toni said, "right now she'd be...?"

She looked at me expectantly. Toni hated math and refused to do even the simplest mental calculations.

"Mid-thirties," I said. My gaze drifted to the house in the photo. "So your dad lives near this place?"

"Not really."

"But you said—"

"I said we pass it on the way." Her tone, suddenly sharp, hit me like a slap.

THE HAUNTED PURSE

Toni didn't like to talk about her dad. She said the subject depressed her. According to the court papers, she and Mason were supposed to spend every other weekend with him as well as two weeks in the summer and half their Christmas vacation. In reality, they rarely saw him, because he was so busy with his two jobs and his new family.

When Toni had found out her stepmother was pregnant with twins, she'd prayed for two boys. She knew what was coming, and she was desperate to hang on to her status as Daddy's Little Girl. Too bad for her. She'd been bumped out of that spot by little Elise.

"Fortune Boulevard. This is where we get off," Toni said as the bus wheezed to a stop.

I grabbed my denim purse from under the seat and slipped the photo into it. My lunch was also inside, but I wasn't worried that either it or the photo would disappear. Nothing had gone missing since Toni's birthday. I was pretty sure the purse had been making things vanish to get my attention. Now that Toni and I had started looking for the girl, it was satisfied. We were doing what it wanted us to do.

The day was humid but overcast, warm and yet breezy, which translated into fairly comfortable walking conditions. The house was three blocks from the bus stop, on Levergood Street. Toni led the way, having a sense of direction I lacked.

We were in a stately older neighborhood. Most of the houses were medium-sized but dignified-looking, with deep front porches and sturdy brick chimneys. The frame models had a thick look, as if the raw lumber they'd sprung from was forever buried beneath countless coats of paint. Each house had a small, immaculate lawn and mature but neatly trimmed shrubbery.

In one of the yards a little girl sat in a turtle-shaped sandbox under a tree, shoveling sand into a bucket. She looked up as we passed, and Toni said *hi there* in her high-pitched baby-talk voice. I just stared, trying to imagine what it would be like to be four and have so much—a sandbox, a yard, a nice big house, probably a mom *and* a dad, plus a quartet of grandparents and maybe a sibling or two. A pet dog or cat. A toy-filled bedroom. All the things I'd grown up without.

That little girl probably had no idea the world contained people like me. When I was her age, I'd had no idea it contained people like her.

"There it is," Toni said, grabbing my arm. I followed her gaze and saw, across the street, the house in the picture. I pulled the snapshot out of my purse and held it up.

The presence of the turret told me this was the right place. Other than that, a lot had changed over the years. The house, formerly a white frame structure, was now tan. A garage had been built next to it, connected by a covered walkway. Trees that were saplings in the photo now sported thick trunks and towered over the house like gargantuan sentries. A wrought-iron fence surrounded the property.

We crossed the street. When we reached the sidewalk in front of the house, I stopped, gazing down at the photo. A shiver went through me as I realized I was standing in the same spot where the girl had stood. I turned to face the street and jutted my hip out, mimicking her pose. Holding the same purse she'd carried, only twenty years later. I could almost feel time sliding away, our separate decades bumping together.

"Libby! Come on," bellowed Toni, thudding up the porch steps.

The front door had a doorbell and a door knocker; Toni used them both. While we waited, we checked out the porch. It looked like a nice place to hang out. There was a wide wooden swing on the left and matching redwood chairs flanking a small round table on the right.

"I don't think anybody's home," Toni said.

She knocked one more time—*clunk, clunk, clunk*. We waited another minute and then turned and clomped down the porch steps.

And almost collided with a lady coming around the side of the house.

"Oh!" all three of us said at the same time.

The lady laid a hand on her chest as if trying to stave off a heart attack, but she was laughing. "Sorry! I was out back. I *thought* I heard someone knocking."

She was too old to be the girl in the photo—her gray hair and crepey skin suggested she was at least sixty. She wore light-blue Capri pants and an oversized cotton shirt. Her hands were hidden beneath filthy gardening gloves.

"What can I do for you?" she asked, looking from Toni to me. She slipped off the gloves and tossed them onto the porch. "I don't think it's the right season for girls to be selling cookies, though I wouldn't say no to a box of those chocolate-mint things."

"Sorry, no cookies," I said with a grin. I held out the photo. "I found this picture inside a purse I bought at the thrift store, and we were wondering—"

"Why, that's my house!" exclaimed the lady, taking the photo from me. "Oh, my! This *is* an old picture, isn't it? Look at the trees—they were barely taller than I am!"

Toni and I made appropriate noises of amazement.

I said, "We were wondering about the girl in the photo. Is that your daughter, or...?"

She shook her head. "This isn't my picture. I've never seen it before. It must have been taken before my husband and I bought the place."

"Oh," I said, disappointed but not really surprised. "Well, do you happen to know who the girl is?"

She pulled a pair of glasses out of her shirt pocket and slipped them onto her face. She squinted at the photo as though even with glasses her vision wasn't quite up to par.

"Why, I believe that's the girl who lived here before us," she said. She handed the picture back to me. "The one who disappeared."

Chapter 13

"If memory serves, the girl went missing twenty years ago, during the summer," said Mrs. Atkins, the lady from the castle house. "I know how long ago it was because my husband and I bought this place shortly before Christmas that same year, just a few months after she disappeared." Her voice softened. "That poor family, what they must have gone through. Probably couldn't bear to stay in the house. Too many memories."

"What do you think happened to her?" I asked. "Could she have run away?"

Mrs. Atkins brushed at a smudge of dirt on her shirt as she pondered that. "Seems unlikely. This neighborhood isn't the kind of place kids run away from. And most young people who run away turn up eventually. This girl never did."

I asked where the girl's family lived now. Mrs. Atkins didn't know. She couldn't even remember their names.

"I believe there was an older sister," she offered. "Oh, and the father owned some sort of business in one of the neighboring towns." She smiled apologetically. "That probably doesn't help, does it?"

She invited us inside for brownies and iced tea, which I thought was a surprisingly friendly and trusting gesture. Where I lived, you didn't invite strangers into your home. Toni and I thanked her but declined. We had more work to do before we caught the bus back to Ashton.

We went to a few other houses, but most of our knocks went unanswered. Of the people who were home, none had lived in the neighborhood long enough to have known the family of the missing girl.

By now it was nearly noon, and we were famished. Toni led the way to a fast-food place that had an outdoor courtyard dotted with small aluminum tables. She bought a milkshake and fries to supplement her peanut butter and jelly sandwich, and it was a good thing she did. A mustached guy in a Burger Wiz shirt kept flouncing outside to chase off people who were sitting at tables without an official BW purchase in front of them. This struck me as totally unnecessary and just plain mean. There were plenty of empty tables.

I placed the girl's picture on the table between us and studied it as I ate. The girl smiled up at me, oblivious to whatever fate was about to befall her.

"What do you think happened to her?" I asked Toni. "Do you think she's still alive?"

Toni swallowed a bite of her PBJ before replying. "No."

My heart sank. "How can you be so sure?"

"Come on, Libby. She's been missing for twenty years. Where do you think she's been all this time if she's not dead?"

The breeze lifted a corner of the photo. I set my purse on the edge of it to anchor it in place. "She could have amnesia. Maybe she hit her head, and somebody found her and took her in."

"And she never got her memory back? And the person who found her didn't bother to check with the police to see if she was reported missing?"

"Then maybe she ran away."

"Mrs. Atkins said she didn't."

"That's her opinion. She doesn't know." I swiped one of Toni's fries and shoved it into my mouth.

"Libby." Toni's tone was firm. "She's dead. It's the most logical explanation."

Anger surged in me, quick as a flash fire. "Stop saying that! They never found a body."

"That doesn't mean anything. Maybe she got lost in the woods and died there. Maybe she fell down an abandoned mine shaft. Maybe she—I don't know—got swallowed up by quicksand."

I raised an eyebrow. "Quicksand? Really?"

"No." She flashed a sheepish grin.

"She's not dead," I said. "How could she be? The purse is trying to get back to her. That's why it gave me her picture." I'd come to that conclusion last night as I lay awake in bed, thinking about the purse, the girl, and all the weird happenings of the past few weeks.

Toni bent over her milkshake and took a good long slurp through her straw. When she came up for air, she said, "Or maybe it's trying to lead us to her body."

I stared at her in outrage. I started to tell her how crazy that was. And then I felt the façade of my certainty crumble. It wasn't that I truly believed the girl was alive. I just didn't want her to be dead. But Toni was right. She probably was. All the evidence pointed that way.

I glanced at the photo, wincing as I imagined that innocent smile twisted into a grimace of pain. Those guileless eyes widened by fear. God, she was so young. An ordinary teenager like me, like Toni.

I said, "Okay. So maybe you're right."

"Of course I'm right. The purse is enchanted. Which means it's alive, in a way. It was probably like a pet. It loved her. So of course it wants the world to know what happened to her."

"But how are we going to find out what happened to her if the police couldn't do it all those years ago?"

"There must be something we can do. Like...hold a séance." She jiggled in her chair. "Yeah, we should try to contact her spirit."

"I thought you didn't believe in séances."

"I didn't believe in lots of things—*before*." She gave me a mock-resentful look. "You and your stupid purse have shattered my whole belief system."

"A séance." I stared into a distant tree line, dredging up everything I knew about séances. And then a truth hit me, one so obvious and yet exhilarating that it made me laugh out loud. "No, no, we don't need a séance. We're already in touch with the spirit world."

"What are you talking about?"

"The purse isn't enchanted. It's haunted. By the girl in the picture!"

Chapter 14

"So you're saying a ghost lives in your purse."

Toni had slid her chair a couple of feet from the table, as if trying to distance herself from the purse. I didn't get her apprehension. Was a haunted purse any scarier than an enchanted one?

"It sounds crazy to me, too," I said, "but yeah, I think so."

The Burger Wiz guy kept one eye on us as he wiped a nearby table. I shoved another fry in my mouth to show him we were still consuming our Burger Wiz purchase.

"You hear about haunted houses and haunted graveyards," Toni mused. "Haunted hotels, haunted mines. But a haunted purse? Is that even possible?"

"Apparently it is. Considering we have one right here in front of us."

Toni's eyes raked across the purse. "Why don't we ever see her? Aren't ghosts supposed to appear to the people they're haunting?"

"Maybe she doesn't operate that way. Or can't for some reason."

Toni dragged her chair back to the table. She reached out a hand, hesitated, and then gave the purse a gentle squeeze. Something rustled inside.

We exchanged startled looks. Toni unzipped the purse and peered into its depths. With a magician-like flourish, she pulled out a copy of our local newspaper, *The Ashton Times*.

"Whoa," I said. "How'd that get in there?"

It was a stupid question. I knew how it had gotten in there.

Toni swept the remains of our lunch to the edge of the table and spread out the newspaper. "It's a clue. Your ghost friend is giving us a clue about her disappearance."

"You sure about that?" I tapped the date at the top of the front page. "This is today's paper. How can it possibly have a clue about a girl who disappeared twenty years ago?"

"There must be something in there, or she wouldn't have given it to us."

I scooched my chair close to Toni so we could look through the newspaper together. The front section included stories about the eruption of a volcano in Hawaii, a couple of foreign wars, and the latest political goings-on in Washington, DC. The Style section contained book reviews, celebrity gossip, TV listings, and a full page of comics and word puzzles. Sports and Local News had their own separate sections. Neither of us spotted anything remotely connected to a missing person's case from twenty years ago.

By now, the Burger Wiz guy had stopped wiping tables and was glaring at us like a bull getting ready to charge.

"We're probably missing something obvious," I said, stuffing the newspaper back into my purse. "I'll go through it again tonight at home. Maybe something will jump out at me."

"I'll do an internet search," said Toni. "Maybe I can dig something up on the missing person's case."

That night, I didn't find anything remotely connected to the girl's disappearance, even though I pored over that newspaper for more than an hour. Toni's internet search was just as fruitless—she found no information at all on a missing girl from Rosedale. Which made us wonder if Mrs. Atkins had her facts straight.

THE HAUNTED PURSE

Ghost Girl needed to cough up some better clues, I thought. Otherwise, our investigation would never get off the ground.

Chapter 15

The day of the dance finally arrived, a welcome distraction from my Ghost Girl mystery. I had an early dinner (half a can of ravioli) and then jogged to Toni's apartment. I told the Moores my mother had to work. Mrs. Moore clucked sympathetically and said it was a shame she wouldn't get to see me in my dance finery. Mason offered to take pictures with his spy camera.

I had already brushed my hair and pulled it into a low ponytail that trailed halfway down my back. As far as I was concerned, I was ready for the dance, aside from slipping on Mrs. Moore's dress.

Toni disagreed. She gave me a long, critical look and said, "Nope." She said, "Mom! Libby needs a makeover."

I protested, but Toni wouldn't back down. "This is our sophomore dance. Don't you want to look your best? My mom used to be a beautician. At least let her fix your hair."

I was already tired of arguing, and we'd barely started. "Fine. She can fix my hair."

Ordinarily I shampooed and air-dried every other night, a regimen that was fuss-free but left my hair flat and dull and a little bit frizzy. I always parted my hair in the middle and let it hang down the sides of my face like coarse, rippling curtains.

When Mrs. Moore got done shampooing and conditioning and blow-drying me, I had the tresses of a model—smooth, glossy, and full of body. She gave me a side part and pulled the skimpy side of my hair behind my ear, anchoring it with a pearl-studded barrette. The fuller side swooped provocatively across my brow. I swung my head from side to side, loving the way my hair bounced across my shoulders, light as butterfly wings.

"Now you need makeup," said Toni.

"Actually, I think I'm good with just the hair," I said.

I never wore makeup. Toni kept offering me hers, but I always said no. To begin with, I didn't think her woman-of-color foundation would cut it for a pale white girl like me. Eye shadow was a different story—it crossed racial boundaries—but I didn't share Toni's tastes. She favored metallics: silver, bronze, gold, rose-gold. Shades that, in my opinion, made it look like a robot was busting out of its fake-human skin.

"You need makeup," Toni insisted.

After a short argument we both knew she would win, I agreed to let her put blush and mascara on me. She talked her mom into plucking some of my eyebrow hairs, a mildly painful process that sleekened my brow line and dramatically accentuated my "natural arch." By this time I'd resigned myself to the makeover and was even a little curious to see what it would do for me.

When we were ready for the dance, we stood in front of Toni's bedroom mirror, arm in arm. I couldn't take my eyes off my reflection. Was that really me? I looked...beautiful.

I also looked more like my mother than ever before.

"See?" said Toni, beaming like I was a piece of art she'd just created. "You look fabulous."

"Well—mostly," I said, wincing as my gaze swept downward.

My fabulosity stopped at my ankles. My feet were humbly encased in a recent thrift-store buy—black flats with lopsided black bows on top, someone's old ballet slippers. At three dollars, they were all I could afford. Mrs. Moore had offered to lend me a pair of her dress shoes, but my feet were half a size larger than hers. I'd tried to cram my feet into those pretty pumps, but the pain of scrunched toes was too much to bear. The black flats would have to do.

Toni and I were still standing at the mirror when her bedroom door flew open. We jumped backwards just in time to avoid a full-frontal whack. Astound-o Man galloped into the room, wielding his spy camera. "Toenail! Liberty Bell! I am Astound-o Man, and I am here to—"

He stopped dead, his mouth dropping open as his gaze landed on me. The kitchen-curtain cape wafted down over his shoulders like an exhalation.

"Liberty Bell..." he said faintly. "Liberty. Libby..." He gulped. "You look—you look—"

"Get out of here, booger brain; you almost knocked us out!" Toni spun her brother around and pushed him toward the door.

Mason craned his neck, continuing to stare at me. He looked stricken, as if he'd suddenly lost the ability to swallow.

Toni shoved him into the hall and slammed the door. She turned to me with a triumphant grin. "How about that. I think little bro is crushing on you."

I hung my head in consternation. "Oh crap."

"No, no, this is a good thing. Now I have something to tease him about."

Chapter 16

"I think everybody in the whole class is here," Toni whispered as we stepped into the gym. "Do you feel like everybody is staring at us? I feel like everybody's staring. Do you think they're making fun of my outfit?"

"Nobody's staring," I said, though I too felt the weight of eyes upon us. "And nobody's making fun of your outfit—you look amazing. And, by the way, ow. You're hurting my arm."

"Sorry." She loosened her grip slightly but continued to clutch my arm. I felt like I was in a blood-pressure cuff.

We moved tentatively across the polished wood floor. Earlier today we'd played volleyball in here. Now there were colorful streamers and strings of white lights, and small tables where foursomes could sit and chat. The gym looked like a nightclub, though the faint scent of sweat and rubber sneakers still hung in the air.

"I'm nervous, too," I said. "Just remember, these are the same people we see in school every day. The only difference is, we're all in one place and everybody's dressed up."

"Everyone looks so different," Toni marveled. "It's almost like we're in Halloween costumes."

I spotted a refreshment stand in the far corner of the gym. A PTA mom was ladling red punch into plastic cups and setting them on the table.

"Come on," I said. "Let's get some punch."

Toni stayed right on my heels, so close she kept bumping into me as I threaded my way across the room. She really was nervous—usually she was the one leading the way.

We saw a few couples, but this was largely a singles event. People stood around in tight clusters of four or five, and a few waved hello as we walked by. We passed a DJ who was setting up his sound equipment.

"People are still staring," said Toni. "It's not my imagination."

"Well, you're staring back." We'd reached the refreshment stand. I took two plastic cups of punch from the smiling PTA mom and handed one to Toni.

As we were sipping our punch, Louie Henry and Charlie Cassidy walked by. And did a double take.

"Oh my God. Libby?" said Louie, grabbing my arm to steady herself. She wore four-inch spike heels. "Look at you, all glammed up!"

Toni pushed forward, grinning. "Doesn't she look amazing? The makeover was my idea. She was going to come to the dance in—get this—a ponytail and no makeup!"

"No!" exclaimed Louie.

I grinned sheepishly.

"Looking good, Dawson," said Charlie, circling me like a buyer appraising a showroom car. "Awesome hair. Kickass dress. The shoes? Total shit, but that's okay. That's not where people are looking."

Louie and Charlie were cousins and best friends. Louie's actual name was Louise, and Charlie's was Charlotte. Their mothers were sisters whose family had a tradition of naming children after dead ancestors. Even the youngest babies had names like Esther and Rosemarie and Roderick. Names as old as some of the thrift-store goods I bought.

THE HAUNTED PURSE

Louie and Charlie weren't considered cool, but they were generally respected by everyone in our class. That was mainly Charlie's doing.

Charlie intimidated people. She didn't mean to, but she did. She was tall and stocky, with limbs as dense as tree trunks. She lumbered around like a bear. Her bushy eyebrows gave her a fierce look, and her short brown hair stuck out like metal spikes. She was about to receive her first letter in weightlifting, a feat few sophomore girls achieved.

As far as anybody knew, Charlie had never committed even a minor act of violence. It was her potential that scared people. Everybody knew she could beat the stuffing out of them if she wanted to.

I'd always liked Charlie. I could sense her innate goodness. And I appreciated her propensity for straight talk. Most people said what they thought you wanted to hear.

Tonight Charlie was wearing a black pantsuit with a plain white shirt underneath. Louie wore a flowered dress in shades of peach and mint green, and her brown hair was French-braided.

"You guys look amazing, too," I said. "Check out Toni. Don't you love her retro look?"

"*Love* it!" said Louie, bouncing for emphasis and nearly falling off her heels. "And that denim tote is the perfect touch. Libby, that's yours, isn't it?"

I nodded.

"Are you sure I don't just look old-fashioned?" Toni asked anxiously.

"No, no, you look amazing," said Louie. "Did you see Madison Chang? She went retro, too."

"Yeah?" Toni perked up, clearly cheered to have her wardrobe choice validated by another dance-goer, one who happened to be the class volleyball star.

"Your outfit's better," said Charlie. "Madison's wearing brand-new clothes with a retro design. You look like you actually raided some old lady's attic."

"Oh. Thanks," Toni said uncertainly.

"Did you hear there's going to be a king and queen of the dance?" asked Louie.

Toni's eyes went wide. "Seriously?"

"It was Amelia Drake's idea, a last-minute thing. She thought it would be fun to have royalty like they do at prom. Since Ms. Eckhart is the advisor for the dance—and you know how tight she is with Amelia—she approved it."

"Wow," I said, digesting this. "So how do this king and queen get picked? Do we vote?"

"Yep," said Louie. "Everybody at the dance gets a vote."

"Amelia knows she'll be voted queen," said Toni. "That's why she suggested this."

"*Of course* she'll be voted queen," said Louie. "She's the coolest of the cool."

I gave a derisive snort. "She's the meanest of the mean, is what she is."

No one disagreed.

Amelia loved throwing parties for the cool kids at her big fancy house, and she always gave out verbal invitations to the chosen few—loudly, so the people who weren't invited *knew* they weren't invited. I often saw her and her friends pointing and tittering over some uncool girl's tattered gym clothes or outdated shirt.

Sometimes that uncool girl was me.

"Still," said Toni. "I guess it makes sense. A queen is supposed to be pretty, and Amelia's the prettiest girl in the class."

"Not tonight she isn't," said Louie, looking pointedly at me.

I shook my head furiously. "That's not true!"

"Oh, it's true," said Charlie. "You have Amelia beat looks-wise—tonight, anyway. What you don't have is the coolness factor."

"That's okay. I don't have it either," Louie told me.

"Amelia will win," Charlie said matter-of-factly, "because this king and queen thing is really just a beauty contest for the cool kids. Nobody else stands a chance."

"Why does it have to be like that?" Toni fumed. "Somebody should do something."

"Blame it on the great social divide," Charlie said. "It's worse here than at other schools."

Our school district comprised two distinct areas: the Hilltop, which was officially known as Kenmore Borough, and downtown Ashton. True to its nickname, the Hilltop sat on top of a hill, and it was where the professional people of our region resided—doctors, lawyers, bank presidents, business owners. The houses varied in size and level of grandeur, but even the most modest ones looked like miniature palaces.

Most of the cool kids came from the Hilltop—the cheerleaders, the sports stars, the kids who starred in the yearly musical. That was because their parents could afford things like gymnastics lessons and basketball camp and voice coaches. The

Hilltop kids were groomed to succeed, in school and beyond. Some were nice, but others saw themselves as above the Downtown kids, and in more ways than geographically.

Charlie and Louie lived in a middle-class neighborhood below the Hilltop, just a few blocks from the senior high school. Everybody called that area the Halfway, though it was technically part of Kenmore Borough. Some Halfway kids got assimilated into the Hilltoppers' group, while others fit in better with us Downtowners. Charlie and Louie were in the latter group.

"So, who do you guys think will be king?" I asked.

Toni and Louie answered in unison: "Connor Tipton." They looked at each other and giggled.

Charlie nodded in agreement. "Connor's got it all—the blond hair, the flirty smile, that bod. Half the girls in the class are crushing on him. Probably half the guys, too."

"I'm pretty sure Amelia's into him," I said. "Did you ever see how she looks at him?"

"Oh, for sure," said Louie. "She probably thinks this king and queen thing will turn them into a couple."

We stood silently, lamenting the realities of the senior high social strata. Then Louie jerked her head toward the far end of the gym. "Mr. Tuttle's setting up his photography booth. You guys wanna go get photographed?"

I followed her gaze and saw Tim Tuttle and his assistant positioning a large backdrop depicting a grove of blossoming trees.

"I didn't know there was going to be a photographer," said Toni. She looked at me. "You want to go over? It's not every day we get dressed up like this."

I pulled my gaze away. "You go ahead. I didn't bring my wallet with me."

That was no lie. But I would have said no even if I'd had my wallet. The truth was, I couldn't afford to throw my money away on something as frivolous as dance photos. Not tonight, not tomorrow, not next month. I just didn't want to admit it. Tonight, for a change, I felt well-dressed, confident, pretty. No need to remind everyone that I was the poorest one in our little group.

"Oh, but you don't have to pay now," Louie told me. "Mr. Tuttle will post the proofs on his website. You go online to check them out and order what you want. Or don't order anything at all if you don't like how they came out."

I thought that over and still landed on no. What was the point of getting photographed if I had no intention of buying the finished pictures? I'd probably be curious enough to check them out online, and what if they came out really, really good? And I couldn't afford to buy any? That would be yet another disappointment, another item for the ever-growing list of things I wanted but couldn't have. Another jab to my deflating inner-city soul.

"Hell, let's do this," said Charlie. She grabbed my arm and propelled me toward Mr. Tuttle's booth. I tried to protest but she ignored me. And she was strong—I couldn't break free. Toni and Louie were right behind us, chattering excitedly. "Does my hair look okay?" "Do you think my purse should be in the picture?" By the time we reached the photo booth, I'd resigned myself to going through with it. I just hoped I'd have the self-discipline to stay off Tim Tuttle's website.

We beat the crowd—the line was just starting to form. Mr. Tuttle snapped some shots of the four of us together, followed by one of just Louie and Charlie, and then one of Toni and me. Then he photographed us individually. I was last.

"You're so lovely, my dear," he murmured, as he adjusted the tilt of my chin. "I wish all my subjects were as photogenic as you. Let's have fun with this, shall we?"

For the first couple of shots, I smiled into the camera. Then Mr. Tuttle had me gaze pensively into the distance. I did a three-quarter turn and glanced provocatively over my shoulder. I held a lacy parasol. I pretend-sniffed a bouquet of white silk roses.

"Oh my God, Libby. That was amazing," Louie gushed when I was done. "You looked like a model at a photo shoot. Did you notice how he took more pictures of you than anybody else?"

I wrinkled my nose. "Really?" More pictures meant more chances that at least one would come out great. I really wanted to see the one with the parasol. Well, maybe I would allow myself a quick look at Tim Tuttle's website. Just one little peek.

Charlie tugged at her cousin's sleeve. "Come on. There's some people we need to see." She turned to Toni and me. "We'll catch you two later, okay?"

She gave an abrupt little salute, like an army officer departing on a reconnaissance mission. Then she and Louie headed into the thickest part of the crowd.

Chapter 17

A shrill whine erupted from the microphone at the DJ's booth. A few people covered their ears. We all crowded closer to see what was going on.

Ms. Eckhart stood with the DJ as he fiddled with the microphone to eliminate the feedback. He handed the mike to Ms. Eckhart, and she welcomed us to the dance, her husky voice booming across the gym. She went over the rules—no leaving the building, no public displays of affection, no disorderly conduct. She urged everybody to visit Tim Tuttle's photography booth. Then she talked about the king and queen contest and said the voting would begin at seven o'clock.

I caught a tiny flash of brightness, like the flicker of a firefly, on the far side of the DJ booth. It was an earring, probably a diamond one judging from the intensity of its sparkle, and it was dangling from the ear of Amelia Drake.

Wow, I thought in begrudging admiration.

Amelia was a golden girl in every sense. She gleamed, she shimmered—her hair, her skin, the twenty-four-karat flecks in her green eyes. Tonight she wore model-grade makeup and a satiny turquoise dress that clung to her narrow body like a mermaid suit. Her blonde hair cascaded to her shoulders in collector-doll ringlets, clearly the work of a skilled stylist. She was listening raptly to Ms. Eckhart. But then her gaze shifted, zeroed in on me. Maybe she'd felt me staring.

She gave a jolt, and those delicate brows knit together in displeasure. She whispered something to Jade Beasley, who stood next to her. The two of them glared at me. I glared back, tossing my head proudly. I knew I looked as good as Amelia tonight. Maybe better, if what my friends had said was true.

The music started. Amelia and her friends dissolved into the milling crowd. A few people drifted onto the dance floor and started dancing, their movements stilted and self-conscious. Others joined them in straggles of twos and threes. After a while people started to loosen up. The moves got wilder. The dance floor filled up.

Toni and I stood on the sidelines, still dance-shy, content to be observers. But three songs in, when we heard the first lively strains of "Uptown Funk," we looked at each other, grinned in mutual surrender, and stepped onto the dance floor. This was our favorite oldie. We couldn't not dance to it.

People grinned and waved as we bounced by, parting to make room for us. They turned to watch us dance. I was glad we'd practiced in Toni's bedroom. When the song ended, Toni yelled "Let's get more punch." The next song had already started.

We were snaking through the crowd, dodging flailing elbows and shimmying hips, when Nicholas Gray and Jared Berzansky stepped in front of us and asked us to dance. Toni answered for both of us with an enthusiastic nod.

We never did get that punch refill. We kept dancing, sometimes with each other, sometimes with our friends, and sometimes with boys who asked us. Toni danced with Downtowners and a few Halfwayers. I was surprised when, three dances in a row, I was approached by Hilltop guys.

THE HAUNTED PURSE

We sat out the first slow-dance. When the laid-back beat of the second slow song started, Tommy Sturgis appeared from nowhere, his arms outstretched, an invitation in his eyes. I stepped toward him because refusing would have seemed rude. I turned to give Toni a quick, apologetic wave. No worries. She was already cheek to shoulder with Jared Berzansky.

As soon as Tommy's arms went around me, I had second thoughts. I'd never slow-danced before! But this was Tommy, my almost-friend, a kid as quiet and as serious about school as I was. Tommy and I had been getting thrown together on scholastic quiz teams since fifth grade. He was a Halfwayer, and I was comfortable with him. And so, mimicking the other girls on the dance floor, I rested my forearms on Tommy's shoulders and let him move me gently in a circle. I started to relax. This wasn't so hard.

"You look really nice tonight," Tommy said, his mouth close to my ear.

"Thanks. So do you," I said.

He wore a white shirt, gray trousers, and a navy-blue tie—colors that coordinated nicely with my dress. If we'd been models for a fashion magazine, we would have been on the same page.

The song was only half over when a figure loomed behind Tommy and tapped him on the shoulder. My throat constricted when I saw who it was. Connor Tipton! Connor made some exaggerated miming gestures that indicated he wanted to dance with me. I'd seen this same scenario played out in old movies on TV. I was pretty sure it was called *cutting in*.

I felt Tommy tense up and clutch me tighter. I could tell he didn't want to turn me over to Connor—which was fine with me, because I didn't want to be turned over. Connor was our class's version of a movie star. The thought of dancing with him terrified me.

I was about to shake my head in an adamant *no thanks* when I saw Amelia Drake slow-dancing nearby with Dylan Reed. She turned her head and spotted our little threesome, her eyes icing over as she sized up the situation. Her gaze seized mine, and the message in those glittering eyes was clear. *Don't. You. Dare.*

A little squirt of mean-juice shot through me, and before Tommy could respond, I slipped out of his arms and stood gazing up at Connor.

"Well, hello there," Connor murmured as he gathered me into his arms. "You're Libby, right? I think you're in my world history class."

"Yes. I am," I said breathlessly.

He leaned close, his lips brushing my ear. "You look amazing, Libby. Whatever you've done to yourself, you should do it every day. Show the world how gorgeous you really are."

I swallowed hard and managed a shaky smile.

Dancing with Tommy had been easy enough; dancing with Connor was effortless. But instead of moving in stationary circles like everybody else, we glided across the floor as smoothly as ice skaters, weaving among the other couples. Connor's body heat, intensified by the exertion, released the scent of his cologne. I got drunk inhaling it.

The dance ended quickly because we'd started so late. Connor released me slowly, as if reluctant to let go. He said, "I'll see you around, Libby," winked, and walked away.

I wound my way unsteadily across the dance floor. Heading for the restroom, I ran into Toni, who grabbed me by both arms.

"Oh my God. Did I see you dancing with Connor Tipton?"

"I think you did," I said dazedly.

"Amelia is going to kill you. Seriously."

I grinned. "I know."

The voting started promptly at seven. The school had an online voting tool, but there hadn't been time to enter all the possible names, so primitive processes were being employed: paper ballots, hand-counting. There were no names on the ballot. You just wrote in the names of the people you wanted to win—one boy and one girl. A dozen PTA moms had shown up to handle the sorting and counting. They promised to work like crazy to get the results tallied before the end of the dance.

"So," said Toni, as we walked away from the voting table, "I'm guessing you voted for Amelia."

"Of course." I shot her a crooked grin. "Actually, I voted for you."

"You did? Well, that's a coincidence. *I* voted for *you*!"

We leaned in for a quick sideways hug.

At eight-fifteen, the lights in the gym were turned up. We all blinked like moles as our eyes adjusted. The school principal, Mr. Peterson, stepped up to the microphone and said he had the results of the vote. Voices buzzed; then everybody quieted down and gathered around the DJ booth. I saw Amelia Drake pushing her way to the front of the crowd, trailed by her ladies-in-waiting, Jade Beasley and Ava Hicks.

"We've never before crowned royalty at a sophomore dance," said Principal Peterson, chuckling at the outrageous irregularity of the situation. "This was Ms. Eckhart's suggestion. She said it was what you, the sophomore class, wanted."

"We didn't want this!" Toni whispered. "It was all Amelia's doing."

"We didn't have much time to prepare," Principal Peterson continued. "Unfortunately, we don't even have crowns. However, each of our two winners will receive a hundred-dollar gift card for the local mall, courtesy of our PTA."

An excited murmur went through the crowd.

"Like Amelia and Connor need a hundred bucks," muttered Toni.

"Well. Without further ado," the principal said, "the king of the sophomore dance is...Connor Tipton!"

"Surprise," said Louie.

People applauded, and a couple of girls yelled "Woo-hoo!" A grinning Connor pushed his way through the crowd, his thick blond hair flopping with every step. I flushed as I recalled the way his body had pressed against mine as he'd guided me across the dance floor. Connor joined Principal Peterson, who handed him an envelope.

I glanced at Amelia. She was biting her bottom lip as she watched Connor.

"Congratulations, Connor," said Principal Peterson.

He turned back to the crowd. "And now. I am pleased to announce. The queen. Of the sophomore dance. Is..."

Amelia edged forward.

"...Libby Dawson!"

My heart bounced against my chest wall. *What?*

"Oh my God!" Toni screeched in my ear. "Libby, you won! Get up there!"

I was vaguely aware of the cheers around me, of the crowd parting for me, people patting my back. Somehow I made my way to Principal Peterson, who congratulated me and handed me the envelope containing the mall gift card. As I took my place next to Connor, reality hit me like a shot of caffeine. I'd won! I'd actually beaten Amelia. When Tim Tuttle stepped up to take a picture, my smile was ready and confident.

"Didn't I tell you?" Connor murmured in my ear. "You look amazing tonight." He grabbed my hand and held it high. My eyes searched the crowd, found the blue-green glimmer of Amelia's dress. The back of it, anyway. Jade and Ava were leading her away. As I watched, Amelia reeled like a funeral-goer overcome by grief. Her friends caught her and yanked her upright.

Hey, Amelia, I wanted to shout. *Still think you're the coolest girl in the class?*

I never made it back to the dance floor. Tim Tuttle whisked Connor and me away to his booth, where he took a bunch of touchy-huggy shots of us, like we were a prom couple. Afterward, people kept coming up to congratulate me. I took my denim purse back from Toni so I could put my prize envelope inside. It kept getting crumpled by hugs.

Toni slipped away to use the restroom. While she was gone, Ms. Eckhart stopped by to say, very stiffly, "Congratulations, Liberty. I hope you can appreciate what a great honor this is."

"Yes, I can," I said, just as stiffly.

She started to walk away, but then stopped, turning her head just far enough to present her profile to me. "The vote was very close. You barely beat Amelia."

"Yeah?" I said. "But I beat her."

I was still staring at her departing back when Louie tottered up and grabbed me in a hug that nearly knocked me off my feet.

"It worked!" she squealed. "Our plan worked! I knew it would."

I blinked at her. "What plan?"

"Operation Cinderella," said Charlie, materializing behind her cousin.

I shook my head, still baffled. "What are you talking about?"

"We're talking about *you*!" declared Louie. "We knew you could beat Amelia—with a little help."

I looked from Louie to Charlie. "Oh, God. What did you do?"

"We asked people to vote for you," Louie said with an elated giggle. "Not Amelia's friends, of course, but pretty much everybody else. You wouldn't believe how many people didn't want Amelia to win. If we hadn't told them to vote for you, everybody would have just voted for their best friend. There would have been, like, a zillion different names on the ballots, but nobody would have had enough votes to beat Amelia."

Charlie grinned slyly. "It didn't take much to convince the guys. They couldn't stop talking about how hot you looked."

They stood there beaming at me.

"No!" I cried. "I didn't ask you to do this. Why would you do this?"

"Oh! You're upset?" said Louie.

I stared at the floor, fighting back tears. "I thought I won fair and square. Now I find out you had to beg people to vote for me!"

"We did not beg," Charlie said indignantly.

"You used me," I went on, my voice breaking. "You didn't want Amelia to win, so you used me to make sure she didn't."

"So?" Charlie raised her eyebrows. "You didn't want her to win either."

"That's not the point! What you did was—was—" I had to grope for the right word; it had been on our history vocabulary list last month. "—*exploitation*! You *exploited* me. You exploited the way I look. If I'd known this was going to happen, I never would have gotten fixed up like this. I would have left my hair in a ponytail. I would have worn my same old thrift-store clothes." I shook my head savagely. "Never again. I will never do this again."

Charlie rotated her spiky head in outrage. "Oh, puh-lease. Don't give me that 'It's a curse to be beautiful' bullshit. When you've got good looks, you make the choice to play them up or play them down. If you play them up, it means one thing—you want people to notice you. And honey, tonight people noticed you."

"Well, I wish they hadn't!" Even as the words came out, I knew they weren't true. Standing next to Connor, listening to my classmates applaud me, had been the highlight of my year. Maybe of my life. This was the first time I'd ever felt special. Singled out. Accepted. Cool. If the way I looked had helped me get there, was that such a bad thing?

I fumbled in my purse and pulled out a tissue. This was all so confusing.

"Libby, I'm sorry," said Louie, sounding genuinely contrite. "We thought we were doing you a favor." She flashed a rueful smile. "Look at it this way—can you use the hundred bucks?"

I blew my nose and nodded heavily. "Yeah. I can use the hundred bucks."

Chapter 18

"I think Mom forgot about us," said Toni. "She probably got busy on her laptop and lost track of time. As usual."

The dance had ended twenty minutes earlier, and we were standing in front of the school with a handful of other people waiting for their rides. Among them were Jade and Ava, who were huddled together looking shell-shocked. They kept throwing murderous looks in my direction.

I'd filled Toni in on what Charlie and Louie had done. She wasn't as upset about it as I was. In fact, she seemed pleased that they'd taken matters into their own hands.

"Maybe we should call your mom," I said, unable to suppress a shiver. Although it was mid-May, the night air was chilly, and I hadn't worn a jacket. The truth was, I didn't own a springtime jacket. I did have a gray hoodie that would have kept me warm, but it was too casual for this occasion.

Toni said, "I'll go see if I can borrow Ms. Eckhart's cell phone. Wait here in case my mom shows up."

Ms. Eckhart stood inside the building, keeping a dutiful eye on us stragglers through the plate glass windows. She turned her head as Toni approached. In that instant, Jade and Ava darted up and, before I could let out a peep, hustled me around the side of the building. They must have been waiting for their chance to get me alone.

"Hey!" I cried, trying to shake free of their grasp. Jade let go, but Ava clutched my arm even more tightly.

"Oh, you think you're pretty special, don't you?" Ava spat. "Queen Lib-er-ty." She drew out the syllables, mocking my name. "Ha! You're not even close to being queen material."

"Amelia deserved to win, and you know it," said Jade.

"If she deserved to win, she would have won," I retorted. "People voted. It was fair."

"Was *not*," countered Jade. "Because your little friends went around buying votes."

"They did not buy votes," I said.

"Then they threatened people," said Ava.

"No, they didn't!" I said, though I wasn't sure about Charlie.

I glanced from Jade to Ava. Wow. Nobody had ever looked at me with such hatred before, not even my mother. My heart thudded as I wondered what they were going to do to me.

"Look," I said, trying to sound reasonable. "I'm sorry things didn't work out for Amelia. I never expected to win. But there's nothing we can do about it now."

"Actually, there is," said Ava.

With one deft movement, Jade wrenched my purse off my shoulder. She turned it upside down and shook the contents onto the grass. Out fell the envelope containing the mall gift card. Jade snatched it up and slipped it into her purse.

"Let's go, Ava," she said. "I'll get my dad to stop at Amelia's on the way home so we can give this prize to its rightful owner."

Ava gave me a violent shove, and I went stumbling across the grass. I managed to stay on my feet, ever mindful that I was wearing a borrowed dress, one I needed to return in pristine condition. Ava took a step toward me, her fists raised threateningly. "If you ever tell anybody what happened here, we will come after you. And we will make you very, very sorry."

They stalked off, disappearing around the corner of the school. I was shaking as I scooped my possessions back into my purse.

Chapter 19

"You need to tell Ms. Eckhart about this," Toni said furiously. "Come on, she's still inside."

"No." Already I regretted telling Toni what had happened. I was embarrassed and humiliated. Ashamed of myself for not fighting back. I didn't want anybody to know about the incident. But as soon as Toni had come outside and seen my face, she knew something was wrong. She wouldn't stop hounding me until I'd blurted out the whole terrible story.

"Just forget about it," I went on. "Ms. Eckhart's not going to do anything. Ava and Jade and Amelia, they're her friends."

"But those shitheads stole your prize!"

A car coughed nearby. We looked up to see Mrs. Moore's battered old coupe pulling up to the curb. Mason was in the front passenger seat.

"Girls, I am so sorry," Mrs. Moore said as we climbed into the back seat. "I was filling out job applications online, and I lost track of time."

"That's okay," I murmured, though it occurred to me that if she'd been on time, I would still have my gift card.

"How was the dance?" Mrs. Moore asked as she pulled away from the curb.

"Mother, please," said Toni." We're tired. Can't you just leave us alone?"

Mrs. Moore sighed.

We rode the rest of the way in moody silence. Mason kept turning around to gaze at me. I shot him daggered looks until he stopped.

THE HAUNTED PURSE

As we turned onto Riverview Lane, I reached into my purse to get the key to my apartment. My hand brushed something thin and stiff and papery. Something that couldn't possibly be in my purse but was.

My prize envelope. I pulled it out and stared at the words on the front. *Sophomore Dance—Queen.* I could feel the hard rectangular gift card inside.

Toni saw what I was holding. She broke into an incredulous grin.

Ghost Girl had worked her magic again.

Chapter 20

"I can't believe you got your gift card back."

This was probably the tenth time Toni had said that. She couldn't stop marveling.

It was Friday, the day after the dance. Lunchtime in the cafeteria. Toni was spooning strawberry yogurt into her mouth while I hunched low over my peanut butter sandwich, trying to avoid eye contact with the lunch crowd.

Every time I looked up, people were staring at me. It was weird and disconcerting. Yesterday at this time I'd been a nobody. Last night I'd become royalty. Today I was a hybrid—half dance-queen Libby, half everyday Libby. I'd washed off the makeup before going to bed last night, but my eyebrows still had that sleek, tweezed shape. My hair, though flattened somewhat from a night's sleep, was still shiny and bouncy. I'd even stuck Mrs. Moore's pearl barrette back in.

"You're so lucky," Toni went on. "I wish I had a ghost-friend looking out for *me*."

"Yeah," I said, "for a dead person, she's pretty great."

"Uh-oh. Here comes another fan," said Toni, her eyes skimming over my head.

I gave my hair a quick fluff with my fingers and ran my napkin across my mouth, just in case the fan was Connor Tipton. A few seconds later I felt a tap on my shoulder. I turned to see Tommy Sturgis standing there.

"Libby, hi. I just wanted to say congratulations. I'm really glad you won last night."

"Aw, thanks, Tommy."

He gave a curt nod and turned to leave. "Hey. Tommy?" I said. "I'm sorry about that slow-dance thing. That was kind of weird. I wasn't sure what to do."

He waved away my apology. "Don't worry about it. It was Connor. You did what any girl in our class would have done."

Toni watched him walk away. "He's nice. Cute, too."

"Yeah," I said. I'd never thought of Tommy as cute before, but he was. He had hair nearly as dark as Toni's and eyes that blazed unexpectedly blue.

No sooner had Tommy left than Ethan McKinney stopped by, stammered out his congratulations, and then turned to flee, running straight into Principal Peterson.

This had been going on all day—red-faced boys congratulating me, girls hugging me in sisterly solidarity. I couldn't believe how many of my classmates were happy I'd won. Mostly Downtowners, but also some Halfwayers, and even a few Hilltoppers. Maybe people were just glad I'd kept Amelia from winning.

Amelia wasn't in school today. Louie had heard she was so upset she couldn't get out of bed. Jade and Ava were here, but they were spatting. More accurately, Ava wasn't speaking to Jade, though Jade kept following her around, trying to make up. Toni and I were among the few people who knew the real story: Ava blamed Jade for losing the gift card.

I'd stashed my prize at home, under my mattress, for safekeeping. If I'd had it with me, I might have been tempted to wave it in Jade's and Ava's stupid, stuck-up faces. Just to see their mouths drop open. That would have been a bad idea. Antagonizing Amelia's gang was like poking a hornet's nest with a stick.

"You'll probably start getting invited to Hilltop parties," Toni said. She spoke in a matter-of-fact tone, but I saw the furrow in her brow. She was afraid I was going to ditch her for the cool crowd. I would have been worried about the same thing if she'd been the one voted queen.

"That's not going to happen," I assured her, though last night as I'd stood next to Connor, listening to all the applause, it had seemed like a real possibility. Of course, that was before I'd found out what Charlie and Louie had done.

"Being dance queen doesn't make me one of *them*," I continued. "I still live where I live. If I showed up at some Hilltop party, the butler would take one look at me and slam the door in my face."

Toni's eyes raked down over my faded Jurassic Park tee. "Yeah, you're probably right."

I crumpled up my lunch bag and threw it at her.

After school I stopped at my apartment long enough to pick up the gift card and then bused myself to the mall for a minor shopping spree. I bought all the things Toni and her mom had used on me the night of the dance—mascara, blush, hairdryer, tweezers. I figured the blush-mascara combo was just enough makeup to polish me up without turning my face into some garish paint-by-number. I also found a pink tee shirt with sparkles along the neckline on a rack marked forty percent off.

It was time Cinderella started looking more like a princess.

Chapter 21

I didn't know why my mother had left me a check instead of cash. Sometimes she did that.

Apparently, she'd dropped it off while I was at school, presumably so she wouldn't have to interact with me. As soon as I realized she'd been in the apartment, I raced around taking inventory. It didn't look like she'd taken any of my stuff.

Sometimes she did that, too.

For the first time in my life, I had possessions worth stealing, things I didn't want to lose. My denim purse, of course, which was with me virtually all the time. But also the items I'd bought at the mall—my makeup, my hairdryer, my pretty new shirt.

I fingered the check pensively. I'd planned to spend the next hour or so poring over the newspaper Ghost Girl had left me, but I really needed to get that check cashed. I was low on groceries and nearly out of cash. The bank closed at four, and it was already three-forty.

I laid the newspaper on the kitchen table so I wouldn't forget about it and headed out the door.

I'd dreamed about her during the night. Ghost Girl. In the dream, she'd stood at the foot of my bed holding the newspaper, her arm outstretched like she was handing it to me. At least I thought it had been a dream. Maybe it was a nudge. My investigation had stalled, and it wasn't going to start up again until I solved the mystery of the newspaper.

It was a lovely late spring afternoon, and the people of Riverview Lane were outside in droves. They loped down the broken sidewalks. They chain-smoked on street corners. They pushed tattered baby strollers. They sat on cracked concrete steps, soaking up the sun like anemic flowers.

This was how my street was all summer—teeming with bodies, like some marketplace in India. Most of the housing units lacked air conditioning, so even on the hottest days it was more comfortable to be outside than in. You could always count on a breeze coming off the river. The smell might gag you, but at least the air was moving.

I cut across a little park near the center of town, a small, square chunk of forest sitting in the midst of the grimy city like an unexpected piece of dessert. It was lush with trees and shrubs and flowers. Wooden benches dotted a winding concrete path.

I stopped to admire a blooming rose bush, the sweet fragrance wafting up my nostrils. Gently I stroked petals soft as a baby's cheek. On a whim I used my thumbnail to sever the slender stem several inches below the bloom. I pricked my finger flicking off the thorns and had to lick the blood away. Then I stuck the bloom behind my ear. The scent floated deliciously around my face.

Belatedly it occurred to me that picking flowers in the park was probably frowned upon, if not outright prohibited. I looked around in mild panic, then relaxed. I was alone. No one had seen me.

I took pains to avoid drawing law enforcement attention to myself when I walked the downtown streets. If I saw a cop heading in my direction, I would veer into a store. Some irrational part of me believed the police had magical powers that enabled them to recognize abandoned minors. I couldn't let them discover my secret.

The bank wasn't crowded, so I was able to get in and out quickly. Walking up the sidewalk, I heard an eruption of male laughter. I glanced across the street and felt an electric jolt shoot through my stomach. There on the street corner stood Connor Tipton and two other Hilltop guys, Evan Romero and Gabe Shannon. They stood in a loose cluster, mock-punching each other. Gabe spotted me and called, "Hey, Libby, looking good!" Evan whispered something to Connor and laughed. Connor shoved him away.

"Whatcha up to, Libby?" Gabe called in a slightly taunting voice.

"Just living life," I called back. I lowered my head and walked faster. I didn't want to get sucked into a chat session with these guys. Especially Connor.

I didn't like the feelings Connor stirred up in me. I kept telling myself I didn't have a crush on him...but maybe I did, just a little. Often, before I went to sleep at night, I'd find my thoughts drifting back to the night of the dance, to our mutual triumph as we'd stood before our classmates, my hand clasped in his. I'd flush at the memory of that slow dance, the muscled warmth of his arms around me. There was an intimacy about those moments that made me feel connected to Connor, though I doubted he felt the same way. Sometimes he said hi to me at school, but aside from that, nothing had really changed between us.

Each time I visited the public library, I used one of the computers to log onto Tim Tuttle's website. I'd spend the whole session gazing at the pictures of Connor and me. We looked like a young celebrity couple glammed up for the Emmy Awards. A notice on Tuttle's website said dance proofs would be available for sixty days. I was seriously considering ordering a photo, just one, to keep as a souvenir of that night. I figured I could afford a five by seven if I lived on ramen noodles for a week. The shots of me by myself were nice, too, but if I could buy only one, Connor was going to be in it.

"Well. *Somebody's* in a hurry," Gabe said loudly.

I kept walking, my eyes purposefully trained on the sidewalk ahead.

I'd gone almost a block when I heard footsteps pattering behind me. I whirled around and saw Connor heading toward me. My heart jangled in a weird mix of dismay and elation.

"Libby, wait up!" he said, grinning as he caught my eye. He trotted to catch up with me. "Damn! You walk fast."

"Where are your friends?" I asked, fiddling with the rose in my hair to hide my nervousness.

"Eh." He spat into the gutter. "Those guys are so immature. I ditched them."

I hoisted my purse strap farther up my shoulder and set off again. Connor stayed in step with me.

"Can you believe school's almost over?" he said. "This year went by crazy-fast. What are you doing this summer? Got any big vacay plans?"

"Nope."

"Just hanging out here? That's cool."

I grunted. There was nothing cool about spending the summer in downtown Ashton, and we both knew it.

"My family's going to Hawaii in a few weeks," he offered. "We have this cottage on Oahu. Well, us and one of the other partners at my dad's law firm. We go every year."

"Lucky you."

"Meh. Hawaii's not that great. You can only go snorkeling and zip-lining so many times before it gets boring."

"Sure," I said, as if I, too, got bored snorkeling and zip-lining in Hawaii. I walked a little faster. Connor upped his stride to match mine.

"I think I can get out of going this year," he said. "See, I got this summer job lined up. I'm going to be working at my uncle's tuxedo rental store in the mall. I figure I can stay with him while the fam's in Hawaii."

I shot him a curious glance. "You got a job? Why?" It wasn't like he needed the money. Not with a lawyer-father who took the family on Hawaiian vacations every year.

"It was my parents' idea." His thick blond bangs were straggling into his eyes. He flipped them back with a jerk of his head. "They think it'll keep me out of trouble. Ha! If I want to get in trouble, twenty hours a week at the mall isn't going to stop me."

"Ha!" I echoed.

"So, do you have a job lined up?" Connor asked.

"Me? No."

"You should get one." His eyes wandered to my tee shirt, thin and misshapen from too many washings. "You could probably use the money, right? I mean, you're so pretty. If you just had some decent clothes..."

I stopped dead in my tracks, speechless and smarting. Connor squeezed his eyes shut and said, "Damn. That didn't come out right."

"It's okay," I said, more humiliated than angry. "You're right. Getting a job would help with a lot of things. We don't have much money, my mom and me. *We've* never been to Hawaii. We never go anywhere. We live in a crappy apartment by the river. I buy my clothes at the thrift store. If I bought them anywhere else, we wouldn't be able to afford food."

There. All the cards were on the table. *You're rich, I'm poor. You're a Hilltopper, I'm a Downtowner. Where does that leave us, Connor? What are you going to do now?*

I had no idea if he was looking at me, because I was staring at the ground. There was a dime in the gutter, half hidden under a weathered sales receipt. I was itching to bend down and pick it up, but my pride wouldn't let me.

Connor was quiet for a while. Then he said, "My mom was poor growing up. We have some poor cousins." Barely before I could process that, he laid a hand on my shoulder. "Hey. You want to get something to drink? My treat."

My stomach did a little flip-flop. "Sure. There's a diner just up the street. Chester's."

Since it was well past lunchtime but too early for supper, the diner was nearly deserted. We sat at a table in the back, and Connor ordered two colas and a plate of fries for us to share. While we ate and drank, we reminisced about the dance and griped about a recent English assignment and discussed a rumored affair between the wood shop teacher and the school librarian. Then the conversation drifted to siblings and pets. Since I had neither, Connor did most of the talking.

THE HAUNTED PURSE

When the last fry was gone, I murmured a thank you and slid off my stool, ready to head to Toni's to tell her about this unexpected rendezvous. I needed her feedback. Was this a date? If so, it was my first one, which was a pretty big deal.

Connor was right on my heels as I pushed through the door. "Wait, I'll walk you home."

"No, no, you don't have to do that."

"Oh, come on." He flashed that lazy smile. "I don't want to say goodbye yet. I'm having a good time. Aren't you having a good time?"

"Yes," I admitted. "It's just..."

The truth was, I didn't want Connor to see Riverview Lane. I was ashamed of where I lived. But that was silly. He already knew I was poor. And he'd taken me to Chester's anyway.

"Come on," I said. "It's this way."

Chapter 22

We turned left on McKinley Avenue. This was a street I generally avoided, but from the diner it was the shortest way home. On the rare occasions when I found myself on McKinley Avenue, I shot up the sidewalk like a panicked bunny. There were three bars within two blocks of one another, and rough-looking men were always staggering out of them. Those men scared me. I didn't like the way they looked at me. I didn't like the things they said to me. "What's up, buttercup?" "Hey, there, honeybunch, need a ride?" "Well, ain't you a sweet thang." Ugh.

But today, with Connor by my side, I felt safe.

"Well, this is it," I said when we'd reached Riverview Lane. I had my arms crossed over my chest, my purse dangling at crotch level, as if by double-covering my private parts I could hide the ugliness of my neighborhood. "Thanks again for the fries and drink. And for walking me home."

"Yeah, no problem." He scuffed at the sidewalk with a designer sneaker. "Whew! I probably shouldn't have gotten that large cola. Can I use your bathroom?"

"Oh." My gaze slid to my shabby apartment building. "That's probably not the best idea. I'm not allowed to have boys over when my mom's at work. If she found out—"

"She won't find out. I'll be real quick."

"The apartment's probably a mess—"

"You should see my house on the maid's day off."

"There's a convenience store two blocks down," I said desperately. "It has a public restroom."

"Two blocks? Come on, Libby. This is kind of an emergency."

I looked up at him, silently begging him to drop this. Knowing he wouldn't.

"Please," he said, and I nodded in resignation.

Mr. Owens wheeled himself off the walkway to let us pass, eying us with interest but keeping his judgments to himself.

While Connor was in the bathroom, I hovered by the front door, twisting and untwisting a strand of my hair. I'd never had a boy in my apartment before. The whole atmosphere seemed different, charged with a foreign energy.

I heard the noisy flush of the toilet followed by the *shush* of running water. Connor stepped out of the bathroom, adjusting the waistband of his shorts.

"Relief," he said with a grin. He took a look around. "So this is where Libby Dawson lives."

I shoved my hands in the pockets of my shorts. "Yep."

"It's very neat."

I shrugged. It was easy to be neat when you didn't have many possessions. Still, I took Connor's words as a compliment. I was a much better housekeeper than my mother had ever been.

"Can I see the rest of the place?"

"I don't think my mom would—"

"Just a quick tour, then I'll go."

"Fine." I tossed my purse onto the couch and gestured around me. "This is the living room." I pointed right. "That's the kitchen." The kitchen and living room shared a space, a not-very-big space, separated by the kitchen counter. "You've seen the bathroom. The bedrooms are down the hall. That's pretty much it."

Connor laughed. "You call that a tour? We didn't even move!"

Before I could stop him, he had stepped into the short hallway on the far side of the living room. He bypassed the bathroom and stopped at the closed door of my mother's bedroom. "Is this your room?"

"No. Hey, don't go in there!" I said sharply as he reached for the doorknob. "That's my mom's room. She's kind of private about it."

I could not let him see that room. The bare mattress, the sparse furnishings, the absence of clutter on the dresser all screamed *nobody lives here.*

"Okay. Sorry." He continued down the hall. "Then this must be your room."

"Yeah, but you really shouldn't—"

He had already disappeared into my room. I hesitated for a moment and then moved down the hall. I stood in the doorway of my room, twisting my hair again as I watched him look around. I tried to see my room through his eyes.

I had to admit, this was the nicest room in the apartment. I'd decorated it myself, with thrift-store buys and castoffs from the neighbors. I'd painted the mismatched dresser, nightstand, and wooden bed frame the same shade of pure-white so they'd look like a set. The focal point, though, was my pale-blue and yellow comforter, which looked brand-new. Selena had let me have it for a steal and had even found a pair of curtains in the same shade of yellow.

"Nice," said Connor. "Your bed looks really comfy."

He reached for my hand and pulled me into the room. His eyes were half-closed as he gazed down at me.

"Well. Here we are. King Connor and Queen Libby." He laughed softly. "It's almost like we're married."

I flashed an uncertain smile.

"You know, you really are the hottest girl in our class," he said in a husky voice, stepping closer to me. "I'll never forget the way you looked at the dance, all fixed up."

"Oh. Thanks," I said, feeling my cheeks heat up. "Toni and her mom—"

And then his arms went around me, and his face moved toward mine, and suddenly he was kissing me.

I had never been kissed before. My initial surprise was quickly replaced by a kind of oozing relaxation as I marveled at how good it felt to be kissing Connor Tipton. All the strength ebbed out of me. I became something soft and gooey, like melted caramel drizzled over warm apple pie.

I became aware that we were moving, ever so slightly. Connor was inching me across the floor. Were we dancing again? His lips left mine and brushed my neck, and a tingle of pleasure shot through me. Our legs bumped the bed, and we toppled onto it. Connor's lips found mine again. He rolled on top of me.

Suddenly there was a loud thud from close by. We jumped like nervous cats and broke apart. I raised my head to see what had caused the thud. It was my denim purse. It had fallen off the dresser.

"Oh my God!" I cried, snapping out of the weird, melty spell I'd been under. I pushed Connor away and leapt off the bed.

"Hey, hey. Libby. What's the matter?"

"This! What we were just doing! It's—wrong!"

He sat up, smiling lazily. "Felt pretty right to me."

"No! I'm not ready for—" I gestured toward him, toward the bed. "—this!"

"Sure you are. You liked me kissing you. I could tell."

"No!" I stumbled out of the bedroom. I heard a creaking noise as Connor got off the bed. I heard his unhurried footsteps behind me.

"You have to leave," I said, yanking open the door to the hall.

He leaned against the wall, his arms folded, his gaze insolent. "What if I don't want to?"

Rage bubbled up in me, so intense it made my voice tremble. "Connor Tipton, if you don't get out of here right now, I will start screaming. I will scream and scream, and everybody in the building will come running, and somebody will call the police, and—"

Actually, I doubted anyone would come. People were always screaming in my neighborhood. Nobody ever investigated.

Connor straightened up, his eyes suddenly cold. "What's your problem? Don't you know the drill? Girls like you, tenement trash like you, you're supposed to be easy."

THE HAUNTED PURSE

"Easy?" I shrieked. "Is that what you think? Well, I'm not easy. And I am not tenement trash! My neighborhood might not be the nicest, but I'm a decent girl, and—and—you're a jerk, and if you don't leave right now—"

"Okay, okay." He raised his hands, shushing me. "I'm going." He shot me a contemptuous glance as he moved toward the door. "I can't wait to get out of here. This place is a dump. I probably picked up some disease just being here."

"Out!" I screamed, giving him a shove. I slammed the door so fast, it hit him in the butt.

Chapter 23

I slid the chain lock into place and leaned against the wall, shaking violently. "I will not end up like my mother!" I screamed to no one. "I will not end up like my mother! I will not end up like my mother!"

And then I pulled my hair so hard it hurt. Just to punish myself for thinking someone like Connor Tipton would ever want me for any honorable purpose. Tenement trash, he'd called me. How many other people saw me that way? My anger receded, replaced by the throbbing stab-wound of rejection, of hopeless inferiority.

There was a sudden pounding on my door. I let out a yelp, my nerves still jangly. I cracked the door as far as the chain would allow, peering out with one eye. There in the hall stood Mason. Today he wore a dark-blue tee shirt, green camouflage-print shorts, sunglasses, and a man-sized fedora he'd probably bought at the thrift store. His posture was bent under the heft of a gray backpack.

"Mason?" I slid the chain off and flung the door open. "What are you doing here?"

Mason's chest was heaving like he'd run up the stairs. "I heard screaming."

I raised an eyebrow. "All the way from your apartment?"

"No." He pushed up his hat, which kept sliding down his forehead. "From out front. Me and that guy in the wheelchair. He said I should make sure you were okay. Are you okay? That boy who was here, the one you were at Chester's with, he didn't hurt you, did he?"

"Chester's? How do you know—?" I broke off with a gasp. "Mason! Have you been following me?"

"Not every day. Just sometimes." He took off his sunglasses and looked up at me. "Who was that guy? Is he your boyfriend?"

I pulled him into the apartment and shut the door. "What's going on? Is this an Astound-o Man thing?"

"No. Today I'm a detective. I follow people. I look for clues."

"A detective," I mused. "What happened to Astound-o Man?'

"He's still around. I keep him right here in my backpack in case I need him. Being Astound-o Man, it gets boring sometimes. There's more to do when I'm a detective. Plus"—his eyes flicked away from mine briefly—"people don't make fun of me as much."

Mrs. Moore must be relieved, I thought, to see her son beginning to phase Astound-o Man out of his life. "Does your mom know where you are?" I asked.

"No. She's at work. I told Toni I was going to Albert's. Toni never asks questions when I go out. She's just glad to get the apartment to herself."

I lifted the brim of his hat so I could see his eyes better. "You realize I'm going to have to tell your mom about this, right? You know she doesn't like you running around town when she's not home."

He shook his head gravely. "You won't tell."

"What do you mean, I won't tell?"

He stared up at me, triumph glinting in his brown eyes. "Because if you tell on me, I'll tell on you. I'll tell how you live here all by yourself, without a mom, which is against the law because you're only fifteen."

"What the hell, Mason!" I yelled.

Mason flashed a placid smile. "See? I know how to find out stuff about people. I'm a pretty good detective, huh?"

"You're a pest, is what you are," I growled.

He slipped his sunglasses back on. "You don't tell on me, I don't tell on you. Deal?"

"Fine! Now get out of here."

After Mason left, I took a long shower and changed my clothes. I found the rose on my bedroom floor. It had probably fallen out of my hair during the kiss. It was wilted, but at least it hadn't been trampled by Connor's sturdy designer sneakers. I stuck it in a glass of water, and it perked up pretty quickly.

It wasn't until much later, when I was in bed for the night, that I realized what the denim purse had done, how it had saved me.

How could it have fallen off my dresser? I'd tossed it onto the couch when I was showing Connor the apartment.

Chapter 24

Going to school the day after my encounter with Connor was tough. I almost stayed home. We hadn't done much more than kiss, but was that what he'd told his friends? Or had he made up a wilder story, not wanting to admit he'd struck out? Clearly he'd had more than fries and soft drinks in mind when he'd followed me up the street. But had Gabe and Evan known his true intentions?

To my relief, everyone at school was acting normal, even Gabe and Evan. Nobody stared at me. Nobody whispered and pointed. Connor, of course, was ignoring me, and I ignored him right back. But I got the feeling he hadn't told anybody anything. Maybe he didn't think people would believe him. Maybe he respected me for saying no.

That same day, we had the end-of-the-year academic awards ceremony. In the individual subjects category, I received two awards, as the top sophomore student in English and math. Charlie received the phys ed award, and Tommy Sturgis got the social studies award. I was happy for them, though Tommy and I both knew the social studies award should have been mine. We'd compared history scores all year, and mine had always been a point or two higher.

Should I challenge Ms. Eckhart? No, I decided. That was a battle I wasn't up to fighting. It wasn't like I had a parent to go to bat for me. Besides, I was the only sophomore to receive two subject awards, a distinction that earned me the Sophomore Student of the Year award. I walked out of the auditorium with two embossed certificates and a gold pin.

See? I wanted to shout to Connor Tipton, who had gotten exactly zero academic awards. *Tenement trash isn't who I am. If anything, it's where I live. It's the second-hand clothes I wear. Nothing more.*

The next day I had my end-of-the-year meeting with Mr. Swartzenfelder, the guidance counselor. Mr. S was a balding man with plump, wormlike lips that parted in frequent, sales-rep smiles to reveal his big yellow teeth. He shook my hand and congratulated me on my awards. We sat across from each other at his wooden desk. A manila folder lay open in front of him.

"So tell me about your future plans, Liberty. What do you want to do with your life?"

"It's Libby," I said, totally unsurprised that he didn't remember that from last year's meeting. "For starters, I'd like to go to college."

The dingy teeth flashed. "Good, good. You're on the right track. I've been reviewing your school record, and I can see that you're an exceptional student. Always have been."

I shrugged. *Thank you* didn't seem like the right response, but I didn't know what was.

"You're definitely college material," Mr. S went on. "We just have to make sure you get there. We don't want you throwing away your potential, now do we?"

"Why would I throw away my potential?"

"Kids like you often do."

"Kids like me?" I felt myself starting to bristle.

He clasped his hands together on the desk. "You live on Riverview Lane. I gather that your parents are...how shall I put this? Of a low income status?"

"Parent," I corrected. "There's just the one. And, yeah, we're poor as shit."

I never talked that way to adults. But if he was going to stereotype me, I might as well live up to the image.

He didn't even blink. He leaned forward, regarding me soberly. "It's imperative that you keep your grades up, Libby. Your socio-economic status puts you at a disadvantage. Girls like you, even the better students, often fall in with the wrong crowd. They use drugs. They get pregnant and drop out of school. They don't live up to their potential, because they let circumstances drag them down."

I sat up very straight, like a military cadet. "I am not going to get pregnant. I don't use drugs, and I don't hang out with people who do."

"Okay, okay, that's good." He smiled again, clearly trying to unruffle my feathers. "Because Riverview Lane? That's a bad area, sad to say. But keep on the straight and narrow, keep those grades up, and you have a real shot at getting a full ride to college."

I blinked at him. "Wait, what?" I knew what *full ride* meant, but I made him explain it anyway, just to hear the words. It meant scholarships, tens of thousands of dollars' worth. It meant getting to go to college for free.

For a kid like me, that was huge.

We fleshed out the class schedule for my junior year. Before I left, Mr. S said, "Let me leave you with this thought, Libby. The world is full of successful people who came from humble beginnings. Doctors, lawyers, corporate CEOs. You have the potential to be anything you want. You just have to be willing to work for it."

That sounded like a canned speech to me, one he used on all the poor-as-shit kids. But I didn't hold it against him, because I heard the truth in it.

Chapter 25

Toni and Mason spent the first week of summer vacation with their dad. Toni threw a major fit but couldn't get out of it.

It was a long week for me. I spent a lot of time reading and cleaned the apartment so thoroughly it gleamed. At least once a day I pored over the newspaper, searching for the clue that had to be there, but I never found anything. Ghost Girl hadn't provided any new clues. I wondered if she was waiting for me to figure out this one first.

Thursday morning, I walked to the library to get something new to read. First, though, I went to the park and swiped a big pink flower from a bush. Then I headed up Dupont Street and stopped in front of a tiny brick house with a sign above the door that said *Jon Horowitz, DDS*. I tossed the flower into the yard and stood on the sidewalk for a minute, my head bowed.

This building hadn't always been a dentist's office. Years ago it had been a home, and it held memories for me—warm, blurry memories of the only true grandma I'd ever known. Mrs. Garcia. I didn't know what cemetery she was buried in, so this was where I came to pay my respects.

Mrs. Garcia had been my on-again, off-again babysitter when I was little. I kept getting kicked out of day care centers because my mother could never manage to pick me up on time. Or pay the monthly tuition bill.

Mrs. Garcia was a widow, and I'd been just three when we met her at a local food bank. When my mother griped about how the latest day care center had wronged us, Mrs. Garcia said she'd be happy to babysit anytime we needed her.

I had a feeling my mother hadn't paid *her* on time either, but she never kicked me out. The two of us bonded instantly. Mrs. Garcia's daughter and the daughter's husband and their little boy lived in Germany, so she hardly ever got to see them. All the love that should have been showered on that grandchild came my way instead.

Mrs. Garcia would sit on the floor and play games with me. In her lilting Hispanic voice she told me stories about Jesus, whose portrait hung in her living room. She kept packages of shortbread cookies in her cupboard because she knew I liked them. And, unlike my real grandmother, she never pinched me or even yelled at me.

Once I started school, she was there to meet the school bus every afternoon. Nights when my mother worked late, I slept at her house, in the tiny spare bedroom under the eaves. This went on until I was in second grade, when Mrs. Garcia died—suddenly, inconceivably—of a heart attack.

My mother had no patience for the tears of a grief-stricken seven-year-old. "Oh, stop crying over that worthless old bag," she'd say furiously. Mrs. Garcia had left her in the lurch, and she couldn't forgive that.

After that, there were other babysitters and a few after-school programs, but none of them lasted. When I was eight, my mother decided I was old enough to be home alone.

THE HAUNTED PURSE

I still grieved for Mrs. Garcia. I didn't know if she could see me from wherever she was now, but if she could, I wanted her to be proud of me.

At the library I slid *1984* down the return slot and pulled *A Prayer for Owen Meany* off a fiction shelf. Both books were on the summer reading list for my English honors program. To get to the checkout counter, I had to pass the seating area near the front windows. A couple of old men sat there reading newspapers.

Newspapers.

Newspapers!

Suddenly I knew why Ghost Girl had left that copy of *The Ashton Times* in my purse. There were no clues hidden among all that modern-day news. No, she was trying to guide me to another newspaper, a much older one. Maybe she couldn't manifest an actual newspaper from twenty years ago, so she'd given me a more recent one in the hope that I'd make the connection and do the legwork myself. It had taken a while, but I'd finally figured things out. And now that I had, it seemed so obvious. Why hadn't I thought of checking old newspapers sooner?

I stepped up to the counter. The clerk, a slender Black lady named Jane, was humming a merry tune like she'd never heard the rule about keeping quiet in libraries.

"Oh, hey, Libby."

The library was another place where they knew me by name.

I handed over the book and my library card, and Jane, still humming, clacked away on her computer keyboard.

119

"Got a question, Jane," I said. "Those newspapers by the windows, the ones the library subscribes to? How long do you keep them?"

Jane tore her eyes away from the computer screen long enough to glance at me. "About a month."

"So you don't have really old ones, like from twenty years ago?"

"No, we have them. They'd be on microfilm. Is there something you need to look up?"

"Yeah, but it happened in Rosedale. Would it be in the Ashton newspaper?"

"Absolutely. The Ashton Times covers news from all over the tri-county area."

She studied her computer screen for a few moments and then hit the enter key. The printer behind her started up with a gasp. "But if you're looking for articles from twenty years ago, keep in mind that Rosedale wasn't called Rosedale back then. It was known as Burnt."

I blinked in surprise. "Burnt? As in *somebody accidentally touched a hot iron*?"

"Burnt as in *burnt to the ground*." Jane pulled the checkout receipt from her printer and slipped it inside the cover of *A Prayer for Owen Meany*. "Rosedale started out as a mining settlement. Burned down twice in its early days. By the time it became a town, everybody was calling it Burnt. The name stuck for a long time. Then, in 2008, a new mayor took office and decided we needed a name with a more positive connotation." She handed *Owen Meany* to me. "I lived there at the time. Had to fill out a bunch of address change forms."

Now I knew why Toni had come up empty when researching missing person cases in Rosedale. Twenty years ago, Rosedale hadn't existed, at least not by that name.

"Our intern can help you with the microfilm," said Jane. "Let me give him a buzz."

A few minutes later I was on the second floor of the library, sitting in front of a microfilm reader, which looked like a morbidly obese computer monitor. Brian, the library's college intern, showed me how to operate it.

"You just stick the film in *here* and turn these knobs *here* to scroll up or down. If you want to print something, press this button. The printer is over there."

"Thanks, Brian." I scooched my butt around to get comfy in the padded office chair and started scrolling through the grainy images of newspaper pages.

According to Mrs. Atkins, the girl had gone missing during the summer. I decided to start with the May 15 edition of *The Ashton Times* and work my way forward. I pulled up the front page and began scrolling.

I didn't find what I was looking for until I got to July 20. The story was on the front page of the Local News section. I drew in a tremulous breath and leaned close to read.

Chapter 26

Burnt teen reported missing

Police are searching for a fifteen-year-old girl from Burnt who went missing after leaving her home Monday evening.

Crystal Callahan is described as Caucasian with long, light-brown hair and hazel eyes. She is five foot four and weighs 105 pounds. She was last seen wearing navy-blue shorts and a blue-and-white-striped tee shirt.

According to the girl's mother, Mrs. Mae Wittmeyer, Crystal left home around 6 p.m. Monday, saying she was meeting a friend. However, the friend later told police that the two girls had not made plans to get together that evening.

Anyone who has seen Crystal or has information about her whereabouts is urged to contact the Burnt Police Department.

A black-and-white photo accompanied the article—a school picture, judging by the speckled background. The girl was even prettier up close, her almond-shaped eyes well positioned below perfectly arched brows, the small nose perched above a set of straight white teeth. In this photo, her hair flowed to her shoulders.

"Crystal Callahan." I said the name aloud, letting the syllables melt in my mouth like meringue.

Ghost Girl had a name. She was real.

When I got back to my apartment building, Mr. Owens was parked in the bald patch of dirt we called a front yard, slouched so low that I feared he would slide out of his wheelchair. He looked up and grunted at me.

"Mrs. Carlson is looking for you."

I frowned. "Mrs. Carlson? What does she want?"

"Wouldn't know." He went back to staring out at the street.

Mrs. Carlson and her daughter, Alyssa, lived in my apartment building, one floor below me. Like Mrs. Moore, Mrs. Carlson was a divorced mom who lived where she did because of the low rent. But you could tell that she considered Alyssa and herself too good for Riverview Lane. Her resolute mouth and sensible black shoes told the world she intended to walk out of this neighborhood just as soon as she could, headed for someplace better.

Alyssa went to school with Toni and me, but we didn't know her that well. We'd invited her to accompany us to the thrift store a couple of times, but her mom always said no. Alyssa wasn't permitted to attend Louie's and Charlie's sleepovers either, because Mrs. Carlson didn't know their parents and was afraid there might be guns in their houses. Or drugs. Or a vicious dog. Or a child-molesting uncle.

Evenings and weekends, Mrs. Carlson and Alyssa were always together. Toni and I sometimes saw them walking through town, Alyssa trailing her mother like a balky terrier on a leash. I got the feeling that Mrs. Carlson regarded the two of them as a best-friends mother-daughter duo, whereas Alyssa just wanted to be free to live her life. One of these days, I thought, Alyssa was going to snap. She'd sneak out of the apartment and end up smoking pot, robbing a convenience store, and getting knocked up. All in the same night.

I rapped on the Carlsons' door. It opened a crack, and a staring brown eyeball appeared, as menacing as a gun barrel. Then the door swung wide open to reveal a smiling Mrs. Carlson. She looked so benign and friendly, I had to wonder whose demon eyeball I'd just seen.

"Libby, hi! Please, come in."

She ushered me to the kitchen, where Alyssa, a hunched, narrow girl with hair the same tarnished-penny shade as her mother's, was seated at the table. Spread out in front of her was an open textbook and several sheets of notebook paper, one of which was covered with Alyssa's tight, tiny scrawl.

Alyssa and I exchanged the awkward hellos of two people who should have been friends but weren't. I slid into an empty chair. Mrs. Carlson set a glass of orange juice in front of me without asking me if I wanted it.

"Your timing is perfect," she said. "Alyssa's doing her homework."

"Homework!" I said. "It's summer vacation."

Alyssa opened her mouth to speak, but her mother beat her to it. "Alyssa's enrolled in a summer school class. She didn't do so well with geometry, so they're making her retake it."

Alyssa sighed tragically. Her eyes were abnormally moist—but then they always looked that way, as if she'd bitten her tongue and it was still stinging.

"This is why I wanted to talk to you." Mrs. Carlson sat across from me and folded her hands primly on the table. "Alyssa told me about the awards you got at school. She said you were named student of the year. That is just so impressive."

"Oh. Thank you," I said, with a modest bob of my head. I took a swig of my orange juice.

"I have a proposition for you," Mrs. Carlson said. "I'd like to offer you a job."

I set my glass down with more force than I'd intended. Orange juice sloshed upward but stayed within the confines of the glass. "A job?"

"I'd like you to tutor Alyssa. I'll pay you fifteen dollars an hour. I'm thinking three one-hour sessions a week for six weeks."

I did the math. Six weeks at forty-five dollars a week worked out to two hundred and seventy dollars. That would go a long way at the thrift store! But the thrift store wasn't where I would go. Once my wallet fattened up, I'd be doing my shopping at the mall.

"Is this really necessary?" Alyssa asked. Her voice sounded strained, like she was being gently strangled. "I'm doing fine. I got a C plus on the quiz yesterday."

"Exactly," said Mrs. Carlson. "A bright girl like you should be making A's."

"But fifteen dollars an hour? How can you afford that?"

Mrs. Carlson reached over to pat her daughter's arm. "Don't you worry about that. I can pick up extra shifts at the hospital.

"I'm a nurse," she told me, though I already knew this, having seen her coming and going in her blue cotton scrubs. "An LPN. For now, anyway. I'm working on a bachelor's degree in registered nursing. RNs make more than LPNs, you see. Of course, I'd be doing just fine if that deadbeat father of Alyssa's was better about paying child support." She chuckled good-naturedly, but darker emotions swirled in her eyes—fury, resentment, loathing.

I smiled tightly and glanced around the apartment. This was the first time I'd been inside. Though furnished shabbily, the place was tidy and pristine—obsessively-compulsively so, it seemed to me. Not a single dirty dish sat on the kitchen counter. The living room was so clutter-free, it looked like a stage set. Only the disorder on the kitchen table suggested that not everything was bliss and perfection in the Carlson household.

"Remember to ask her about Jared," Alyssa said.

"Right," said Mrs. Carlson. "Libby, you know the Berzanskys, don't you?"

"I know Jared."

Jared Berzansky usually sat in front of Toni and me on the school bus. He was a big, beefy kid with a booming voice, and like Charlie, he tended to intimidate people. But Toni and I got along with him just fine. Especially Toni. In fact, toward the end of the school year, it had seemed to me that Jared and Toni weren't chatting so much as flirting.

"Jared and Alyssa are in the same summer geometry class," said Mrs. Carlson. "I work with Jared's dad, and he's looking for a tutor, too. Same deal—three hours a week, fifteen bucks an hour. Can I give him your number?"

And just like that, my salary doubled.

"You can start now if you'd like," said Mrs. Carlson. "Alyssa could probably use some help with her homework."

I walked out of their apartment fifteen bucks richer.

That evening as I was finishing the dishes, I heard a metallic rattle from the hall. The door swung open, and in walked my mother.

THE HAUNTED PURSE

She waved an arm ambiguously—did it mean *hello* or *don't bug me?*—and went into the bathroom, slamming the door behind her. She was in there for maybe five minutes. Then she screeched, "Oh my God. Oh, shit, shit, shit!"

I scurried down the hall and rapped on the bathroom door. "What's going on in there? Are you okay?"

"No." She opened the door. She was holding a slender object that looked like a digital thermometer.

"Are you sick? Do you have a fever?" I asked.

"No, you idiot. This is a pregnancy test. I'm pregnant!"

Chapter 27

My mother flung the pregnancy test toward the waste basket. It bounced off the rim and skidded behind the toilet. She pushed past me without so much as a *pardon me* and headed into the living room, where she belly-flopped onto the couch.

I lowered myself into the flaccid depths of our one and only easy chair, eying her prone body. "Are you sure?"

"Yes, I'm sure!" Her voice was muffled by the lumpy maroon couch pillow. "I got a plus sign. Plus means pregnant. Go see for yourself if you don't believe me."

"I believe you," I said. I folded my hands in my lap. "So, when would you be having this baby?"

"I don't know. I might be three months along. Maybe four. My period's never been regular. I don't even keep track. But yesterday it hit me how I haven't had one for a while."

She sat up, swiping her hair out of her eyes. "Arthur is going to freak. He is going to have a shit fit."

"Maybe not," I said. "It's his baby, too. He might be happy about it."

She looked at me sharply, and I cringed as I waited for her to call me an idiot again. But all she said was, "Trust me, he will not be happy."

"Okay, maybe not at first. But he'll get used to the idea."

"No! He's going to dump me. I just know it. Are you ready to get your old roommate back?" She attempted a laugh, but it turned into a sob. "Ready to share your room with a new little brother or sister?"

THE HAUNTED PURSE

My heart sank at the thought, and I realized that as much as I lamented my mother's chronic absence, I was far happier when she wasn't around.

"Arthur doesn't even know about *you*," my mother said, her voice a teary warble. "When he finds out I'm pregnant *and* I have a fourteen-year-old—"

"Fifteen-year-old," I corrected.

"And I'm going to get fat again. God, I hate that!"

Tears spilled out of her eyes. She stood up, plastering her silky shirt against her stomach. "Look. I'm already showing."

"Uh, not really," I said. Her usually concave stomach was now flat. But nobody would have suspected pregnancy.

"I should get rid of it." She threw me a rueful glance. "I almost did that with you. But I kept putting it off, and then they wouldn't let me because it was too late."

I'd heard that story so many times, it had lost its power to hurt me. But I felt a rush of pity for the innocent creature growing in my mother's belly. I wasn't sure which fate was worse—having your life brutally snuffed out, or being born to a mother who didn't want you.

"Christ. I'm going to be late for work," she muttered, striding to the door.

"Oh." I stood up. "So you don't want...anything else?"

"What? No, I just came to use the bathroom. I can't take a pregnancy test at home. If that nosy housekeeper Lily got hold of it, the whole damn world would know. Same deal at work. No privacy."

The door slammed before I could even say goodbye.

Chapter 28

Crystal had started leaving me little gifts. A stub of a pencil, striped neon-pink and orange. A half-roll of hard cherry candies covered in lint. A tiny brown purse, just the right size for a twelve-inch fashion doll. I had a feeling that some of these items had been in the purse long ago, and I was touched that she wanted me to have them. Maybe she was rewarding me for figuring out the newspaper clue.

The purse seemed to be growing more active. Restless, almost. I wondered if Crystal's ghost was somehow drawing strength from my belief in her, my commitment to helping her.

She came to me in dreams, a friend, a blood sister. We roamed the downtown streets, propelled by the mighty horsepower of our own legs. We called boys we liked and hung up when they answered. We frolicked together in sunlit oceans, letting the waves pummel us like liquid wind—and somehow I knew what that felt like.

We had sleepovers. We pinky-swore to be best friends forever.

She smelled like the purse, like the perfume I'd had so briefly and then lost. Sometimes in the mornings as I swam up out of sleep, I could smell her. But the scent always vanished with an almost audible pop as I opened my eyes.

Oh, Crystal. Where are you? What happened to you?

Toni got back on Saturday evening, a day early. Little Eliot had an ear infection, a devastating medical crisis that required the undivided attention of both parents. That was how Toni put it, anyway. She came over to my place on Sunday afternoon. We sat at the kitchen table drinking lemonade I'd made from a powdered mix.

According to Toni, the visit with her dad hadn't been all bad. At the beginning of the week, she, Mason, and Mr. Moore had left Jan and the twins behind and gone off on a four-day vacation that included an afternoon at the beach, a day at an amusement park, a visit to a museum, and a hike to a waterfall. Those had been the good days.

Then they'd returned to Mr. Moore's house for the remaining days.

"Jan hates me. She really, truly hates me," Toni declared.

"I'm sure that's not true," I said, though I really had no way of knowing. I'd never met Jan. Or Mr. Moore, for that matter.

"She can't stand it when Mason and me are there. You know where she was most of the time? In her bedroom with the door shut. She claimed she had a headache. Seriously? A three-day headache that just happened to flare up on the exact days of our visit? What are the chances?"

"Have you talked to your dad about this?"

"Yeah. He says Jan's an introvert. Having visitors stresses her out. She needs lots of alone time to—what did he call it? 'Recharge her battery.' "

"Well, she spent *some* time with you, right?"

"I mean, we all had dinner together every night. One afternoon Dad and Jan and Mason and me played board games while the twins were napping. That's about it."

I thought this over. "So you're upset that you didn't get to spend more time with her?"

"Hell, no. I don't want to spend time with that bitch."

I almost laughed. Instead, I sat quietly, letting her comment hang in the air. After a few seconds, she let out a long, unhappy sigh.

"Look, I don't love her, okay? And she doesn't love me. We're not even related. She's just some woman who married my dad."

"Yes," I said, pouncing on that. "She married your dad. And he loves all of you. It probably kills him that you don't get along. Maybe you should try harder, for his sake."

She swirled her straw violently through her lemonade, making the ice cubes tinkle like wind chimes in a storm. "Why should *I* try harder? Jan should be the one to do that. She's the grown-up."

"You should all try," I said. "I'm sure Jan can tell that you don't like her. She's probably scared to even talk to you. Why don't you reach out to her, try to be friends? Like, sometime when you're visiting and she's shut in her room, knock on the door and say, 'Hey, I just baked some cookies. Why don't you come out and have some?' "

"I don't bake," Toni said scornfully.

"Well, just talk to her, then. Ask her questions about herself. Share something personal."

"Personal?" She spat the word out.

"Yeah, you know. Have a heart-to-heart. Try to form a bond."

Toni was picking up her glass and setting it down at random spots on her napkin, creating a tangled web of damp rings. She shot me a dark look from beneath her eyelashes and said, "I wish you'd stop doing that."

"Doing what?"

"Acting wiser than your years. It's annoying."

I settled back in my chair. "Hey, I'm just trying to help."

"Well, thank you for that."

I couldn't tell if she was being sincere or sarcastic.

"Enough about Jan," Toni said. "What's new with you? Did you miss me? What did you do all week?"

"What did I do all week?" I squinted into the empty space above her head as if trying to remember. "Well, I got a job—two, actually. Oh, and I dug up a newspaper article about the missing girl. Her name is Crystal."

Toni's eyes bulged. "Why didn't you say so? Tell me everything!"

I filled her in on my tutoring gigs and then fetched the article about Crystal's disappearance. Toni snatched it out of my hand.

"This is good," she said when she'd finished reading. "Really good. Now we have some names to work with. Crystal Callahan. Mae Wittmeyer. Weird that their last names are different, though."

"Yeah, I'm guessing Crystal's parents got divorced and then her mom married somebody else."

"So what do we do now?"

"Track down the mom."

"And then what?"

"Tell her we found a picture of Crystal in a thrift store purse. Ask if she wants it back. But hopefully we'll be able to get some information out of her, stuff that might help us with the case."

We agreed that an internet search would be the best way to find Mae Wittmeyer. I didn't have a computer, so Toni jogged back to her apartment to get her mother's laptop ("She's at work; she'll never know, and I bribed Mason not to tell"). We found a white pages directory, and Toni entered Mae's name, town, and state in the search box.

We got results, but they weren't helpful. The most important details—address, phone number, and email address—had been strategically redacted.

Mae Wittmeyer, ### Xxxxxx Street, Ashton, OH

*Addresses (current and former): Ashton, OH * Burnt, OH * Hoboken, NJ*

Related to: Peter Wittmeyer, Lauren Appelbaum, Crystal Callahan

Phone numbers: 740-###-####, 740-###-####

Email address: xxxxxxxxxxx@xxxxx.com

"At least we know this is the right Mae Wittmeyer," I said, trying to stay hopeful. "Though I'm surprised Crystal's name is listed, considering how long she's been missing."

"Peter Wittmeyer," mused Toni. "That's the Car King guy. Do you think him and Mae are married?"

"Mrs. Atkins did say the dad owned a local business. I think he might be the stepdad, though."

When Toni clicked on "Unlock Mae's full report," a pricing page came up.

"Shit," she said. "We can't get the good stuff unless we pay."

A one-time price of $11.99 included all contact information and a background report for a single record, while a $5.99 monthly subscription provided access to twenty records each month. There was also a five-day trial membership that cost $1.00. That was the link Toni clicked on. She said she would put it on her mom's credit card. She didn't have the card with her, but all the information was stored on the laptop.

"I'll just have to remember to cancel before the five days are up. When Mom wonders about the charge, I'll tell her it was Mason playing detective. He'll deny it, but she won't believe him."

"Aw. Poor Mason," I said. It didn't seem fair to frame him.

Toni gave me a withering look. "Don't 'Poor Mason' me. The kid's a jerk. He has it coming."

We flipped a coin to see who would make the call. I won—or lost, depending on how you looked at it.

My apartment had a landline phone, which I was pretty sure my mother had forgotten about. I kept it hidden behind the couch so she wouldn't notice it and take it away. It was the old-fashioned kind, with a receiver tethered to the base and the base wired into the wall. I would have loved to have a cordless model or, better yet, a cell phone, but there was no way I could afford an expenditure like that. Up until now, anyway. My tutoring gigs were opening up a whole new world of purchasing possibilities.

I set the phone on the coffee table and dialed the first number in Mae's record.

"Hello?" said a gruff male voice.

That took me by surprise. "Um...hi. Is this—is this Peter Wittmeyer?"

"Speaking."

"I'm trying to reach Mae Wittmeyer. Is she there?"

There was a short silence. "Who's calling?"

I glanced uneasily at Toni, who nodded her encouragement. "My name is Libby Dawson, and I—"

"Who?"

"Libby Dawson."

"Olivia Dawson?"

"No, Libby. L-I-B-B-Y. If I could just speak with Mae—"

"What do you want with Mae?"

"Um..." My hands were getting sweaty. I had to tighten my grip on the phone to keep it from slipping. "Actually, I'm doing research on Crystal's disappearance, and I just wanted to—"

"Research!" The word exploded in my ear. "So you're a reporter."

"No, no, I just—"

"How *dare* you," Peter Wittmeyer snarled in my ear. "Why can't you people leave us alone? Do you have any idea how painful it is to have my stepdaughter's disappearance dredged up every couple of years by some rookie reporter looking to titillate readers with a sensationalistic cold-case story? What you're doing is harassment, young lady, and I will file charges if it continues."

"I'm not a reporter. I'm fifteen, and I just wanted to see if—" I said in a rush, but Peter Wittmeyer had already hung up.

"Wow," I said, as I placed the receiver on its base and wiped my sweaty hands on my shorts. "Peter Wittmeyer is *mean*."

Chapter 29

"Why'd you tell Peter Wittmeyer you were researching Crystal's disappearance?" Toni asked as she refilled our lemonade glasses for the third time.

"I didn't mean to. I was nervous, and it just came out."

"Well, you sure made him mad."

The directory record for Mae Wittmeyer included her address: 723 Regent Street, Ashton, Ohio.

"That's on the Hilltop," Toni said. "We should go there and talk to them in person."

I wrinkled my nose. I had no desire to insert my inner-city self into a ritzy Hilltop neighborhood. Plus, I didn't think Peter Wittmeyer would be any nicer in person.

"Let's wait a while and try to call back," I said. "Maybe Mae will answer. She's the one I want to talk to, not him. He's just the stepdad."

It was nearly five o'clock and we were starving, so I heated up a can of condensed chicken noodle soup and opened a pack of saltine crackers. I dug right into the soup while Toni picked the tiny chunks of meat out of her bowl and deposited them on a saucer, rejects that would not be consumed. She said they looked like pieces of rectum.

"Peter Wittmeyer," she mused. "Did you ever see his commercial on TV?" She lowered her voice to a gravelly growl. " 'I'm Peter Wittmeyer, owner and general manager of Wittmeyer's Auto Sales, and I guarantee we'll give you a square deal every time.' " She cleared her throat, reverting to her girl-voice. "Then he draws that square in the air with his hands?"

I shook my head. I hadn't seen the commercial, mainly because I didn't watch much TV. I had the cheapest cable package, which meant I got only a smattering of channels. It was hard to find shows worth watching, so most nights I just curled up with a book.

"Anyway," said Toni. "He's a lot nicer on TV."

"Of course he's nice on TV. He's trying to get people to buy his cars."

After we did the dishes, Toni dialed Mae Wittmeyer's number again. I watched her expression change from resolute to surprised to outraged.

"That blistering bucket of pus!" she said, slamming down the receiver. "He blocked your number."

"You wanna try calling from your place?"

"No, he'll just block that number, too."

"But—"

"If we want to talk to Mae, we have to go see her. We just have to do it when the almighty Car King isn't around."

I let out a soft, defeated sigh. When Toni got this determined, there was no arguing with her. We were going to the Hilltop whether I liked it or not.

We made plans for Thursday afternoon.

Chapter 30

On Thursday afternoon I slipped on my sparkly pink tee shirt and a pair of gray twill shorts that I'd found at the thrift store with the original tags still attached. They weren't designer clothes by any means, but at least they didn't scream *tenement trash*.

At two o'clock I was out on the sidewalk, the denim purse slung over my shoulder. While I waited for Toni, I paced up and down the sidewalk, kicking litter into the gutter.

I spotted something tiny and white at the edge of the sidewalk, its purity a contrast to the mottled gray concrete beneath it. I bent down and picked it up. It was a doll shoe, the kind of open-toed high heel meant to be worn with a formal gown. If I was the fanciful type, I might have thought a twelve-inch-tall Cinderella had lost her shoe and it had stayed lost.

What would have happened, I wondered, if the fairytale had gone that way? What if the prince had never found the lost shoe, or the girl who'd stolen his heart? Would Cinderella have wasted her life slaving away for a stepfamily who despised her?

No, I decided. Somehow she would have gotten away. She would have made a good life for herself—one that might or might not have included a prince.

I took a couple of steps up the street and laid the shoe on top of a fire hydrant. Maybe the little girl who'd lost it would come back this way and spot it. More likely not. Chances were, the next hard rain would wash it into the gutter, and from there it would be swept into a sewer. Already this tiny shoe was forever lost to its owner.

I turned to see Toni jogging up the sidewalk. I opened my mouth to ask what had taken her so long, but she was already talking.

"What are you doing out here? I tried to call you, like, five times. I can't go right now. Mom had to work late, so I have to watch Mason. We'll have to wait till after dinner."

"After dinner? But Peter will probably be home then."

"Maybe not. It's Thursday, remember?"

"Thursday? Oh, right." Every Thursday, all the downtown businesses stayed open until eight p.m.

"Or we could wait till next week. My mom's working a later shift starting Monday, so I'll be free in the morning."

I thought that over. "No, let's do it today." Now that I'd committed to going to the Hilltop, I just wanted to get it over with.

Chapter 31

"We have to make sure we're back here by seven twenty-five," Toni said. "That's when the last bus leaves."

That didn't give us much time. It was already a little after six.

The bus had dropped us off at the western end of Kenmore Borough, a commercial district that boasted a handful of upscale boutiques, two gas stations, a couple of restaurants, an ice cream parlor, and an L-shaped shopping plaza that contained a mega grocery store and a bunch of smaller shops. We bypassed all that and walked east, into the heart of the residential area.

All the houses were huge. I wanted to call them mansions but wasn't sure that was correct. Where was the dividing line between *large house* and *mansion*? Twelve rooms? Fifteen? Twenty?

"How do you know where you're going?" I asked as we race-walked around a corner. I gawked at the multi-gabled brick behemoth we were passing. It seemed to be frowning at me. All the houses were. *You don't belong here*, they said. They didn't seem particularly friendly to each other, either. Each one was centered on a green lot the size of a horse pasture, so far from its nearest neighbor that the residents would have had to use megaphones to talk to each other. If they even wanted to talk. Tall fences separated most of the houses.

"Mom used to have a friend who lived up here. Sometimes when we visited, I'd go out for a walk. That's where Jade lives," she said, pointing to a stone-fronted monstrosity with a circular fountain in the front yard.

"Let's go faster," I said, ducking my head.

We walked on. It seemed weird that almost nobody was outside on this summer evening. But it was hot. Maybe rich people didn't like to sweat.

"Regent Street," Toni announced at the next intersection. We turned left and found 723 in the middle of the block. Set back from the street, the house was a big, beautiful tan brick structure with coffee-brown shutters and lots of gleaming windows. Trees lined the front yard, their trunks as straight and evenly spaced as bars on a jail cell.

We glanced at each other uncertainly. Up until now, we hadn't been nervous. Suddenly, we were.

"You got the picture of Crystal?" Toni asked.

"Right here." I patted my purse.

Her gaze moved to the house. "You think Mae's home?"

"There's no way to know."

"I just hope Peter Wittmeyer isn't here."

"You said he wouldn't be," I reminded her.

"I said *probably*. Just because the car place is open late doesn't mean he has to stay. He's the boss. He can leave whenever he wants."

"Toni!" I said in exasperation. "I only agreed to do this because you said—"

But she was already striding down the driveway. "There's a window on the side of the garage. Let's see if the Car King's car is in there."

"What? No!" I ran up and grabbed her arm. "Let's just go up to the door. They've probably seen us coming."

She squirmed out of my grasp. "Look at this place. If anybody's home, do you think they're standing around staring out windows? No! They're probably watching movies in their media room or working out in their exercise room, or doing whatever else rich people do inside their fancy-shmancy houses."

"We can't just march up there and start looking in windows!"

"It's one window. It'll take, like, two seconds."

"But what if—"

"Libby! Grow some balls! God, you're such a baby."

"You know what? Do what you want," I said angrily. "You always do. But just so you know—I am not getting in trouble over this. If somebody comes outside and wants to know what you're doing, I'm out of here. You'll be on your own."

"Okay, whatever," she said, rolling her eyes as though *I* was the unreasonable one. She left the driveway and headed into the side yard, which sloped gently downward as it approached the backyard. I felt exposed standing in the middle of the driveway, so I darted after her, crouching low like somebody on a SWAT team. I didn't stop at the garage, though, but continued to the rear corner of the house.

I took a look around the backyard. Directly in front of me was a rectangular in-ground swimming pool with a curvy slide at the far end. A large deck extended from the rear of the house, overlooking the pool. Across the yard was a big, square patch consisting of orderly green rows, obviously a vegetable garden. A six-foot-high white vinyl fence surrounded the property on three sides, providing privacy.

I planted myself at the corner of the house, keeping Toni in sight. But I was ready to bolt at a moment's notice.

Toni pressed her face to the garage window, her hands cupped around her eyes. "Crap. The curtains are closed. I can't see a thing. Who puts curtains in a garage?"

She took a step back, surveying the window. Then she put both hands on the lower pane and pushed, grunting a little. With a jerk, the window slid upward.

"Toni, no!" I whispered. There was no point in saying it louder. She wouldn't have listened even if she'd heard me.

Toni bent at the waist and thrust her upper body through the open window. A few seconds later, she wriggled back out, her cornrows in disarray.

"Well, there's only one car in there, and it's not the Car King's car." She glanced around. "Libby?"

I waved solemnly from the rear corner of the house. Toni clucked in irritation. "What are you doing back there?"

Before I could reply, a car's motor purred alarmingly close by. I couldn't see the driveway from where I was, but Toni could. She whirled in that direction with a gasp. The motor shut off abruptly. A car door slammed.

"Hey!" a male voice yelled. "What the hell are you doing in my yard?"

Panic erupted in my chest and spread through me like a quick-acting drug. I dashed into the backyard, glancing around wildly. There was no escape here because of the fence. My only option was to find a place to hide.

THE HAUNTED PURSE

Directly below the deck was an outdoor storage room, its walls made of latticed wood strips. I skirted this structure until I found a door. Once inside, I threaded my way past a pile of inflated swimming pool rafts, a jumbled collection of lawn chairs, a riding lawnmower, a coiled-up garden hose, and a stack of firewood. I crouched behind a snow blower, clutching my purse to my chest and breathing in ragged gasps.

The Wittmeyers' yard was visible through the gaps in the lattice. I caught a movement to my right. There went Toni sprinting toward the fence in the side yard, her cornrows streaming behind her. She leapt up and grabbed the top of the white vinyl fence, her short legs scrambling as she tried to scale the slick surface. She clung there for a few seconds and then dropped back to the ground. Immediately, she got up and jumped again—frantically, like a trapped fly buzzing against a windowpane. Again she fell. The fence was too high, she was too short, and she didn't have the upper body strength to hurl herself over the top.

A sob of horror rose in my throat. I clamped a hand over my mouth to stifle it.

A man came into view, presumably Peter Wittmeyer. He strode toward the fence, barking into a cell phone. "Yes, a trespasser. A young girl. Caught her breaking into my garage. Seven twenty-three Regent Street. Can you send an officer right away?"

Chapter 32

The police came. I couldn't see their car, but the flashing red and blue lights were reflected in the shiny surface of the side-yard fence. All the action was taking place out front, too far away for me to hear anything. After maybe fifteen minutes, the lights stopped flashing, and I heard the police car drive away. I figured Toni was inside, on her way to jail or reform school or wherever else they took fifteen-year-old criminals.

A wave of relief washed over me. I'd been worried that Toni would rat me out, that the police would storm the backyard looking for me. The fact that they'd driven away without doing that suggested that Toni hadn't mentioned me. I felt a rush of gratitude toward her.

It was too bad Toni was in trouble. It really was. But for me the trouble would have been much worse.

If the police had caught me, the first thing they would have done was try to contact my mother. Good luck with that! Even I didn't know how to reach her. I didn't know Arthur's phone number, or even his last name. And my mother had never given me her work number because she claimed she wasn't allowed to get calls at the nightclub.

The police weren't stupid. They would have figured things out and turned me over to Child Protective Services. Within a day or two I'd've have been living with strangers, probably in a whole different school district. Sharing a cramped bedroom with some other unwanted kid.

THE HAUNTED PURSE

Anyway, I wasn't out of the woods yet. I was still trapped under the Wittmeyers' deck. At some point I was going to have to make my way back to the street. The thought made me shudder; I did not want to risk an encounter with Peter Wittmeyer. Of course, if I waited till dark, I could probably slip away unseen. The bad news was, there would be no more buses to the downtown area. I was going to have to walk home, a distance of maybe four miles. In the dark. Through some pretty unsavory neighborhoods, including my own.

I inhaled deeply, drawing in the intermingled smell of raw earth and swimming pool chemicals. Well, if I was going to be here for a while, I might as well get comfy. At least this enclosure was cool, almost like a basement. I spotted a folded plastic tarp and laid it on the bare ground behind the snow blower. I lowered myself onto it, situating my denim purse on my lap like a small child. It felt good to sit down. I could only hope bugs wouldn't crawl up my shorts.

I leaned against the foundation of the house, the cement cooling my back through my tee shirt. Now that I had a plan, I felt calmer. Relaxed. Sleepy, even, now that the adrenaline rush had subsided...

I didn't realize I'd dozed off until I was jolted awake by a clomping noise from above. Someone was walking across the deck. The footsteps thudded down the stairs, and someone stepped into the yard.

Peter Wittmeyer. The man who'd yelled at me on the phone. The man who'd called the police on Toni.

I rose up on my knees, hugging my purse to my stomach as I stared in fascination. He stood at the edge of the pool, his posture tall and proud, like a land baron surveying his property.

He turned his head to the right and then to the left, displaying a profile as sharp as a hawk's. Because he was shirtless, I thought maybe he was going to take a swim. Instead, he turned and started walking back toward the house. Straight toward my hiding place.

I gasped and ducked behind the snow blower. The door of the latticed room creaked open. I squeezed my eyes shut and held my breath. My leg itched, but I didn't dare reach down to scratch it.

I heard rummaging noises from the front of the structure, clanks and clunks and a heavier thump as something fell. Then the door banged shut. I waited a minute and then rose up, peering through the latticework into the backyard.

Peter Wittmeyer was cleaning his pool. He held a long pole with a shallow net on the end, and he was using it to skim debris from the surface of the water. I watched as he repeatedly swirled the net across the pool and then tapped it on the ground to dislodge the gunk. There was a rhythm to the process that I found hypnotic. *Swirl, lift, tap, tap. Swirl, lift, tap, tap*. When he was done, he let the net clatter down on the concrete that framed the pool. He turned toward the house, his hands on his hips as he gazed up at the deck. I took this opportunity to study him.

He was, I guessed, around sixty, a tall, muscular man with short gray hair that was thinning on top. He projected an air of authority, the kind you'd see in an army commander or a police sergeant. There was something inscrutable in his expression that made me wonder what secrets he kept.

THE HAUNTED PURSE

Something crept down my forehead. I swiped at it and realized it was sweat. Why was I so warm? You'd have thought I was standing next to a raging fire. My stomach was especially hot where my purse was pressing against it...

Holy crap. The heat was coming from my purse! Involuntarily, my hands flew up, and the purse slipped to the ground with a soft plop. I saw steam rising as it hit the cool earth.

I eyed the purse fearfully, wondering if it was about to burst into flames. When nothing happened, I reached down and laid my hand on it. The fabric was feverishly warm, as if its interwoven threads were veins coursing with blood.

"Crystal?" I whispered. Was she reacting to the nearness of her stepfather? Was she trying to tell me something about him?

When I looked up, Peter Wittmeyer was moving toward the storage room, the swimming pool net in his hands. I dropped to a crouch just before he opened the door. I heard clinks as he maneuvered the long pole into the room. Then the door clicked shut. He stomped up the steps and across the deck. A door slid open and then shut. The purse grew cool.

I watched the sun set over the Wittmeyers' backyard fence. The sky turned a brilliant orange, then hot pink, then dull lavender. The air took on the grainy gray look of an old movie. Lightning bugs flashed, as fleeting as meteors. Finally, I deemed it dark enough to leave my hiding place. But before I headed to the street, there was something I needed to do.

I peed. Right there, in the Wittmeyers' yard, squatting in the grassy stretch where the outer wall of the storage room met the rear corner of the house. I couldn't hold it any longer, and I knew I wasn't likely to stumble across a public restroom anytime soon. My bladder was so full, it took half a minute to empty.

I felt hot with shame as I slunk up through the side yard. I was no better than the drunks I saw late at night from the window of my apartment, peeing into the gutter.

I hadn't counted on a motion detector light. It caught me in its accusing glare as I cleared the front of the house. My heart seized up, and I sprinted the rest of the way to the street. But no one came bursting out of the house. No one pursued me. I was safe, at least from Peter Wittmeyer.

Now I just had to make my way home.

Chapter 33

I needed to get back to the familiar territory of the shopping center. The problem was, I had no idea which way to go. I hadn't paid attention to all the twists and turns Toni had taken to get us to the Wittmeyers' house. All I could do was head west, which was easy at first because the sky still held a faint glow where the sun had set. But the light faded rapidly, and soon that part of the sky was as dark as the rest.

The air was still warm and muggy, and I quickly worked up a sweat. I tried to keep my eyes fastened on that now indistinguishable western horizon. But some of the streets curved in unexpected ways, and before I knew it, I'd lost all sense of direction. I kept going, hoping I was heading the right way.

As I passed a huge, stone-fronted house with a fountain in the front yard, I realized I'd seen it before. This was Jade's house! I came to a halt, staring pensively up the driveway. If I went to the door and begged for help, Jade would tell me how to get to the shopping center. Wouldn't she? Okay, maybe not. Jade wasn't the type to let go of grudges.

The porch light was on, its dim yellowish glow illuminating two figures on the porch swing. I heard whispery voices, the rhythmic creak of the swing. A girlish squeal of laughter rang out, unmistakably Jade's. Then came the low murmur of a boy's voice, followed by a husky laugh. I froze. The boy sounded like Connor Tipton.

I took a few steps into the darkened yard, squinting. It *was* Connor. I could make out his thick blond hair shining under the porchlight. Jade sat next to him, the long line of their thighs touching. As I watched, Connor pulled Jade's head toward his, and their faces mashed together in a kiss.

I felt a pang of some unpleasant emotion—disgust, or dislike, or maybe a residual bit of jealousy. Yes, jealousy. Although the feelings I'd had for Connor had been superficial and fleeting, they had, after all, been feelings. Connor Tipton would always be the first boy I'd ever kissed. I wished I could undo that, but I couldn't.

Anyway. I shook off my distaste like a coat that no longer fit and focused on the juiciness of this development. Were Connor and Jade a thing? How did Amelia feel about this? Did she even know?

A movement from the porch interrupted my thoughts. Connor had left the swing and was trotting down the porch steps.

"Text me when you get home!" Jade called, and then she disappeared into the house.

Connor was heading my way. I stepped into a small jungle of shrubbery at the front of Jade's yard and crouched against a scratchy bush. The scent of blooms wafted around me, settling on my skin like perfume. Connor walked past without seeing me. He loped down the street and disappeared around a corner. I crawled out of the shrubbery and stepped onto the sidewalk.

All was quiet except for the soft chirping of crickets. I gazed upward. The sky was very dark, with a generous sprinkling of stars and barely any moon. I walked into the middle of the street and turned slowly in a circle, studying what I could see of the horizon. Beyond the houses at the far end of the street was a subtle silvery glow that I thought might be the lights from the shopping center. I set off in that direction.

Ten minutes later, I rounded a corner and saw the neon lights of the ice cream parlor ahead. Relief swept through me. Now I knew where I was. All I had to do was walk two blocks to Frontier Street and then follow it to the downtown area. With any luck I'd be home in an hour or so.

Chapter 34

The first section of Frontier Street meandered down a gentle slope through a residential area with well-maintained sidewalks and evenly spaced streetlamps. The houses here were technically part of the Hilltop but weren't nearly as fancy as the ones in the Wittmeyers' neighborhood. They were smaller, older, crowded close like old friends. Instead of doctors and lawyers, they were inhabited by accountants and teachers.

Traffic was fairly light. Every few minutes a car or two would swish by, generating a rush of air that cooled my skin. I felt an occasional mild sting on my neck or my arm and swatted at it too late. Damned mosquitoes.

As I walked, my thoughts strayed to Toni. Where was she now? Still in police custody? Mrs. Moore would have been contacted by now. I wondered how she'd reacted. At the very least, Toni would be grounded, and in my opinion, she deserved it. Her actions tonight had hurt not just herself but me too.

It was her fault I'd had to cower under the Wittmeyers' deck for hours. Her fault I had to hike home in the dark. And her fault I'd had to pee in the Wittmeyers' yard like some old drunk. If we'd done things my way, if we'd knocked on the Wittmeyers' front door, we could have avoided all this trouble. Sure, we would have tangled with Peter Wittmeyer, and he probably would have shooed us off his property. But we might have had a chance to speak with Mae, and maybe she would have talked her husband into letting us stay.

THE HAUNTED PURSE

I heard the thumping bass of the car's radio before I heard its engine, a frenzied heartbeat of sound coming up behind me. The car slowed as it approached. The music cut off. A male voice cried, "Woo, mama, check this out!"

I glanced over. Creeping along beside me was an older-model white car crammed with guys in their early twenties. The one in the front passenger seat, a beefy guy with long, stringy hair, hung out the window, leering at me.

"Hey, darlin', you look like somebody who could use a ride."

"I bet that's not all she could use!" said a voice from deep in the car, and raucous male laughter rang out.

I walked faster, ignoring them. The car rolled along beside me. I could smell somebody's b.o., pungent and sour like a new variety of cheese.

"Well. Looks like we got us a stuck-up bitch," said a guy in the back seat. "What's your problem, sweetheart? Think you're too good for us?"

"Don't be that way, honey. Come on over—we just want to show you a good time."

"A *real* good time."

"We got lots of room. You can sit on Russell's lap."

Every nerve in my body was jangling an alarm, but I didn't know what to do. Should I run to the nearest house? I glanced to my right, but the house I was passing was dark. Either no one was home, or the residents were in bed.

I looked behind me, relieved to see headlights approaching. A pick-up truck rolled up behind the white car, got right on its bumper. When the white car didn't speed up, the driver of the truck honked.

The guy driving the white car stuck his arm out the window and waved the other driver around him. The truck didn't budge. Instead, the driver honked again.

"Asshole!" muttered the driver of the white car. He hit the gas and the car roared away, the truck right on its tail.

I stood stock-still on the sidewalk, watching the two vehicles move down Frontier Street. After a few blocks, the white car slowed and then turned left onto a side street. The truck whizzed past it with an impatient roar of its engine. A moment later I saw the white car backing out onto Frontier Street. The guys were turning around. They were coming back.

I didn't think they could see me from this distance, especially since I was in a darkened spot between two streetlights. I raced across the street and into the nearest yard. A cluster of shrubbery encircled a tree. I leapt into it and scrunched myself into a tight ball, holding my breath as I heard the white car approaching. The engine revved twice, and then the car came to a stop.

Oh God. Were they going to hunt me down on foot? How many of them were there? Five? I wouldn't stand a chance.

"Where'd you go, princess?" one of the guys called out the window. "You playing hide and seek?"

"Hey, Bones, a couple more cars are coming," somebody said.

"Shit!" said Bones. With an angry squeal of the tires, he peeled away.

I didn't waste a second. I took off like a cheetah, sprinting from yard to yard, scrambling over an occasional low fence. Every time I heard a car approaching from either direction, I ducked behind the nearest large object—a bush, a garden shed, a tree, a car. I didn't know how persistent the guys were, how long they were going to look for me. If they thought I lived in this neighborhood and had made it home, they would give up. But if not—I couldn't bear to think about what might happen to me.

It was easy enough to conceal myself here, in this residential neighborhood. But soon enough the houses would vanish as the road cut into a steep hillside that fell just short of being vertical. There were no sidewalks along that stretch, only a guard rail situated at the cliff-like outer edge of the road. The inner edge hugged a rocky cliff wall going up, up, up.

That section of Frontier Street was maybe half a mile long, and it was all downhill as it approached the downtown area. But it might as well have been ten miles long. If the guys came looking for me there, they would find me, because there was nowhere to hide.

Emerging from a cluster of trees in an overgrown front yard, I realized I'd reached the Halfway. Two blocks ahead was the street my school was on, followed a block later by Belmont Street, where Louie and Charlie lived. I'd been to their houses plenty of times for birthday parties and sleepovers and group study sessions that never involved much studying.

"Louie and Charlie!" I said aloud, thumping myself on the forehead. Why hadn't I thought of them sooner? Louie and Charlie would save me. One of their parents could drive me home. And if for some reason that wasn't possible, I could sleep over and catch a bus home in the morning.

I released a long, shaky breath. Salvation was just a few blocks away.

The hike to Belmont Street took longer than it should have because I had to keep hiding. A couple of times I peeked out of my hiding place to get a glimpse of the passing vehicles. One car was white, but I couldn't tell if it was the car of my pursuers. I shuddered with relief as I finally turned the corner and left Frontier Street behind.

Louie and Charlie lived two blocks down, in a modest but well-kept neighborhood dotted with trampolines and above-ground swimming pools and intricate wooden swing sets with forts on top. As I approached the cousins' nearly identical frame houses, I was cheered to see lights on in both.

But when I knocked on Louie's door, nobody answered. I pounded again, louder, straining my ears for some sign of life from within. Nothing moved. Louie's dog didn't even bark. An absolute stillness emanated through the walls, as if the house was nothing but a vacant shell.

The same thing happened at Charlie's house. Clearly, no one was home at either place. I sat on Charlie's front porch steps jiggling my knees as I tried to decide what to do. Wherever they were, the families were bound to come home eventually. But when? Should I wait?

I heard the rhythmic bounce of a basketball from across the street, four houses down. I turned my head, zeroing in on the sound. That was where Tommy Sturgis lived. I could see someone in the driveway, shooting baskets, but I couldn't tell whether it was Tommy or his older brother.

I jumped up and jogged down the street. "Tommy?"

He whirled around, dropping the ball as he spotted me. It bounced several times and rolled into the grass.

"Libby! What are you doing here?" His blue eyes, wide with surprise, took me in.

"Hi!" I said, ignoring his question. "Hey, do you happen to know where Louie and Charlie are?"

"Louie and Charlie? They went to Virginia Beach."

"Oh, no! Both of them?"

"Yeah, their families go on vacation together every summer. I think they're coming back on Saturday."

"Their lights are on," I said faintly. "I thought they were home."

"They want it to look that way," Tommy said. "You know, to discourage burglars." He reached over and pulled a twig out of my hair. "Is everything okay?"

"Oh, yeah. Yeah. I was just...I was, uh—"

"In the neighborhood?" Tommy suggested, with a trace of a grin.

"Yeah." I grinned back. "I was in the neighborhood, and I, uh... Actually, I wanted to see if one of their parents could drive me home. It's a long story"—I rolled my eyes in an *I won't bore you with the details* way—"but I was over on Frontier Street, walking home, when this carload of guys..."

To my dismay, my voice started to tremble. "These guys, they were, like, yelling things out the windows, trying to get me to go with them. And they drove away, but then they turned around and came back. They stopped the car, and they were calling for me, and I was hiding, and I was scared... I was so scared they would—"

Suddenly, I was crying. All the stress and horror of the past few hours burst from me like a rainstorm, the kind that bubbles out of rainspouts and sweeps teeny-tiny doll shoes into sewers.

"Hey, no, no. Don't cry," Tommy said in alarm. "It'll be okay. My brother can drive you home."

"He can? Oh, thank you!" I shook my head helplessly, apologizing for the tears I just couldn't stop.

"Come on up on the porch," Tommy said, placing a hand on my back. "Eric's in the shower, but he'll be out soon."

I let him guide me to the porch, where he got me situated on a cushioned glider. He disappeared into the house and came out with a glass of water and a box of tissues. I took both gratefully.

"I'm sorry," I said, my voice still wobbly. "I don't know what's wrong with me."

"Hey, you don't have to apologize," said Tommy. "I'd be crying too if a carload of girls was after me." He gave a crooked grin. I grinned back through my tears.

He sat down next to me and started telling me what some of our classmates had been up to since school had let out. His monologue was a blessed distraction that calmed me. I was impressed to hear that Nathan Ferguson had saved a little kid from drowning at the community pool. Ethan McKinney had broken his arm skateboarding. Danielle Fleegle was away at archaeology camp.

"Oh, and Nicholas Gray's family is moving to Wisconsin in August," Tommy finished. He fell silent, easing the glider gently to and fro with a sneakered foot. He didn't press me about what I was doing so far from home at this time of night. We just sat quietly, taking in the nighttime sounds of the neighborhood.

THE HAUNTED PURSE

A TV chattered companionably through an open window of the house next door. Down the street, kids squealed as they chased lightning bugs. Somewhere in the distance a dog barked.

"Are you sure your brother won't mind driving me home?" I asked Tommy.

"Are you kidding? Eric's only had his license for a few months. He never turns down a chance to drive."

Across the street, an outdoor light flicked on. Someone came outside with a broom and started sweeping the driveway.

"Who's working outside so late?" I asked. "Is that Angelina Fetzer?"

Angelina was a year older than us. I'd met her at one of Louie's parties, but I didn't know her very well.

"No. That's Emma," Tommy said.

"Emma Randall? I thought the Fetzers lived there."

"They do. Emma's their foster child."

Emma Randall was a classmate of ours, a pretty girl who rarely spoke and had no friends as far as I could tell. She'd joined our class in January, but I'd never known where she came from, where she lived. I'd had no idea she was a foster child.

"We call her Cinderella," Tommy went on grimly. "The Fetzers work that girl to death. They go around bragging about how they just wanted to help a kid in need. But really, they were just looking for slave labor. That and the money they get from the state each month for keeping her."

A chill juddered through me. This was precisely why I couldn't let anyone find out about my living situation. I did not want to end up like Emma Randall.

Eric came out of the house, toweling his hair dry. He had Tommy's blue eyes, and those eyes lit up when Tommy asked him to drive me home. Tommy came along. We sat together in the back seat, and Eric joked about being our chauffeur.

"You sure you're okay?" Tommy asked as we pulled up in front of my apartment building.

"I'm fine. Thanks again, both of you. You totally saved me."

Tommy walked me to the door of my building. By now it was after eleven o'clock, and even Mr. Owens had gone inside. I could hear the usual drunken laughter from down the street. Closer by, through an open window of a nearby apartment building, a couple screamed swear words at each other. A baby wailed. A siren shrieked, the sound ear-piercing even from blocks away.

This was the roughest neighborhood I'd been in all night, but I was very glad to be back.

Upstairs in my sweltering apartment, I headed straight for the bathroom and stripped off my sweaty clothes. I was more exhausted than I'd ever been in my life. I managed to brush my teeth and give my body a quick wipe with a wet washcloth. Then I slipped into my well-worn summer nightie and collapsed into bed.

Things didn't stop happening just because I was asleep. Somewhere in those dark and silent hours I found an answer to the big question that was bothering me.

What happened to Crystal?
Peter Wittmeyer murdered her.

Chapter 35

I awoke with a gasp, as if from a nightmare. But it wasn't a nightmare that had awakened me. It was a thought, and that thought pulsed in my head like a migraine. I must have been thinking about Crystal all night, my brain working on the case even as I slept. And this was what it had come up with.

Peter Wittmeyer a murderer? Wow. That would explain why the purse had heated up like a feverish puppy when he got close to it. It would explain the secretiveness I'd sensed in him. And it would explain why my phone call had made him so angry. But how was I going to figure out his motive, let alone prove his guilt?

Sunlight streamed beyond the filthy pane of my bedroom window. I glanced at the clock on my nightstand. The digital display read 10:47. I couldn't believe I'd slept so late! I slid out of bed. I needed to get my day started.

In the shower, my thoughts shifted to Toni. What was she doing right now? How much trouble was she in? She would probably call me today to make sure I'd gotten home okay. I decided not to go all *I told you so* on her, but she would definitely be getting a blow-by-blow account of the ordeal I'd gone through last night. She owed me that much.

After breakfast I lugged my overstuffed laundry basket to the laundromat, two blocks down the street. No one else was inside, though a dryer was running, the tumbling clothes visible through the porthole-like window in front. A child's pink sock lay forgotten on the floor, half-covered in fluffy dryer lint.

I rooted through my laundry basket until I found the clothes I'd worn yesterday. There were a couple of dirty marks on both the shirt and the shorts. I sprayed them with a stain remover and prayed to the laundry gods for absolution.

Mason showed up as I was stuffing my laundry into a washer. He wore his detective clothes, the oversized fedora obscuring the top half of his face. I gave him a look of irritation.

"What are you doing here, Mason?"

"Looking for clues."

"What kind of clues?"

"Won't know till I find them."

"Is your mom working today?"

"Yeah."

"So Toni's in charge? Where does she think you are?"

"Albert's."

"Then get your butt over to Albert's."

"My butt would rather be here." He leaned against the rumbling dryer and tipped his fedora back so he could see me better.

I narrowed my eyes at him, trying to look menacing. He smiled charmingly in response.

"Are you having a nice day? I'm having a nice day. I found a quarter on the sidewalk. Here." He threw it at me. Instinctively I ducked, and the quarter clattered to the floor. "You can have it. For the washer."

I bent down and snatched up the coin. "Fine. But this doesn't make up for blackmailing me."

Mason pulled a big red sphere of bubblegum out of his shorts pocket and popped it in his mouth. He chewed it into a soft pink mass and said slurpily, "Toni's grounded. But I guess you knew that."

"How would I know that? I haven't talked to her today."

His eyes were locked on me, his gaze too shrewd for a ten-year-old. "Whatever she did to get in trouble, I think you were in on it."

I chose to neither confirm nor deny that. I poured a capful of detergent into the washer's dispenser drawer and turned the knob to start the cycle. The sound of gushing water filled the air. "So you don't know what she did?"

"Nobody will tell me. I just know it was something bad. We had to go down to the police station last night to pick her up."

I pulled *A Prayer for Owen Meany* out of my purse and sat down on the wooden bench next to the washers.

"My dad's coming to get her tonight," Mason went on. "Mom says she can't trust her to be home without a grown-up anymore. She has to go live with my dad and Jan for the rest of the summer because Jan's a stay-at-home mom and can keep an eye on her."

I stared at my book, trying not to let my dismay show.

"Toni's pretty upset," said Mason. "I heard her crying in her room."

Jan probably wasn't jumping for joy, either. "What about you?" I asked. "Who's going to watch you when your mom's at work?"

"Nobody." He tilted his chin up proudly. "I'm going to be eleven in September. Mom thinks I'm mature enough to stay by myself. I just have to check in with her every two hours."

I snorted in disdain. "You're not mature. You lie to Toni all the time about being at Albert's."

He gave me a taunting look. "You going to tell on me?"

"No, I am not going to tell on you!" I raised my book so I couldn't see his smug little face.

I got so engrossed in *Owen Meany* that I didn't hear Mason leave. When I got up to transfer my damp laundry to the dryer, he was gone. The other dryer had stopped running, but no one had come to claim the clothes inside. I winced in sympathy, imagining wrinkles setting in like fissures in a rock. Somebody was in for a lot of ironing.

When I reached into my purse to get quarters for the dryer, I felt a flash of pain, as if a tiny animal had bitten my finger.

"Ow!" I yelped, dropping the purse.

There was a fine, straight line of blood on the side of my pinkie. A paper cut. But what had cut me? Warily I picked up my purse and peered inside. A photograph was tucked behind my wallet, its long, sharp edge protruding.

Gently I slipped it out. It was a five-by-seven photo of Crystal. But not just any photo. It was her school picture, the same one from the newspaper article about her disappearance. Unlike the newspaper photo, this one was in color.

Why was Crystal showing me this photo? I'd already seen it. I turned it over, thinking maybe there was a message written on the back. But the smooth white surface was unmarked.

It wasn't until I got home, when I opened my purse to get out my key, that I found the second photo. This one was even more perplexing than the first.

Chapter 36

I stood at the kitchen counter, gazing down at the two photos that lay there. Each featured a smiling, brown-haired girl. Each was a five-by-seven school photo with a mottled blue-gray background. The difference was, one of the pictures was twenty years old, while the other had been taken less than a year ago.

The girl in the second photo was me.

Goosebumps rippled across my skin as I glanced from Crystal's face to mine. The arrangement of our photos side by side seemed to erase the time and space that separated us, making us seem like classmates. Maybe even sisters.

I took a minute to study my picture. This was the first time I'd seen it. I never saw any of my school pictures, except in friends' yearbooks, because my mother never purchased them. She wouldn't even spring for the cheapest package, the one that consisted of a single four-by-six and four wallets. Not that I cared. If I wanted to see my own face, all I had to do was look in the mirror.

Like Crystal, I'd taken a good tenth-grade picture. Toni had braided my hair that morning, and that smooth, tight braid flowed down the right side of my neck, disappearing below the frame of the picture. My eyes were clear and wide, meeting the camera head on. Same with Crystal's eyes.

Two girls, born two decades apart. One alive, one dead.

What was Crystal trying to tell me?

Chapter 37

It was mid-afternoon, and Toni still hadn't called.

I had stopped being mad at her. In fact, I was feeling pretty bad for her. She'd gotten herself into a heap of trouble—with Peter Wittmeyer, with the police, and with her parents. The last thing she needed was a best friend who couldn't forgive and forget. I plopped down on the couch and dialed her phone number.

She answered in a toneless mumble. "Hello."

"Hey, it's me. I ran into Mason, and he said you—"

Click.

I stared at the receiver. Had Toni just hung up on me? Surely not. I dialed the number again.

"Hello."

"Hey, I think we got cut off. I just wanted to say hi and see how you're—"

Click.

I uttered a small noise of frustration. Something was up. I called back a third time, swinging the coiled phone cord in agitation.

"Don't hang up!" I said when she answered. "You have to tell me what's going on. Are you mad at me?"

"*Mad* at you?" she said icily. "Why would I be *mad* at you? Just because you deserted your so-called best friend at the worst moment of her life—"

"What?" I blinked in outrage. "I told you you'd be on your own if you got caught. *I* should be mad at *you*. You're the one who dragged me into that mess. Do you have any idea what I went through last night?"

"What *you* went through," she said shrilly. "Did you get stuffed into a police car and taken to police headquarters?"

"No," I yelled. "I almost got gang-raped and murdered!"

Toni made a contemptuous *puh* sound. "Gang-raped and murdered? Seriously? Oh, this I gotta hear."

I stood up and paced half the length of the couch, which was as far as the phone cord would stretch. "Okay, well, I was walking home, or trying to, all by myself in the dark. I missed the bus because I had to hide under Peter Wittmeyer's deck till dark. It took me a long time to even find my way back to the shopping center, because—"

"Just get to the raped and murdered part."

"Okay! It happened when I was walking down Frontier Drive. This carload of guys came by, and they were yelling things at me—like, trying to get me to go with them. They kept turning around and coming back, and I had to hide in shrubbery—"

"Wait a minute. Some guys in a car yelled things at you? How do you get 'almost gang-raped and murdered' out of that?"

"You weren't there," I snapped. "You don't know. It was the scariest thing that ever happened to me."

"Yeah? But in the end, you didn't get murdered, did you? You didn't get raped. Your story had a happy ending." She let out a short, bitter laugh. "My ending? Not so happy. I got hauled away by the police, like some criminal. And now I have to go live with my dad and *that bitch* for the rest of the summer."

"I know." I bowed my head, my anger dissipating. "Mason told me."

"If you'd just stuck with me, we could have gotten away. Both of us. I tried to climb over the fence in the Wittmeyers' yard, but I couldn't do it. I'm too short. If you'd been there, you could have given me a boost."

"And who would have given *me* a boost?" I wondered.

"That's the thing—you probably wouldn't have needed one. You're tall enough that you could have gotten over by yourself." Her voice got quieter, though the bitterness lingered. "Where were you, anyway? Hiding somewhere, watching the whole thing?"

I didn't answer. I felt a flush spreading across my face.

"Yeah. That's what I thought. Well, I hope you enjoyed the show. I'm gonna go now. Don't call back."

"Toni, wait. I know you're upset—"

"You got that right."

"Call me when you calm down?"

There was a long pause. "I don't know if I *will* calm down. I don't know if I can get past this. There's, like, this side of you I never saw before, and I don't know if I want to be your friend anymore."

I tried to speak—to protest, to beg—but I couldn't. My throat had gone dry. My vocal cords were frozen.

"Just so you know," Toni went on, "I wouldn't have abandoned you, no matter what. Friends stick together. They don't ditch each other when things get tough."

Shame seeped through me, hot and slow like melted tar. My perspective rotated a hundred and eighty degrees, and suddenly I saw things from her point of view. She was right. I'd totally abandoned her. I'd left her to fend for herself while I focused on saving my own skin.

"Oh, Toni," I said, my voice cracking. "I'm so sorry. You're right. I should have tried to help you. But I had a reason for hiding. A really good reason."

"Ooh. This I can't wait to hear."

I squeezed my eyes shut in torment. "I can't tell you."

She made a sound of disgust. "Goodbye, Libby."

"Wait! Okay, I'll tell you, but you have to promise not to tell anyone, ever. Because this is huge."

"Fine. I promise."

"If you tell anyone, my life will be destroyed. Seriously. You'll never see me again."

I could practically hear her curiosity buzzing across the phone line. "Okay, okay, I said I wouldn't tell. What's the big secret?"

So I poured it all out. I told her how I lived alone. I said if the authorities ever found out, I'd be thrown into foster care. I told her how I couldn't risk drawing attention to my situation, and that was why I had to avoid run-ins with the police at all costs.

Toni didn't say a word the whole time I was talking. When I finished, she was silent for so long, I thought she'd hung up. Finally she said, in a tone of mingled admiration and envy, "You are so lucky! I wish *my* mom would move in with some guy and leave me behind. But not Mason. She can take Mason with her."

Chapter 38

Toni wasn't in as much trouble as she might have been in, because Peter Wittmeyer had chosen not to press charges.

"What did you tell him?" I asked, switching the phone receiver to my left ear because my right one was going numb. "What did you tell the police? Didn't they want to know why you opened the Wittmeyers' garage window?"

"I said I liked this boy in the neighborhood and I thought the Wittmeyers' house was where he lived. I said he was a couple of years older than me and had his driver's license. I said I was checking to see if his car was in the garage, because I wanted to know if he was home."

"And they bought that?"

"Drew Bowers lives three doors down. He's seventeen. I said I got the wrong house."

"So." I paused uncomfortably. "Everybody thinks you were there by yourself? Stalking some guy?"

"Yeah. Peter Wittmeyer never saw you. Nobody asked if anyone was with me, and I didn't tell."

"Thank you," I said. "You're a good friend."

"Damn right I am."

"So did you see her? Mae?"

"Yeah, she's really nice. She brought me lemonade while we waited for the police."

Before we hung up, I told Toni about the photos I'd found in my purse. She was as mystified as I was. I also told her I thought Peter Wittmeyer had murdered Crystal.

"The man does have a temper," she said. "But murder his own daughter? Do you really think he'd go that far?"

"She wasn't his daughter, remember? She was his stepdaughter."

"Oh, good point. Stepparents are way different from parents. I can totally see Jan murdering me." She paused. "Still. Why would Peter Wittmeyer murder Crystal?"

"I don't know. Maybe she found out something bad about him."

In the background, I heard Mrs. Moore yelling at Toni to get off the phone.

"I gotta go," Toni said. She sighed heavily. "I sure am going to miss playing detective with you."

"Me too. I don't know if I can do this on my own."

"Sure you can. Call me at my dad's if you ever want to talk things over."

Chapter 39

I didn't do much of anything over the next two weeks except read and tutor and watch way too much TV. I was on vacation, taking a badly needed break from all the craziness. The denim purse sat limply on my closet floor, emptied of my day-to-day possessions. When I had to go out, I took the old black purse with me, safety pins and all.

Then one day I woke up ready to get back to work.

I winced as I pulled the denim purse out of my closet, expecting to find a backlog of clues I'd have to figure out. But there was only one—a snapshot of Crystal standing in a doorway with a brown purse looped over her shoulder. The purse looked like a life-sized replica of the tiny doll purse she'd left me. That had to mean something, though I didn't know what. I zipped the photo into one of the larger compartments of the denim purse. That was where I was keeping all the things Crystal had left me.

It had rained in the night. The streets were littered with drowned worms, sodden trash, and rancid brown puddles of indeterminate depth. The weather gurus were predicting sunshine by midmorning, but when I walked to Wittmeyer's Auto Sales around ten, a thick layer of clouds still hung above the city, brushing the tops of the tallest buildings. I had the sense of being indoors, a prisoner trapped in a vast, low-ceilinged dungeon.

THE HAUNTED PURSE

I approached the dealership from the rear, creeping down the edge of the alley. I was wearing gray shorts and a camouflage tee shirt, which was as close to invisible as I could get. I'd left both purses at home. They would only slow me down if I had to flee suddenly.

My mission: to find out whether Peter Wittmeyer was at work today. If he was, I would bus myself to the Hilltop and knock on Mae's door.

"Well, hey, if it isn't Libby Dawson."

Already on edge, I nearly jumped out of my skin. Mr. Abrams stood at the rear of his lot, his three chins grinning at me as he dropped a bag of trash into a big square dumpster.

"Whatcha up to, girl?"

"Oh, hi, Mr. Abrams. Just—on my way to the library."

Crap. As much as I liked Mr. Abrams, I couldn't afford to be sidetracked today. I kept walking, trying to convey *girl in a hurry.*

"I hate to tell you this," Mr. Abrams said. "But you're going the wrong way. Unless they moved the library without me knowing about it."

"Ha-ha, no, it's still in the same place." I pivoted and started walking backwards. I was still moving away from him, but at least I was maintaining eye contact, which, I hoped, made me seem less rude. "Actually, I have to stop off at—" Quick, what was down this way? "—the drugstore to pick up some, uh, ibuprofen and emery boards for my mom."

"Where's your little friend? I hardly ever see one of you without the other."

"Toni? She's visiting her dad."

"Ah, spending some quality time with those adorable little twins." His voice was getting progressively louder as I moved farther down the alley. "She must be so happy."

"So happy," I called back.

"Nice family, the Moores. Jack Moore is one of my best customers. Say, could you use some scallions?"

"Some what?" I yelled. So much for being invisible. The whole block had to know I was here.

"Scallions. Green onions. From my garden. Got a bumper crop this year, thanks to all the rain. I brought some in for the folks in my office, but I've got plenty to spare. Come on over. You can take your pick."

"Thanks," I shouted, "but I really don't like scallions. Nice talking to you, Mr. Abrams. Gotta run."

Then I turned and broke into a trot.

I kept glancing over my shoulder until I saw Mr. Abrams slogging back to his office, as ponderous as a hippo. I beamed a mental apology in his direction and turned my attention to the task at hand.

I was looking for the Car King car. I slumped in discouragement as I surveyed the area behind Peter Wittmeyer's building. There were a zillion cars back here, split among several different parking lots on both sides of the alley. Some were undoubtedly employees' cars, some belonged to customers, and some were used cars available for sale. Still others probably had nothing to do with Wittmeyer's Auto Sales but belonged to employees or customers of other nearby businesses. I didn't know which lot Peter's car might be in, so I would have to check all the cars in every lot.

THE HAUNTED PURSE

My search took nearly half an hour. The big garage door of Peter Wittmeyer's service department was open, and I could see the mechanics inside, tinkering under the hoods of cars. I crept quickly past the taller vehicles and bent low behind the shorter ones to avoid being seen. I didn't want anyone to think I was breaking into cars. It wouldn't be the first time one of the neighborhood teenagers had done that.

The Car King car was nowhere to be seen.

As I wound my way out of the last parking lot, the sun emerged from the clouds, bright as a police spotlight. I trotted across the alley and stashed myself in the shadow of a dumpster while I thought things over. Maybe Peter Wittmeyer hadn't arrived yet. Maybe he was taking the day off. Maybe he'd parked somewhere else. Maybe he was driving his wife's car.

I decided to hang out for a little while longer. If he didn't show up soon, I would try again tomorrow.

"Hi, Libby."

The voice came from close behind me, nipping at my left ear. I was so startled, I choked on my own spit as I whirled around. There stood Mason, in full detective regalia.

"Mason, for God's sake!"

"What are you doing back here?"

"Nothing." I bit the word off abruptly. "I'm on my way to the thrift store."

"No, you're not. You're just standing there, staring at the car place. Before that, you were walking around the parking lots looking at all the cars."

I clutched my head with both hands. "Oh my God, you have got to stop following me! You can go to jail for stalking people. Did you know that?"

"Well, *you're* stalking somebody. Aren't you?"

"I'm not stalking him. I'm just—"

"Aha! You said *him*." He pointed triumphantly at me. "Who is it, Libby? Some car salesman? Are you in love with some car salesman? Are you trying to get him to take you on a date? Did you put a love note on his car?"

I glowered at him. The kid was so relentlessly exasperating, it was almost funny. "I am not in love with some car salesman."

"Then why are you—"

"Shhh! Keep your voice down. You're practically yelling."

He went a notch lower. "Why do I have to keep my voice down? We're outside."

"I'm trying to be—stealthy. Do you know what stealthy means?"

"Yeah. It means sneaky." His face lit up. "Are you spying on somebody?"

There was no point in denying it. I didn't have a good cover story, and even if I'd had one, Mason wasn't likely to believe it.

"Yes," I said. "Trying to, anyway. But it's not going very well."

He looked up at me with big, earnest eyes. "I can help. I won't even charge you." He pulled a three-inch pencil and a small, tattered notepad out of his shorts pocket. "What's the subject's name?"

I eyed him thoughtfully. Mason took his detective work very seriously. And he was good at it. After all, he'd uncovered my biggest secret.

"Peter Wittmeyer," I said. "The subject's name is Peter Wittmeyer. He owns Wittmeyer's Auto Sales, in case you didn't figure that out. I need a way to tell when he's at work. If you could find out where he parks his car, that'd be great. It's big and black, and the license plate says Car King."

Mason made notes on his notepad. I appreciated the fact that he didn't ask why I was keeping tabs on Peter Wittmeyer. He said, "Let's go out front. You can wait for me on the bench by the thrift store."

He seemed so competent, so in-charge, almost like a grown-up. Meekly I followed him up the side alley. I watched him tug open the heavy glass door at the front of the car dealership and slip inside.

I crossed Linden Street and sat on the weathered bench outside the thrift store, chewing my bottom lip. What was Mason going to do in there? What if Peter Wittmeyer confronted him? What if Peter Wittmeyer found out he was Toni's brother? What if Mason was forced to confess that I'd sent him in there?

Chapter 40

The exterior of the car showroom was mostly glass, but I couldn't see inside. Instead, I saw the reflection of the sunlit scenery outside, including my own staring self. It was as if Mason had slipped beneath the murky surface of a lake. Five minutes passed, then ten. I stared harder at the door, willing him to reappear.

I caught a movement from up the street. Tim Tuttle was outside picking up litter with a pointy metal stick and stuffing it into a small trash bag.

His face brightened as his gaze fell on me, like he'd spotted an old friend. He crossed the street, stopping in the middle to impale a paper cup and a crumpled cigarette pack. I smiled politely as he worked his way toward me, though I kept one eye on the front door of the car dealership.

"Hi there, young lady. Looks like it's clearing up."

"Finally."

"That was quite a rain we had last night. Did you hear all the thunder?"

"No."

"Lucky you. The storm went on for hours. Kept me up. Might have to grab a nap at lunchtime."

In rapid succession he stabbed a cardboard juice box and two french fry cartons and deposited them in his bag. Then he reached down to peel a rain-soaked piece of business paper off the pavement. He wrung it out and dropped it into the bag.

"That's really nice of you," I said. "Picking up litter like that."

"Just doing my civic duty. I'm not the only one who does it. All the business owners pitch in. We take pride in our neighborhood."

"That's great," I said. "I wish people on my street would do that."

Riverview Lane was an eyesore, its litter as plentiful as autumn's windswept leaves. Part of the problem was that there were hardly any public trash cans. It was as if the local authorities had given up on the poor end of the city.

"Which street is that?" Tim asked, sitting on the bench next to me.

"Riverview Lane."

"Ah, Riverview. You must go to Greater Ashton Senior High. You look familiar. Have I taken your school picture?"

"Yeah, a couple of times. Plus, you were at our sophomore dance in May."

"Ah." The word rode out of him on a big gust of breath. "That's where I know you from. You're the girl they voted queen."

His eyes flicked from my face to my faded camo tee to my black canvas sneakers with the matching holes where my toes had poked through. Then back to my face. "You live on Riverview Lane? I had no idea. That night at the dance—" He broke off, his gaze shifting to a passing car.

I knew what he was getting at. The night of the dance, I'd been somebody different, Cinderella at the ball. A confident, silky-haired girl in a stylish dress. Tim Tuttle had probably assumed I was a Hilltopper. But now he knew better, and I didn't like the way his face had changed when he figured it out.

"Your classmates have excellent taste," he said, as if he thought a little flattery might repair the damage. "I would have voted for you, too." He looked at me again, his gaze suddenly thoughtful. "Have you ever considered going into modeling?"

"Me? God, no!"

If he was startled by the vehemence of my reply, he didn't show it. "Don't be so quick to rule it out. A pretty girl like you? Once you get established, you could make hundreds of dollars per photo shoot. For maybe an hour or two of work. I do shoots for some teen fashion magazines. If you're interested, I'll set something up."

My heart sped up. "Hundreds of dollars? What's the catch?"

He laughed. "There's no catch. Modeling pays well." He leaned close to me, as if about to impart a valuable secret. "If you live on Riverview Lane, I'm guessing you could use that kind of money."

For a moment, I just looked at him, at his up-close face, the three-dimensional mole near his nose, as his words spread through me like bee venom.

In his own way, he had just called me tenement trash.

I stood up, my fists clenched at my sides. "For your information, I already have a job. I'm a tutor. No, it doesn't pay hundreds of dollars a session, but I'm good at it. And, yeah, I live on Riverview Lane, but that won't be forever. I'm going to go to college and get a good job, and once I leave this dump of a city, I'm never coming back. So do I want to flip my hair around and smile pretty for the camera? No, thank you. That's just not me."

By the time I finished my tirade, Tim's smile had vanished. He no longer looked like the friendly, charismatic photographer everybody knew. His posture had stiffened, his eyes had gone cold, and his lips were pressed together like a well-sewn seam.

"I only wanted to help you," he said, tying his litter bag shut with an abrupt movement. "Whether you know it or not, I care about the kids in this community. But if you think you're too good to model—fine. I know plenty of girls who will jump at the chance you just turned down."

He got to his feet.

"Wait," I said, suddenly mortified at my own behavior. "It's not that I think I'm too good to model. I just meant—"

"Oh, I know what you meant," said Tim Tuttle. "I'm very sorry to have bothered you."

He strode across the street and went into his studio.

Chapter 41

Hundreds of dollars—for an hour or two of work? That was a lot to throw away.

Had I made a mistake? Was I being too sensitive about the whole tenement trash thing? Should I have asked for time to think things over?

If I went crawling back to Tim Tuttle, would he let me change my mind?

I was still agonizing over the encounter when Mason loped out of Peter Wittmeyer's building. He'd been inside for nearly half an hour. I ran across the street to meet him. He led me into the alley between the car dealership and Apex Insurance.

"That window right there?" he said, pointing to the last window on the first floor of the Wittmeyer building. "That's Peter Wittmeyer's office. When you want to see if he's there, just walk by and take a peek. Looking for his car won't work, because he doesn't park outside. He has his own private garage inside the building."

I stared at him in amazement. "How'd you find that out?"

"I asked him."

"You talked to Peter Wittmeyer?"

"Yeah. It took a while to find him. There were lots of people in there. Customers looking at cars, salespeople helping them. The place was so busy, nobody paid any attention to me. I walked around till I found an office with a sign on the door that said Peter Wittmeyer General Manager. He was in there working. So I went in and talked to him."

"Wow, Mason," I said. The kid had a lot of nerve.

"I told him I like his commercials on TV. I said I bet he had a really nice car, since cars are his business. He took me to the garage and showed it to me."

"He showed you his car?"

"Yeah. I want to get a car like that someday. He said to come back when I get my driver's license and he'll give me a square deal."

"Stay away from Peter Wittmeyer," I said sternly. "He is not a nice man."

"If you say so. But he was nice to me."

"Hey. Mason," I said before we went our separate ways.

"What?"

"I want you to stop following me."

"Yeah, okay."

He started down the alley. I grabbed a fistful of his shirt and pulled him back. "Seriously. I want you to look me in the eyes and promise you're not going to follow me anymore."

"Okay!" He yanked himself away and gave me a sulky look. "I promise I won't follow you anymore."

Chapter 42

It was almost lunchtime, too late for a morning trip to the Hilltop. I decided to delay my trip till early afternoon. I went home and fixed myself a tuna salad sandwich, which satisfied my hunger but left an unpleasant metallic aftertaste in my mouth, as if I'd chewed up part of the can. No name-brand tuna for me. I bought only the cheapest varieties, just a step up from cat food.

After lunch, I brushed my teeth and changed into my most recent mall purchases—a white button-down shirt, indigo jeans, and reddish-brown loafers that looked like leather but weren't.

These clothes were much classier than what I usually wore. They suggested I was someone polished, sophisticated, cultured. I felt a little bit like an imposter, though, because I really wasn't those things. Not yet, anyway. The clothes were going to help me get there. I intended to have a whole new wardrobe by September, one that reflected the girl I aimed to be.

I'd been working with Alyssa and Jared for three weeks, and my wallet was plumping out nicely. So was my tutees' understanding of geometry. Alyssa had gotten an A on the last test, and Jared had scored a B.

On my way to the bus stop, I swung by the car dealership and walked down the alley. Peter Wittmeyer was still in his office. Through the window I could see his drill-sergeant head bobbing emphatically as he spoke to someone on the other side of his desk.

THE HAUNTED PURSE

Last week I'd picked up a complimentary city map from the downtown welcome center, so once I got off the bus, I was able to find my way to Regent Street. I even managed to steer clear of Jade's street.

For a long time, I stood on the sidewalk behind the Wittmeyers' stately trees, staring at the house. I couldn't shake the bad association this place had for me. I wanted to bolt, to run back to the shopping center and catch the next bus home. But backing out wasn't an option, because Crystal was counting on me. So I steeled myself for whatever was to come and strode up to the house.

Mae herself opened the door. I knew her at once, even though we'd never met. She was short and plump, a summertime Mrs. Santa Claus, though her pleasant face was scored with more lines than a woman her age should have had. Grief had done that, I thought.

"Hi! Are you Mae Wittmeyer?" I asked.

"Yes." The brown eyes were friendly and curious.

I opened my mouth to introduce myself. Instead, I burst into tears.

Chapter 43

"I'm so sorry," I said, my voice a whispery gasp. "This is—embarrassing."

"It's quite all right, dear," said Mae. "Please come in. Let me get you some lemonade."

I followed her to a large kitchen gleaming with stainless steel appliances. She poured lemonade from a pitcher in the fridge. I took the glass she handed me and gulped gratefully. Mae's lemonade was much better than the powdered-mix stuff I made. She probably used actual lemons.

"Let's go to the family room," said Mae. "We'll be more comfortable there."

The family room was twice as large as my whole apartment and was decorated in soothing shades of pale blue and sage green. The seating area—consisting of an L-shaped sectional sofa, two easy chairs, and a couple of tables—formed an island in the middle of the room, anchored by a patterned area rug and surrounded by a sea of open space.

Paintings, mostly landscapes, drew the eye upward. A massive stone fireplace jutted into the room, a work of art in its own right. At the far end of the space, a double set of sliding-glass doors opened onto the deck. The very same deck I'd hunkered beneath not so long ago.

I sank down in the nearest easy chair. Mae placed a box of tissues on the small table next to me and sat on the sofa facing me.

I took another sip of lemonade and set the glass on a coaster next to the tissue box. Mae sat on the sofa watching me, hands in her lap. She had to be wildly curious, yet she didn't say a word as she waited for me to settle down. I supposed that when your daughter had been missing for twenty years, you got very good at being patient.

"You must be wondering what I'm doing here," I finally said. "And why I'm crying. And who I am."

"Let's start there," said Mae. "What's your name, dear?"

"It's Libby. Libby Dawson. And I'm here because I have some things that belong to you."

I reached for the denim purse, which was slumped at my feet like a dozing cat. As I pulled it onto my lap, I felt the warmth emanating from it. The same warmth I'd felt when Peter Wittmeyer had gotten too close for comfort.

Involuntarily, I pulled my hands away, confused and mildly alarmed. Why was the purse warming up *now*? Had Peter Wittmeyer come home, silently and unannounced? I looked around in panic, but the man was nowhere to be seen.

I stole a glance at Mae. Had she somehow been involved in Crystal's disappearance? No. That simply couldn't be. More than likely, the purse was reacting to the fact that this was Peter's home. For all I knew, the chair I was sitting in was his favorite roosting spot, its fabric teeming with his DNA.

Ick. I suppressed the urge to leap out of the chair and sit somewhere else.

"Oh, my heavens!" Mae was staring at my lap. "That purse! Crystal—my daughter—had one just like it." Her voice went low and tremulous. "My Cryssy, she disappeared a long time ago."

"I know." I forced myself to meet her tormented gaze. "I'm so sorry. Actually, this is her purse. Crystal's. I bought it at Second Life, the thrift store downtown."

"Crystal's purse!" Mae half-rose, her eyes sopping up the purse as if it were Crystal herself. Which in a way it was. Then she sank back into the couch. "The thrift store. Of course. Lauren, that's my other daughter, she took a box of Cryssy's things there a few months back. Said I'd kept them long enough. I didn't realize the purse was in that box."

Her eyes, soft with thoughts of her long-lost daughter, flicked back to my face. "Honey, it was sweet of you to come by, but I don't want the purse back. It's yours now."

"Oh," I said, nonplussed that she'd misunderstood my intentions—and relieved that she wasn't going to snatch away my most prized possession. "Actually, I'm here because of what I found inside." I reached into one of the butt pockets and drew out the three photos. Crystal by the turreted house, Crystal's school picture, and Crystal holding the brown purse. "I thought you might want these back."

I laid the photos on the coffee table.

"Oh my," murmured Mae. Her eyes brimmed with tears. "Oh, my baby. My Cryssy."

I slid the tissue box across the coffee table. Mae plucked out a tissue and used it to dab at her eyes. She studied the pictures for a long time, each one in turn. Then she looked up at me.

"But how did you know this was Crystal? How did you track me down?"

I'd already decided I wasn't going to mention the supernatural goings-on, because I didn't know how open Mae was to that sort of thing. I also thought it would be best to leave

Toni out of the story, considering her recent encounter with the Wittmeyers. So I said I'd recognized the turreted house in the photo and had paid the owner a visit. After learning of Crystal's disappearance, I'd gotten Mae's name from a newspaper article I'd looked up at the library. I paused as I debated whether to mention my phone conversation with Peter and then decided there was no reason to leave it out.

"I'm sorry I made your husband mad," I said when I'd finished. "I didn't mean to. I was just trying to find you."

She smiled ruefully. "No need to apologize. Peter's bark is worse than his bite. He tries to shield me from people who want to talk about Cryssy." She leaned forward, looking earnest. "The thing is, I love talking about her."

"Me, too!" I said. I stroked the purse. It was less feverish than before but still warmed my hand. "I dream about her sometimes. A lot, actually. Ever since the pictures turned up, ever since I found out she disappeared—" To my dismay, a clump of emotion lodged in my throat. I tried to swallow it. "Ever since then, I've felt like I knew her. Like—like she was my friend."

My voice, which had been getting progressively shakier, fractured on a sob.

"Oh, honey. Come on over here," said Mae.

I went to sit beside her on the sofa. She put an arm around me and pulled me against her fleshy side, hugging me like a grandma would.

"I want to know more about her," I said, blotting my eyes with my damp, crumpled tissue. "That is, if you're sure you don't mind talking about her."

She patted my leg. "Honey, I do not mind at all."

Chapter 44

Mae said that her first husband, Crystal's father, had died in a car accident shortly before Crystal's birth. She'd met Peter when Crystal was a year old and her other daughter, Lauren, was three. The two of them were married six months later. Peter, who until then had been childless, quickly bonded with Mae's girls, loving them like they were his own. That was what Mae said, anyway. I nodded like I was buying it.

From the time she was about eight, Crystal had loved spending time at the car dealership. Peter often took her to work with him, and she'd spend the day in an unoccupied office, reading mystery books or writing stories. Mae's only rule was that Crystal had to stay inside the building. She didn't want her daughter roaming the downtown streets alone.

Crystal imagined herself an investigator. She'd started out playing detective but by age ten had decided to be a journalist instead. Mostly she investigated neighborhood "cases"—a broken basement window, a prize pumpkin stolen from someone's garden—and wrote about them in a newspaper she typed up herself. Peter ran off copies at work, and Crystal sold them to neighbors for a quarter apiece.

As she grew older, she became interested in police cases. She loved to watch crime shows on TV and kept a folder of newspaper clippings about local crimes. She dreamed of a career in journalism or possibly law enforcement.

To me, Crystal sounded like the teen-girl version of Mason. Because I had such high regard for her, I suddenly saw Mason in a different light. Like Crystal, he was simply following his passion.

According to Mae, the denim purse hadn't been Crystal's only purse. There'd also been a small brown purse she'd carried with her during her investigations—her "reporter's bag." It held her camera, a magnifying glass, a small pair of binoculars, a flashlight, and a notebook. The purse had vanished the same evening Crystal had gone missing.

I picked up the photo of Crystal with the brown purse slung over her shoulder. Mae's eyes zeroed in on it.

"That's it," she said. "That's her reporter's bag."

"You think Crystal was investigating something when she disappeared?"

"I know she was. She told me so, though she didn't offer any details. At first I assumed there was something going on in the neighborhood—a lost dog, kids soaping people's windows. But now I think it was something more sinister than that."

She looked so troubled that I felt compelled to ask, "Like what?"

She glanced around as if she wasn't entirely sure we were alone. "Drug dealing. That's my guess."

"Drug dealing," I repeated. "Was that a big problem where you lived?"

"Not a big problem, but we had our share of it. A few months before Cryssy disappeared, a boy from her school died of a heroin overdose. He was just a classmate, not a friend, but she was upset about his death. She was very anti-drug, my Cryssy was."

"So, do you think—" I began.

"I'll tell you what I think." She was talking faster now, like she'd been holding these words in her mouth for a very long time and couldn't wait to spit them out. "I think she went looking for the drug dealer, the one who sold that boy those drugs, and tried to catch him in the act. Only he caught her and—" She gulped in a deep breath that turned into a sob. "—murdered her."

Is there any chance that drug dealer was Peter Wittmeyer?

I thought it but didn't say it.

Before I left, she handed the photos back to me. "You may keep these if you wish, Libby. I have plenty of pictures of Crystal. But thank you for thinking of me."

She invited me to lunch on Monday, three days from now. "My daughter Lauren is coming for a visit. I know she'd love to meet the girl who ended up with Crystal's purse." She pulled me in for another squishy hug. "You're so much like my Cryssy, honey. Pretty. Smart. Sweet."

Chapter 45

During the bus ride home, hiccuppy sobs burst from me every few minutes, like unexpected rain showers. The middle-aged guy in the seat across the aisle kept glancing up from his phone to eye me in concern, or maybe irritation. I caught his eye and shrugged an apology. I was powerless to halt the meltdown.

I'd absorbed so much of the love and pain and sadness that filled Mae Wittmeyer that it was leaking out of me—my eyes, my nose, my very pores. Having finally met Mae, having been wrapped in those warm maternal arms, I felt closer to Crystal than ever. Now I mourned her like a sister.

On top of that, I was dealing with a brand-new anguish.

I didn't know whether to continue my investigation. I knew that Mae longed to find out what had happened to her daughter. But what if Crystal had in fact been murdered, and what if the murderer turned out to be Peter Wittmeyer? Mae would be devastated. Was it right to expose the man if that meant inflicting a new round of pain on his wife, who'd already suffered so much?

Could ghosts read minds? Was Crystal aware of my dilemma? I groped through my purse, looking for some new communication from the spirit realm, something that would tell me what to do. But there was nothing.

I was still fretting as the bus chugged up Lincoln Avenue toward Riverview Lane. And then I got an idea.

If Crystal could communicate with me by leaving things in the purse, maybe I could communicate with her the same way.

We were nearing my stop. Hastily, I tore a page out of the little notepad I kept in my purse and wrote on it, "Should I keep investigating your disappearance?" I tucked the note deep into the purse.

As soon as I got home, I called Toni to tell her about my visit with Mae. I'd barely gotten the first few words out before she cut me off.

"I can't talk now. Jan and I are baking pies for the community picnic."

I let out a surprised laugh. "You don't bake."

"Jan's teaching me."

"Wow," I said, looping the phone cord around my forefinger. "So you and Jan are baking buddies."

"I wouldn't go that far. Hey, the timer just went off. I gotta take these pies out of the oven. Call me later, okay? I want to hear how things are going. But not tomorrow. We'll be at the picnic."

"Okay. When will you be—" I started, but she had already hung up.

I had a tutoring session with Alyssa from six to seven. When I got home, I couldn't wait any longer. I emptied my purse onto the kitchen table and spread out the contents.

The note I'd written was gone. But nothing was there in its place.

Not yet, anyway.

Chapter 46

It wasn't until the next morning, after my tutoring session with Jared, that I found Crystal's response.

She'd left me a street map, a lopsided rectangle maybe eight inches by four inches that had obviously been torn from a larger map. It looked old. The paper was full of soft wrinkles, as though it had been crumpled up and smoothed out multiple times. There were brown splotches where some liquid—coffee? blood?—had been spilled. A sharp crease down the middle of the paper was beginning to tear at the top, like a zipper creeping down.

The map showed Linden Street—specifically, the block between Lincoln and Jefferson Avenues. The buildings were represented as squares or rectangles, and each business was labeled. Wittmeyer's Auto Sales. Tuttle Photography. Apex Insurance Agency. I thought I knew Linden Street pretty well, but there were some names I didn't recognize: Meyers and Kovich Attorneys at Law, George's Pet Supplies.

Also on the map were several smaller unlabeled squares that might have been smaller shops or even houses. Two squares filled the space where the thrift store should have been. That baffled me until I realized this wasn't a recent map.

It was a map from the year Crystal had disappeared. That was my guess, anyway.

I took a moment to marvel over Crystal's growing strength. Two months ago, she'd been unable to manifest a twenty-year-old newspaper. Now she had no trouble producing a map that was just as old, not to mention the other items she'd given me in recent weeks.

I wasn't surprised to see Wittmeyer's Auto Sales on the map, though it didn't seem to answer the question I'd asked Crystal. Nothing on the map did.

I turned it over. The back was blank, a uniform yellowed-white except for light brown splotches where the spilled liquid had seeped through.

Well. If something was there, it had to be in the tiny print on the front of the map. I fetched a small plastic magnifying glass from the kitchen junk drawer. It had been a prize in a cereal box, but it worked well enough. I moved it methodically across the map, squinting like a jeweler. Some of the lines were blurry, especially in the splotchy areas, and almost all of the printed letters had faded to gray. Oddly, three of them were a sharp, vivid black. The *e* in *Linden*. The *S* in *Sales*. The *y* in *Photography*.

e-S-y.

S-y-e.

y-e-S.

For the longest time, I stared at those letters, unable to believe what I was seeing. I hadn't expected the answer to come so quick and easy. But there it was.

Should I keep investigating your disappearance?

Yes.

THE HAUNTED PURSE

I patted my chest, trying to settle my racing heart. If Crystal could answer that question, she could answer others. I wrote down the first one that popped into my head—*Were you murdered?*—and slipped the note into my purse.

Within an hour I had a response. This time she'd left me a torn-out newspaper ad for ladies' handbags, one of which looked a lot like her reporter's bag. Certain letters in the ad were darker than the others, just like on the map.

y-e-s

The word sent a chill through me, followed by a wave of grief and then a crazy rush of elation as I thought, *Holy crap. I'm communicating with a ghost!*

Which question should I ask next? It was time to brainstorm. I tore a new slip of paper out of my notepad and started scribbling.

Who murdered you?
Where is your body?
Where is the brown purse?
How did you die?
Why were you murdered?
Were you investigating a drug dealer when you disappeared?
Is Peter Wittmeyer a drug dealer? Is he that drug dealer?
And some questions unrelated to the murder.
Will you always be in the purse?
Why can't I see you?
What's it like to die? To be dead?
Should I tell your mom you live in my purse?

There really was no contest. That first question was the most important one. I needed to find out if Mae's husband was, in fact, a murderer. Whether he was or wasn't, learning the identity of Crystal's killer would help me figure out what to do next.

I printed my question on a new sheet of notepad paper. Then I slipped the note into a zippered compartment and set the purse in a quiet corner of my bedroom to marinate.

Chapter 47

Crystal had always worked in piecemeal fashion, leaving me one thing at a time. But that evening when I checked the purse, I found six items.

What she had left me were six five-by-seven school pictures. I spread them across the kitchen table in two rows of three. Several of the faces were startlingly familiar—Toni, Charlie, Mason. There was another picture of me, this one from seventh grade. And two girls I didn't recognize—a sullen-looking bleached blonde and a pretty brunette. The muted colors in the last two photos told me they were much older than the others. Who were these girls? Friends of Crystal's? Addicts who'd bought drugs from her stepfather?

I bent over the table, studying each picture in turn. They didn't seem to answer my question: *Who murdered you?* Of course, a yes-or-no response was one thing. It might be harder for a ghost to answer open-ended questions. Maybe the photos were simply more clues. But how could photos of Toni, Charlie, Mason, and me be clues to a murder that had happened twenty years ago?

I slipped the photos back into my purse. I had to believe I'd eventually figure things out. Maybe the answer would come to me in my sleep, like my revelation about Peter Wittmeyer.

Monday morning around eleven I boarded the bus to the Hilltop, wearing my new jeans and the sparkly pink tee shirt. I was eager to see Mae again and to meet Crystal's sister. I wanted to show them the latest pictures Crystal had left me, the ones I couldn't identify. Maybe they could tell me who the two girls were.

This time a younger woman answered the door.

"Libby? Hi, I'm Lauren, Mae's daughter. Come on in!"

She was a slender woman with chin-length, wavy brown hair and intelligent hazel eyes. I saw Crystal in the shape and color of those eyes, but aside from that, there wasn't much resemblance. Lauren's face was thinner, her mouth wider. Her smile was warm like Mae's, though something in her demeanor suggested she was shrewder, more confident. A woman who was used to taking charge.

Mae hugged me like I was a long-lost friend and made me sit at the kitchen table while she and Lauren finished the lunch preparations.

"I used a new recipe for the crab cakes," Mae said. "I hope they're not too spicy."

"Oh, wow!" I said when I saw the spread. Aside from the crab cakes, there were tacos, pizza, macaroni and cheese, potato salad, raw veggies with two kinds of dip, fruit salad, and a lemony cake-like dessert.

"Mom tends to go overboard when she gets company," Lauren said with an indulgent roll of her eyes.

"I don't know what Libby likes," Mae said defensively. "I wanted to give her plenty of options."

"Well, everything looks great," I said, my eyes lingering on the crab cakes. The only seafood I'd ever had was canned tuna.

I helped Mae and Lauren carry the food to the table on the back deck. Mae had decided we should eat outside to enjoy the pleasant weather.

As Lauren passed me the potato salad, her gaze strayed to my purse, which sat next to me on my chair.

"It's nice to see someone using it again," she said.

I nodded. When my arm brushed the purse, I felt the warmth radiating from it.

"So, do you live around here, Libby?" Mae asked.

I live in the Halfway area.

I almost said it. It wouldn't have been the first lie I'd ever told. I lied about my mother all the time because I had to. But a liar wasn't who I was, not deep down. And I wouldn't have felt right misrepresenting myself to these ladies.

"I live downtown," I said, jutting my chin out in mild defiance. "By the river. I ended up with Crystal's purse because the thrift store is pretty much the only place I shop. We don't have much money. My mom works as a server. I don't have a dad."

I looked from Mae's face to Lauren's, trying to gauge their reaction. Trying to see if those friendly exteriors were actually masks that hid stuck-up, snooty underneaths. To my relief, Mae nodded sympathetically, and Lauren said, "There's no shame in being poor."

"I'm not always going to be poor," I said. I told them about my academic awards and my tutoring gigs. My plans to go to college. I wanted them to know I was somebody smart and ambitious, not tenement trash.

"She's so much like Crystal," Mae said, leaning toward Lauren. "Doesn't she remind you of Crystal?"

"She does," murmured Lauren, her bright eyes on me. She fingered a locket at her throat, a heart-shaped silver pendant the size of a nickel. I wondered if Crystal was inside.

Lauren told me that she and her husband lived in Rosedale, not far from her childhood home. She taught English at Rosedale Junior High.

Aha, I thought, a teacher. That explained the glint of steel I detected beneath the soft exterior. I had no doubt that Lauren was a fair and reasonable instructor, but I would have bet she didn't put up with any nonsense. Her good students—the engaged, obedient ones—probably adored her. The badass kids probably hated her. No one would dare try to deceive her, because those shrewd eyes would see the truth.

I pried my gaze away from hers, wondering if she could read my mind.

After lunch, I helped clear the table and load the dishwasher. Then the three of us went into the family room. I bypassed the Peter Wittmeyer DNA chair and plopped my well-fed self onto the short end of the L-shaped sofa.

"There's something I need to ask you," I said to the ladies. I pulled the two mystery photos out of my purse and placed them side by side on the coffee table. "These were in the purse with the photos of Crystal. Do you know who these girls are? Were they friends of Crystal's?"

"More pictures!" exclaimed Lauren. "I thought I'd emptied everything out before I took that purse to the thrift store."

"It's easy to miss stuff," I said. "Especially since the purse has so many compartments. It happens to me all the time."

Mae and Lauren, seated next to each other on the long arm of the sofa, bent forward to study the photos. Mae picked one up, the photo of the blonde girl.

"This one, I think she might have gone to school with Crystal. Am I right, Lauren?"

Lauren took a closer look. "She does look familiar."

"Well, if they went to school with Crystal, they'd be in her yearbooks, right?" I glanced from Lauren to Mae. "Do you still have her yearbooks? I'd really like to get their names."

Lauren settled back into the sofa, her cast-iron gaze pinning me in place. "Why do you want their names? Does it matter who they are?"

"She wants to know about Cryssy's life," Mae said. "She feels close to her since she has her old purse. Isn't that right, honey?"

I nodded. But Lauren didn't. She said, "As far as we know, these girls weren't part of Crystal's life. They weren't her friends. They were probably just classmates, if that."

"But their pictures were in her purse," I said. "They must have been there for a reason."

"I suppose," said Lauren. "Still. Why do you want to know who they are?"

Her gaze was still fixed on me, tight as teeth. I could see that she wasn't going to back down. Well. I supposed I owed these ladies something. If not the whole truth, then at least a partial truth.

So I blurted it out. "I'm investigating Crystal's disappearance. I know that sounds crazy, maybe even childish, like a little kid playing detective. But I can't stand not knowing what happened to her."

"Oh, honey," Mae murmured.

"Wow," said Lauren, though it didn't sound like a thumbs-up kind of wow. She folded her arms, and I could see her gearing up to dissuade me.

"I want to find these girls," I went on. "I want to talk to them. Who knows? Maybe the police never questioned them. Maybe they know something that would help solve the case."

"Libby, we appreciate what you're trying to do," said Lauren, "but it's been twenty years since Crystal disappeared. You don't honestly think you're going to get anywhere, do you?"

"I probably won't," I said. "Still, I have to try. It's like your mother said—I feel close to Crystal. I want to do something to help."

"See?" Mae said to Lauren. "She's playing detective, just like Cryssy used to do."

Lauren shot her mother a sober glance. "Playing detective probably got Cryssy killed. We don't want the same thing to happen to Libby."

"It won't," I assured her. "If I find out anything important, I'll go straight to the police, I promise."

Lauren studied me for a long moment. Then she said, "I'll get the yearbooks."

She returned with several slim gray volumes. I slid in between Lauren and Mae on the sofa and flipped through pages in the one from twenty years ago until I got to the sophomore class. Row by row I went, moving my forefinger methodically across the pages.

"Here's one of them!" I said, pointing to a face in the fourth row of the third page.

The pictures matched exactly, the miniature black-and-white in the yearbook and the five-by-seven color both showing the sullen-looking blonde.

"Calliope Mendelhoff," mused Lauren, her breath wafting across my cheek like a breeze. "I remember that name. I always liked the way it sounded. Kind of rhythmic, like a poem." She glanced at her mother. "She wasn't a friend of Cryssy's, though, was she?"

"Not that I know of."

We never did find the other girl, the pretty brunette. Mae and Lauren both said they'd never seen her before.

"Calliope Mendelhoff," I said. "I should write that down." I scooted to the far end of the couch to grab my purse. It was still warm. I gave it a reassuring pat.

Easy, girl. He's not here. Peter Wittmeyer isn't here.

But a few minutes later, he was.

Chapter 48

"I should go," I said, glancing at my watch. "I have a tutoring session in an hour."

Lauren and Mae walked me to the front door.

"Thank you so much for lunch," I said. "Everything was great. Especially the crab cakes."

"You're welcome, sweetheart." Mae wrapped her fleshy arms around me. "Please come back soon. Bring your swimsuit next time. We hardly ever use the pool. It would be nice to see a young person splashing around in it."

"Thanks. I'd like that," I said. I didn't own a swimsuit. I'd never owned one. Maybe I could get one on sale at the mall.

Lauren leaned in to hug me. "Honestly, Libby, we're touched that you want to find out what happened to Crystal. But please be careful. Whoever's responsible for her disappearance might still be out there. And if that person finds out you're nosing around, you could be in danger."

"Don't worry. I'm only going to—" I began.

The front door swung open. Peter Wittmeyer stood on the other side of it. All the breath whooshed out of my throat as I gaped up at him.

Mae gasped. "Peter! What are you doing home?"

"Fetching some documents I left behind this morning." He looked from Mae to Lauren to me. "Who's this?"

Mae and Lauren exchanged nervous glances. Mae said, "This is Libby. Libby Dawson. Libby, this is my husband, Peter Wittmeyer."

"Nice to meet you, Mr. Wittmeyer," I managed to croak. "I was just leaving."

"Hold on," said Peter Wittmeyer, blocking my way. "What's your business here? Are you selling something?"

"No," I said, mortified at the way my voice cracked.

"She found a stray cat up the street," Lauren said quickly. "She thought it might be ours."

I nodded, perfectly willing to go along with this lie.

"We don't have a cat." Peter Wittmeyer peered down at me, his bird-of-prey face even more intimidating up close. "Olivia Dawson, you say? Do you live around here?"

"It's actually Libby," I said. "L-I-B-B-Y. And, no, I live...someplace else."

Peter Wittmeyer's face tightened up. "Libby Dawson? Damn it! Now I know why that name sounds familiar. You're the girl who called here a couple of weeks ago, asking about Crystal!" He seemed to grow beefier, like a porcupine whose quills were puffing out. "Didn't I tell you not to bother my family?"

"Peter, please," said Mae. "She's just a kid. She meant no harm."

"How do you know what she meant? I explicitly told her not to bother us, but she came here anyway."

Lauren stepped between me and Peter Wittmeyer. "Dad, stop. She wanted to return some pictures of Crystal to us, that's all."

"Pictures of Crystal? How the hell did she get pictures of Crystal?"

Mae grabbed her husband's sleeve and tugged him down the hall toward the family room. I could hear him raging all the way. Lauren ushered me out onto the porch, closing the door behind us.

"Libby, I am so sorry about that. Even after all these years, any mention of Crystal turns him into a raving lunatic."

I tried to speak but couldn't. I was shaking all over. I leaned against the banister to steady myself.

"He really is a good guy," Lauren continued. She let out a short, mirthless laugh. "Well. I guess you'll have to take my word for it."

No, Lauren. Peter Wittmeyer is not a good guy. He murdered your sister. I can't prove it yet, but I will.

"Crystal's disappearance affected us all in different ways," she said, twisting her locket around and around on its chain. "Mom still has a room upstairs decorated for a teenage girl. Pink eyelet curtains, stuffed animals on the bed. It's like she thinks Crystal is going to come back any day now and she'll still be fifteen."

A cloud of grief dulled her eyes. "Then there's me. I'd just graduated from high school when Cryssy went missing. Talk about self-absorbed! I never had a minute to spare for my pesky little sister." She drew in a short, gasping breath that was almost a sob. "If only I'd tried to talk to her once in a while, maybe she would have confided in me. Maybe I could have stopped her from going wherever she went the day she disappeared."

"It wasn't your fault," I said.

"I know it wasn't. Rationally, I know that. And yet, it feels like it was." She bowed her head, a woman bent beneath a sorrow I couldn't begin to comprehend. When she finally looked up, her eyes were bright again. "Hey," she said. "Let me give you my phone number. Call me anytime you want to talk. About Crystal, about anything. If you want to see my mom, the three of us can meet at my place."

I got a pen and my notepad out of my purse.

"Can you write it down for me?" I asked. "My hand's shaking too much."

That night Peter Wittmeyer infiltrated my dreams, a monster-man with fangs and a spiked tail. He had slithered out of the river and was scaling the outside of my apartment building, intent on devouring me.

I woke up screaming, but no one was there to comfort me.

Chapter 49

I would have expected Calliope Mendelhoff to have a different name by now. A husband's name—Smith, Cooper, Kleinschmidt. But when I typed her name into a browser on a library computer, I immediately got results: *Calliope Mendelhoff, Ashton, OH.* The name was unusual enough that I knew there couldn't be two Calliope Mendelhoffs in the world, let alone in Ashton. This was the woman I was looking for.

I couldn't get a phone number without paying for it, but one of Calliope's social media posts gave an address, which she'd advertised while trying to sell a used TV a few months back. I jotted it down and set out to visit her.

My section of the inner city spilled across the river into an area known as Prospect, and that was where Calliope lived. Her neighborhood was even seedier than mine. Bars outnumbered churches five to one, and every street had its share of porn shops, liquor stores, and pawn shops. There was even a fleabag hotel. The only wholesome establishment was a dollar store, which I visited when I needed something the thrift store didn't carry, like underwear or cheap canned goods. But I made sure to go only in broad daylight and always with a small can of bug spray in my purse to use as a makeshift weapon. So far, I'd never had to spray anybody.

Calliope's apartment building was a big brick structure that had once been a jail. I arrived a little after five on Tuesday afternoon, but when Calliope opened the door, she looked like she'd just rolled out of bed. Her face was as thin and angular as in her high school photo, but weathered now, like an old barn nobody had ever bothered to paint. Her stringy hair was still bleached-blonde, brittle as frostbitten wheat. She wore a short, satiny purple bathrobe and had a cigarette pinched between two fingers.

Before I could get a word out, she rasped, "I don't buy none of that shit you kids sell."

"I'm not selling anything," I said. I waved the photo in front of her face. "I just want to know: is this you?"

She bent in close to study the photo and let out a croak that might have been a laugh. Her breath was fouler than the Arihanna River. I took a discreet step backward. "Gawd! What was this—like, ninth, tenth grade? Must've been, 'cause I dropped out at the beginning of eleventh."

"It was tenth grade," I said.

"Where'd you get this?" She took the photo from me.

"It was in an old purse I bought at the thrift store. I thought you might want it back. Also, I wanted to see if you could tell me anything about Crystal Callahan. She was in your class at school."

"Crystal Callahan." She blew a puff of smoke in my face, her eyes dead as peach pits. "Oh. The girl that went missing."

"Did you know her? Were you friends?"

"Hell, no. I didn't run with that crowd. I wasn't the goody-goody type, even back then."

"Well, do you have any ideas about what might have happened to her?"

"Why would I have ideas about that? I told you, I didn't hang with the girl. Look, my shift starts at five. I gotta go get ready."

"Oh, sorry. Are you a server?" I asked, trying to be friendly.

She let out a scornful laugh. "No, honey, I ain't no server."

She looked at the photo again, her mouth curving downward in bitterness, or maybe regret.

"Right here," she said, tapping the photo with a ragged fingernail. "Right here's where things started to go bad. Tenth grade." Her bleary eyes found mine. "You're about that age, ain't you? Don't make the same mistakes I made. Somebody comes up to you offering you the moon? Run away. Run like hell. Don't let him ruin your life."

She handed the picture back to me and started to close the door.

"Wait," I said. "What do you mean? Who ruined your life? Was it a drug dealer?"

Our eyes locked. Hers, suddenly wide, said *me and my big mouth*. "I don't mean nothing," she growled. "Just forget it."

"No," I said. "You have to tell me who you're talking about."

"I ain't talking about nobody!" she screeched. "Now, go away."

She slammed the door shut and wouldn't open it again, even though I pounded on it for five minutes.

Fine. I would come back tomorrow, and the next day, and I would keep coming back until I wore her down, got her to confide in me. I had a feeling her refusal to talk went beyond a mere reluctance to dredge up bad memories. But where was it coming from? Shame? Hopelessness? Fear?

When I got home, Mr. Owens was parked in the front yard, magazine pages fluttering in his lap like tethered birds. We exchanged amiable grunts, and I stomped upstairs.

THE HAUNTED PURSE

As I reached into my purse and unzipped the small pocket that held my key, I heard an odd clank—metal bumping metal. It was a sound that made no sense, because there was nothing in that compartment for my key to bump against. Or shouldn't have been, anyway.

Tentatively I reached inside and drew out two objects. The key to my apartment. And a second key.

The second key looked old. Antiquish, even. It was a tarnished gold, heavier than my apartment key, as if made from a better grade of metal.

But before I could even speculate about what it might unlock, I heard my phone ringing. I rushed into the apartment, making sure to close and lock the door behind me, and picked up the receiver.

It was Toni. She was crying so hard I couldn't understand a word she was saying.

Chapter 50

"Toni, calm down!" I said, a tight knot of dread already forming in my stomach. "Take a breath and tell me what's wrong."

I heard her suck in a few desperate gulps of air, the way people do while thrashing in deep water. Then she lost it again.

I clenched the phone cord in frustration. I'd never heard her so upset before. Had somebody in her family died? Was she being sent to reform school? Was Jan pregnant again?

I pressed the phone tight against my ear, trying to pick out words. All I could make out was "So so so so..."

"So so *what*?" I demanded. "Toni, come on. You're scaring me."

"So, so—*sorry*!" she whispered. "I am so, so sorry!"

The sobs continued.

"Sorry about what?" I asked. "Toni, you have to tell me what's going on."

She took a couple of hiccupping breaths. I thought I heard her slurping some liquid. When she spoke again, she was still crying, but her words had lost that blurry edge. "I—I told Jan about you. How your mom...isn't around."

"What?" A great shudder racked my body. "No, no, you can't do that."

"But I did. I told Jan, and she called Child Protective Services, and they're going to be coming for you. They're coming to get you, Libby. Like, soon."

My bones dissolved. I collapsed onto the couch. "Oh my *God*. Do you know what this means? How could you do this to me?"

She sniffed loudly. "I didn't mean to. Jan and me, we finally bonded. We took a walk today, and we were just talking, telling stories about ourselves. She told me how she got in trouble when she was sixteen because her parents trusted her to stay home alone overnight while they went someplace, and her friend talked her into having this party, and things got crazy, and the police came, and... Anyway. I didn't have any stories like that, so..."

"So you used mine," I said flatly.

"I wasn't thinking! It just came out. You're the one who told me to bond with her."

I said, in a high, tremulous voice, "You have destroyed me. Do you realize that? Do you know what's going to happen to me now?"

She hiccupped again. "I know. And I'm so, so sorry. But seriously, Libby, it's for the best. You're fifteen. You shouldn't be living by yourself."

"Oh my God, you sound like one of *them*," I cried. "I've been doing just fine on my own. I buy groceries, I pay the bills. I was student of the year, for God's sake."

"You're still a kid. You need to be in a house with grown-ups."

"Do you know what kinds of grown-ups become foster parents? Child abusers. Pedophiles. People looking for easy money."

"Jan says they screen those people really carefully."

"But they don't. There are too many kids and not enough decent families to take them in. Look at Emma Randall. She's a slave. A modern-day Cinderella. Except she won't be going to the ball anytime soon, because fairy godmothers don't exist."

"Foster care isn't forever, Libby. CPS always tries to get kids back with their real families."

"Oh, like that's the answer," I snapped. "You think I want to live with my mother? You don't even know her. You have no idea what a bitch she is. I don't need her. I don't need anybody."

A sudden pounding at the door made me jump.

"Libby Dawson?" a woman called. "Child Protective Services. Open the door, sweetheart."

I dropped to the floor, squatting between the couch and the coffee table. As if CPS could see through walls. "They're here," I squeaked. "I have to go."

"Libby, I—"

I pressed the disconnect button and dropped the receiver onto the couch.

"Libby?" the CPS woman said, rattling the doorknob. "I know you're in there. Your neighbor saw you come home. Open the door, hon. I just want to talk to you."

Sure you do, I thought, sucking on my kneecap.

"If you won't let me in," the woman continued, "I'll have to come back with the police, and they'll break the door down."

Holy crap. In the blink of an eye my life had become a TV melodrama.

Chapter 51

I stayed put for ten minutes. I wanted to be sure the CPS lady had left, but I didn't want to give her enough time to come back with the police. I crept down the stairs, hugging the wall to minimize the creaking of the old wooden steps, and peeked out the front door. So far so good. There were no police cars in sight. Mr. Owens was still in the yard, his back to me.

I eased the door shut behind me and tiptoed down the front steps. Then I slipped into the tight space between my building and the one next door. That passageway spat me into a narrow alley that ran along the river. A two-foot-high concrete barrier separated the alley from the sloping river wall. Once or twice a year, some drunk would tumble over the barrier and have to be fished out of the river by the fire department. Sometimes alive, sometimes dead.

The sky had clouded over, imbuing everything around me with a gloomy pewter light. That suited me just fine. Considering how my life was falling apart, the last thing I wanted to see was cheerful sunshine.

I stayed in the alley for half a block. Then I veered into a narrow walkway between two buildings and made my way to Riverview Lane. As I crossed the street, I glanced toward my building. Nothing seemed to be happening. Not a police car was in sight.

A comforting numbness had spread through me, a self-generated anesthetic that was keeping me from losing it completely while I figured out what to do. I needed help, but who could I turn to? My mother? Not in a million years! Even if I knew how to contact her, she would probably jump at the chance to dump me into foster care.

How about Mrs. Moore? Louie and Charlie? Tommy? Alyssa and her mom? Selena from the thrift store? Mae? Lauren?

No. They were all either respectable adults or kids who lived with respectable adults. None of them would be willing to harbor a CPS fugitive.

I was going to get caught. It was just a matter of time.

Tears of despair blurred my vision. Once I got whisked away to foster care, I wouldn't have the freedom to roam around town as I worked on Crystal's case. My investigation would come to a halt. And I probably wouldn't be able to visit Mae or Lauren.

I couldn't bear the thought of letting Crystal down. Now that I had the key, I was closer than ever to solving the case. Closer to finding evidence that would incriminate her murderer. I had to keep going. I had to elude the authorities long enough to wrap things up. Even if that meant being on the run for a while.

I reached into my purse, just to make sure the key was still there. And then I headed for the door I knew it had to fit.

Since it was after five o'clock, all the downtown businesses were closed. Linden Street was eerily free of both pedestrians and traffic, making me feel like the sole survivor of an apocalypse. I went straight to the main door of Wittmeyer's Auto Sales and tried to insert the key. It wouldn't go in past the first notch.

That was okay. The building had other entrances; I was surprised by how many. I found one on each side of the building and three in the back. Just as I reached the door to the service department, I heard a car cruising down the alley. I dropped to the ground, flattening myself behind a low brick wall that separated the service entrance walkway from the parking lot. When I peeked over the top, I saw a police car rolling slowly by, the two officers inside peering methodically left and right.

Were they looking for me? Probably.

As soon as the police car was gone, I jumped to my feet. The key didn't fit the service department door. And within minutes I found that it didn't fit any of the other doors, either. I glanced down the length of the building, baffled and discouraged. If this wasn't the right place, then what was? *Where, Crystal? Where should I go?*

I searched my purse, but there were no new clues. Apparently, Crystal felt she'd given me everything I needed.

All I could think to do was to reexamine the clues she'd left me, one by one. Maybe I'd missed something—a hidden meaning, a subtle connection.

I trotted across the alley to a tiny concrete yard at the rear of an old house. This house, like many others in the downtown area, had been repurposed as a business office. Two parking spaces abutting the alley had signs advertising "Parking for Customers of Paul Gingrich, CPA." Closer to the house was a fake-wood picnic table where employees could eat lunch while enjoying the lovely urban scenery. I seated myself at the table and pulled Crystal's clues out of my purse. Then I arranged them in chronological order.

Clue number one was the snapshot of Crystal by the turreted house. Next came the newspaper. Then the pencil, the roll of cherry candies, and the fashion-doll purse. Crystal's tenth-grade photo. My tenth-grade photo. The snapshot of Crystal with the brown purse. The map. The ad for ladies' handbags. The batch of school photos. And, finally, the key.

I decided to eliminate items that had served their purpose so I could focus on the remaining clues.

I immediately put the pencil and cherry candies back in my purse, because they weren't really clues, just little gifts she'd left me.

The first picture of Crystal had led me to Mrs. Atkins, who'd told Toni and me about the disappearance. As a clue, that picture was done, used up like a chewed stick of gum, so I slipped it back into the purse. Same with the newspaper. It had prompted my search for the article about Crystal's disappearance, which had provided the names I needed.

I herded the fashion-doll purse, the snapshot of Crystal with her reporter's bag, and the handbag ad into a little pile. They were essentially the same clue repeated, and I'd gotten the message loud and clear. Crystal wanted me to find her missing reporter's bag. The handbag ad had served a dual purpose, since it had also answered my question *Were you murdered?* I put those items back into the purse.

A rush of wind twirled around me like playful fingers, snatching up the torn map and spinning it into the air. The photos went scuttling across the table. I reached out with both hands, grabbing, clutching, recovering my precious clues. I gathered the photos into a loose pile and set my purse on top of them. Apprehensively, I glanced upward. The sky was looking more ominous, the clouds as resolute as hardened concrete. I should probably try to find shelter. But first I needed to finish what I'd started.

The map was the next clue. Crystal had used it to answer my initial question—*Should I keep investigating your disappearance?* Into my purse it went.

That left the school photos. One picture of Crystal, two of me. The others of seemingly random kids. People I knew, people Crystal had known. Kids from at least two different schools, decades apart. What did they mean? What was the common element tying them together?

The last batch of photos had appeared after I'd asked, "Who murdered you?" Yet they didn't answer that question, at least not as far as I could tell. Crystal had literally spelled out her responses to my first two questions, and I'd expected the same this time. Was I missing something? Maybe a name scrawled in tiny, penciled lettering on the back of one of the photos?

One by one, I turned them over. In every instance, the smooth, white surface was unmarked. I checked the fronts, too. There was no writing. In fact, the only lettering anywhere was *Tim Tuttle Photography*, embossed in gold at the bottom right corner of each photo.

I stared at those golden letters. *Tim Tuttle Photography.*

My breathing slowed to a stop. That wasn't just the name of a business. It was also the name of a person.

And suddenly it became the answer to a question.

Who murdered you?

Tim Tuttle.

I sucked in a gasp of air so huge, my lungs couldn't process it. I spent a minute coughing my guts out.

Chapter 52

Could this be true? Could Tim Tuttle be Crystal's murderer? Had Crystal even known him, other than as a school photographer? I pulled the map out of my purse, even though I knew what it showed. Tim Tuttle's studio had been one of the Linden Street businesses twenty years ago. And Mae had said Crystal spent a lot of time at Peter's car dealership, a few doors down. What if she hadn't stayed inside like Mae believed? What if she'd gone outside and snooped around the neighborhood, playing reporter? Her path could have crossed Tim Tuttle's, and she might have learned something about him—something so incriminating that it had gotten her murdered.

But damn. I'd been so sure Peter Wittmeyer was the murderer.

My eyes drifted to the rear of the Tuttle building. It was an old house, just like the CPA's building. But it was much larger, both wider and deeper. A mini mansion of yore.

I shoved the photos and map back in the purse and snatched up the key. After checking for police cars, I made my way to Linden Street.

Through a picture window at the front of Tim Tuttle's studio, I saw a dim light. After glancing around to make sure I was alone, I scurried up the steps to the front porch and peered in the window.

Inside was the reception area, a spacious room with an office desk, a seating area, and a couple of potted plants. Magazines were fanned out on a small table. Portraits covered the walls—blushing brides, tousle-haired teens, giggling toddlers. Samples of the fine work Tim Tuttle did. All was still and quiet inside. The light had obviously been left on to discourage break-ins. But that wasn't going to keep me out. Not if the key worked.

I tried it in the front door. It didn't fit into the lock. I kept my hopes up by reminding myself that the house also had a back door. But if the key didn't fit there, I was back to square one, out of ideas. At that point, I might as well turn myself in to CPS.

I left the front porch and waded through the narrow side yard, the unmowed weeds tickling my calves. A few preliminary raindrops pelted me, big as thumbs. I hurried up the steps to the back porch, grateful for its roof.

The porch looked unused. Forgotten, even. The weathered wood of the floor and railing were splotched with green mold. The floor dipped in one spot where the boards were rotting through. Piled against the house was an assortment of junk—an old stove, a cracked toilet, a stack of mildewed cardboard boxes.

I pushed past all the junk and yanked open the old wooden screen door. A little pile of last October's leaves disintegrated with a crunch as the door raked over them.

I could barely see the keyhole in the shadows of the covered porch. And my hand was trembling, which didn't help. After a few tries, I hit the right spot. The key slid in. I turned it and twisted the doorknob, and the door opened.

Chapter 53

I was standing in a small kitchen crowded with dingy white appliances. The linoleum was cracked and stained and looked even older than the prehistoric stuff on my own kitchen floor. A mug with a brown smudge at the front, where mouth met rim, sat on the counter next to a coffeemaker. A snapshot of Tim Tuttle accepting some kind of award was magneted to the fridge.

A shiver went through me, but it wasn't because I was scared. No, it was because I was cold. I gave a jolt as I realized the coldness was coming from the purse, seeping through my clothes to chill me. I plucked at the strap, trying to hold the purse away from my body.

I thought back to the times at the Wittmeyers' house, the way the purse had heated up. And suddenly it all made sense. Crystal hadn't been trying to tell me her stepfather had murdered her. She'd been showing her love for him, and for the rest of her family. Warmth meant love. I should have realized that.

Here there was no love. Here there had been only terror and pain and death. This was a cold, sinister place, and Crystal was expressing that through the purse.

I moved deeper into the house. Beyond the kitchen, through an arched doorway, was a large dining room furnished with a wooden table and six chairs. The table looked cheap, its surface as thin as a worn-out shoe. A small TV, the old-fashioned cube-shaped kind, sat on a fold-out tray in the corner.

I exited the dining room through a side door and found myself in a hall. I opened a door and saw dirty wooden steps leading down into the dark. Cool air wafted past me, making its escape, and the smell of damp earth filled my nose. I caught another smell too, subtle but putrid. A broken sewer line? Rotten potatoes? I shuddered and closed the door. Unless Crystal insisted, I was not going down those steps.

At the front of the house was a bedroom, its door closed but not locked. It contained a bed covered with a crushed-velvet crimson bedspread, along with a dresser and nightstand. The room had an unoccupied look, like my mother's room. I wondered whether Tim Tuttle slept here on nights when he worked late and was too tired to drive home.

Across the hall from the bedroom was the reception area, which I'd seen from the porch. An open doorway at the rear led to the photography studio. There were lights of varying sizes on tripods and several expensive-looking cameras, also on tripods. A backdrop hung along the rear wall. The scene showed a stone path lined with summertime trees and flowers. A small desk with a computer on top was rammed squarely into a corner.

A door at the rear of the studio led to a smaller room with no windows. I flicked on a switch, and a light came on. From what little I knew about photography, I suspected this had been a darkroom back in the days when photographers had to develop their own film. Nowadays most photographers used filmless digital cameras.

THE HAUNTED PURSE

The space had been repurposed as a storage room. There were several filing cabinets and a shelving unit containing office supplies. I opened one of the filing cabinet drawers and found packets of photographs inside, organized behind alphabetized tabs.

The only remaining room downstairs was a tiny bathroom containing a toilet and sink.

I stepped into the hallway, looking around. This was a two-story house. Where was the staircase to the second floor?

There was one door I hadn't checked, at the front of the house. I'd assumed it led to a coat closet. There was a short, flat metal bar across the edge of the door with an unlocked padlock stuck through it.

I removed the padlock and opened the door, revealing an enclosed wooden staircase leading to the second floor. My heartbeat quickened. If Tim Tuttle sometimes padlocked this door, it had to mean there were things upstairs he didn't want his employees or customers stumbling upon.

The staircase was dark. I fished my mini flashlight out of my purse and headed up, each stairstep creaking beneath my feet. The purse was still icy-cold. It pulsed against my hip as if a disembodied heart was inside, pumping blood to nowhere.

When I reached the top of the stairs, I gasped in revulsion. I had seen this sort of thing on TV shows, but never in person.

The hall was filled with...stuff. You couldn't even categorize it, because there was a little bit of everything. Boxes, bags, shoes, boots, piles of ladies' dresses, moldering old magazines, rotting draperies, stacks of newspapers, and broken chairs. Chipped knick-knacks and dented saucepans and wall art and couch pillows and lamps. Handbags and books and window screens and folders bulging with papers. And much more. The stuff was stacked nearly to the ceiling, a teetering pile of human trappings that made me worry I might be buried alive at any moment. A cleared space maybe a foot wide allowed passage between the stacks of junk.

The upstairs was so different from the downstairs, it seemed like a separate house. The house of a hoarder.

I gritted my teeth and pressed on, turning left into the upstairs hallway. This passage was slightly wider than the one to the right, giving it a well-trodden feel. I entered the first room I came to. It was probably a bedroom, though if there was a bed in there, it was hidden under stacks of junk. A narrow path led to a wide space in front of a tall chest of drawers. I turned to leave and heard a click from my purse, the same sound a camera might make when someone snapped a picture.

I saw it as I moved my flashlight toward the purse—the corner of a photograph sticking out of one of the butt pockets. It was a picture of the chest of drawers in this very room.

"Something's in there?" I said. I opened each drawer, working from bottom to top. They were all empty.

"I don't understand," I said. "You have to give me more."

The throbbing of the purse had sped up. I sensed Crystal flickering, straining to become solid, but limited by forces I couldn't comprehend. I felt her presence as strongly as if she had been standing next to me. We were partners from different worlds, amateur detectives working together to catch a killer. And neither of us could do it without the other.

The purse clicked again, the new photo edging up out of the butt pocket like a sheet of paper emerging from a printer.

This picture showed the same chest of drawers, but it had been pulled away from the wall. Behind it I could see the frame of a door.

I grabbed the edges of the chest and tugged. It was a sturdy thing, made of wood, but because it was empty I was able to slide it away from the wall. Behind it was a door, just as the photo had promised. I turned the knob and pushed.

The room was pitch black. I stepped inside and fumbled for a light switch, and a neon light buzzed on. What I saw was so horrific, it left me paralyzed. I could only stare.

Chapter 54

All four walls of the room were papered in photographs. Eight-by-tens mostly, but also some eleven-by-fourteens and a few five-by-sevens. What they had in common was their content. They all featured nude young people.

Teenagers, preteens, even younger children. Mostly girls, but a smattering of boys. All of them naked. I turned my head right and then left, trying to escape the sight of all that innocent flesh. But it was everywhere. This was a trophy room, showcasing what Tim Tuttle considered his finest work.

This was what had gotten Crystal murdered. Tim Tuttle was a child pornographer, and Crystal had uncovered his filthy secret.

Was she here, in this little room? In dread I searched the walls. Crystal wasn't there, but I did find three other familiar faces—a young Calliope Mendelhoff, the unidentified brunette whose picture was in my purse, and, to my horror, Emma Randall.

I needed to get out of here. I needed to contact the police. I backed out of the room, shuddering, and pushed the chest of drawers back into place.

Click. There in one of the butt pockets was a close-up photo of a brown purse. Crystal's reporter's bag.

In my horror over the photos, I'd forgotten about the missing purse. But Crystal hadn't. She wanted me to find it. Because even though the hidden room contained enough evidence to prove Tim Tuttle's involvement with child pornography, there was nothing to link him to the murder of Crystal Callahan twenty years ago.

The purse would provide that link.

It struck me how Crystal had been in this house twenty years ago. Maybe standing in this very spot. Like me, she'd come looking for evidence of Tim Tuttle's criminal activity. But she'd had the bad luck to run into Tuttle himself. Maybe she'd dashed through the maze of junk and managed to hide the purse before Tuttle caught her. Had he even noticed she had a purse? If he'd searched for it, he probably hadn't found it. How could anyone, unless they knew where to look? This place was an indoor junkyard.

"Where?" I asked, my voice as thin as paper. "Tell me where to go."

My notepad jutted insistently out of the purse. I saw words scrawled lightly on the topmost sheet. God, she'd grown strong. I could almost feel her beckoning me out of the room.

Go right, the spindly writing on the notepad said, so I turned right into the clogged hallway.

Hurry, she said.

I moved down the hall as fast as the narrow passage would allow. Every room I passed was filled with junk.

Here, she said, after I'd rounded a corner. I stepped through a doorway, and my flashlight beam played across yet another craggy mountain range of junk. *Click.* Sliding up out of the purse was a photo showing four cardboard boxes stacked along a wall. A long pink bathrobe trailed down their sides.

I groped for a light switch on the wall just inside the door. But when I found one and flicked it, nothing happened. The overhead bulb had probably burned out long ago, and Tim Tuttle had never bothered to replace it. Or couldn't reach it because of all the junk.

Although it was only early evening, the room was nighttime dark. I couldn't see the windows, but I could hear them rattling in the wind. I heard the spatter of rain against the glass. I heard creaks and thumps from the aching bones of the old house.

I shined my flashlight around. This was the largest room on this floor, so big that it had two doors along the same wall, one at each end of the hall. Accordingly, it contained the most junk. I set off into the cave-like maze of passages. I had to backtrack a couple of times when I reached dead ends. Finally, I saw a flash of pink ahead. The bathrobe, draped over the boxes. Just like in the photo.

I assumed the purse was in one of the boxes. The top one was too high for me to reach. And the others were inaccessible, each crushed by the weight of those above it. I tried to push the whole stack over, but too much other stuff was in the way.

I huffed in frustration and took a closer look at the photo. No, this wasn't about the boxes. The focal point was the bathrobe.

I flew to the side of the boxes where the bathrobe hung, cozy and comforting, like a grandma. It made me think of Mae. I groped up and down the chenille fabric until I felt something bulky. This bathrobe had a hood, and nestled in that hood was the reporter's bag.

I let out a sob of elation and shoved it into the denim purse.

THE HAUNTED PURSE

Crystal's icy breath engulfed me. A new note was creeping up out of the purse, rushing to meet my hand.

This time the writing was firm and dark.

LIBBY RUN

Chapter 55

I stumbled toward the doorway, the one closest to the staircase. Before I could get there, a light jittered from the hallway and spilled into the bedroom. A figure loomed before me. Tim Tuttle.

In his khaki pants and polo shirt, his hair dampened by the rain, he looked like the benign, friendly photographer everyone knew. But that man no longer existed—and probably never had. The real Tim Tuttle was a monster.

"Well, well. What have we here?" The flashlight beam moved up and down the length of me and settled on my face. "Oh. It's the girl from the bench. The one who thinks she's too good to model."

I gaped at him, blinking against the light. I was in the same dire danger Crystal had been in twenty years ago. Alone in a house with a man who had a secret worth killing for. Of course, I had an advantage Crystal might have lacked. Tim Tuttle didn't know I knew about his criminal activity. And he didn't know I'd just recovered Crystal's purse.

Maybe I could get out of this alive.

"I'm really—I'm really—" My voice was barely a squeak; I had to clear my throat to make myself heard. "—sorry about coming in here. It started raining—like, hard. I didn't have any place else to go."

Tuttle lowered his flashlight beam. His face glowed in the ambient light, pale and inscrutable. His eyes were locked on mine. Time ticked by—five seconds, ten seconds, fifteen. Still he stared. What was he thinking? Why didn't he say something?

I made an awkward gesture, indicating the junk piled up around us. The situation was so glaring, the elephant in the room, that I felt I had to comment on it. "Looks like somebody's a hoarder," I said, trying to sound unworried, conversational, almost teasing. Like this was his big secret.

His upper lip curled in disgust. "Not me. This was my mother's doing. The house used to be hers. She died twenty-five years ago, but I've never gotten around to clearing out all her shit. Downstairs was just as bad. Had to clean it out before I could move my photography business in."

I felt a surge of hope. We were conversing, like two acquaintances who'd met on the street and stopped to chat. I needed to keep the talk going. I needed to distract him from the larger issue, to ease his suspicions. To make him see that as trespassers went, I was harmless. Just an inner-city girl who'd come in to get out of the rain.

But before I could think of something else to say, Tim Tuttle took a step deeper into the room. "Did you think I wouldn't know you were here? My security system gave you away. See, the alarm doesn't go off here. It sends me a phone alert. Happened once before. Someone broke in, thought he could steal my cameras. I caught him in the act. Held him at gunpoint till the police got here."

"I didn't come here to steal anything," I said, struggling to keep the tremor out of my voice. "I'm not interested in cameras. The truth is, I'm running away from home. I was looking for a place to crash for the night. Your back door was unlocked, so I came in."

"Really," said Tim Tuttle, looking down his nose at me. "That's odd, because I never use that door. Ever. I lost the key years ago. That door is always locked."

"Well... somebody must have unlocked it. One of your workers." I tried to swallow, but my throat was too dry. "Look, Child Protective Services is after me. That's why I'm hiding out here. Give them a call if you don't believe me. Ask them about Libby Dawson."

PLEASE give them a call. PLEASE tell them Libby Dawson is here.

"You know, I might have believed that," Tim Tuttle said, "if you hadn't been so sloppy."

A jangle of panic went through me. "Sloppy?"

He made a tsk-tsk noise, the kind a parent might make after his child forgets to put the milk carton back in the fridge. "You didn't push the chest of drawers close enough to the wall. I know you were in that room. The old nursery. You've been snooping, just like that other girl did all those years ago."

I didn't even try to deny it. He had to see the dismay in my face, the horror. "Crystal Callahan," I whispered. "She was the other girl."

He looked surprised. "You know about her?"

The purse was pulsing, pulsing, pulsing at my side, a panicked heart beating in sync with my own.

"Peter Wittmeyer's girl," he said. "She was pretty like you. But I never approached her about modeling. Wouldn't have dared. She wasn't the type. Too strong, too sure of herself. You're the same way. I should have realized that sooner."

"I won't tell anybody what I saw," I said, hating the tinny, desperate sound of my voice. "It doesn't matter to me what kinds of pictures you take."

"Well, that's good to know," Tim said with a gracious bow. "Thank you for being so reasonable."

For a moment, he seemed like the old Tim Tuttle—popular photographer, pillar of the community. I actually thought he was going to let me go. Then I realized he was toying with me. I saw the gun in his hand; he'd pulled it out of thin air. My heart quivered, anticipating the bullet. I squeezed my eyes shut.

And then a mighty rumbling began. Tim Tuttle looked around in alarm, unable to pinpoint the source of the commotion. But I knew at once where it was coming from. I felt the jack-hammering at my hip. The rumbling got louder, stronger, shaking the floor like an earthquake, threatening to topple the precarious piles of junk. And then a piercing, other-worldly moan rose from the depths of the purse. On that moan floated a single word.

MURRRR-DER-ERRRR...

Tim Tuttle stumbled backward, his eyes widening as they landed on my purse. He half-fell into a stack of junk.

I didn't waste a second. I turned and dashed into the passageway behind me, threading my body through those tight spaces as I tried to make my way back to the hall. Tuttle's footsteps lumbered behind me. I heard him grunting as he squeezed his bulky man-body through the narrow passages. I heard objects falling in his wake.

My heart dropped as I rounded a corner and came to a dead end. Directly in front of me was a stack of women's clothing as high as my head. I grabbed a laundry-load's worth of it and threw it on the floor behind me. Then I heaved myself over the remaining pile and tumbled heavily into the passage on the other side.

Tim Tuttle swore as he tripped over the clothing on the floor. I heard him go down, the thud muffled by the layers of fabric he landed on.

Ahead was the door to the hall. I dashed out and turned right. Rushed to the end of the hall and turned left. Saw the rectangular dark hole that was the staircase. But just as I reached it, I tripped over an errant piece of junk on the floor.

The momentum propelled me headfirst into the stairwell, and I went bumping down the steps. My head crunched into the door frame at the bottom. In the split second before darkness took me, I smelled the bitter scent of my own doom.

Chapter 56

I wasn't out for long, probably just a few seconds. As I came to, I heard Tim Tuttle thudding down the stairs. I was sprawled face down in the hall, mere feet from the front door. Blood dripped from a stinging wound on my cheek. I belly-crawled toward the door, knowing I'd never reach it but determined to try. I hurt all over and wasn't sure I could stand, let alone run.

"You stupid little bitch," said Tim Tuttle. "Did you really think you were going to get away?"

I rolled onto my side and raised my head. He was pointing the gun at me again. A wave of grief swept over me. I was going to be murdered, just like Crystal. Nobody would ever know what had happened to me. People would assume I'd run away to avoid foster care. Toni would blame herself.

"Please," I whispered. "Please don't shoot me."

His mouth twisted into a smirk. "Shoot you? I'm not going to shoot you. You think I want a bloody mess in my entrance hall?"

He laid the gun on a narrow table along the wall and strode into the first-floor bedroom, the one with the crimson bedspread. He came out holding a purple silk scarf.

The purse, still pressed to my side, gave a small hiccup, reminding me that I wasn't in this alone.

"She's here, you know," I said, rashness displacing terror for just a moment. "In the purse. You heard her yourself, upstairs. She's a ghost. Crystal Callahan is a ghost, and she's come back to get you."

Tim Tuttle's gaze flicked to the purse. The look of fear and confusion returned to his eyes, but only for a second.

"I don't believe in ghosts," he said scornfully, though I got the feeling he was trying to convince himself more so than me. "I don't know what you heard upstairs. *I* heard the wind wailing. And there might have been a minor earthquake, but it's over now."

He took a step toward me, the scarf stretched taut between his hands. "It didn't have to be this way," he said. "You shouldn't have come here tonight."

And then, impossibly, a small figure in a checkered cape leapt over me and kicked Tim Tuttle in the groin. Tuttle doubled over, yelping in pain.

"Mason?" I said with a gasp.

"The name's Astound-o Man," Mason said breathlessly.

He raised his arm and sprayed Tim Tuttle in the face with pepper spray. Tuttle screamed. Mason followed up with a kick to the knee that sent the man crashing to the floor like an axed tree.

Tim Tuttle curled in a ball, clutching his groin with one hand and swiping at his eyes with the other. He didn't have a hand to spare for his injured knee. Mason slipped off his backpack and pulled out a roll of duct tape. He wrapped it around and around Tuttle's ankles and then sliced it from the roll with a pocketknife.

"Libby," he said. "Can you sit on him while I do his hands?"

I dragged myself over, wincing in pain. The idea of having physical contact with Tim Tuttle made my stomach lurch, but we needed to immobilize him. With a grunt, Mason flipped him onto his stomach. I sat on his upper back while Mason wrenched his arms behind him and duct-taped his wrists together.

We pushed Tuttle's body into the stairwell. Mason slammed the door and slid the padlock into place. He clicked it into the locked position. We could hear Tuttle screaming and swearing behind the door.

Mason pulled off his cape and told me to press it against the gash on my cheek.

"Can you stand up?" he asked.

I gave it a try, leaning heavily on him. Together we limped to the front door.

"Hey, Libby," chirped Mason. "Aren't you glad I didn't keep my promise about not following you?"

Chapter 57

The ER doctor said I had a concussion, bruised ribs, a broken wrist, and too many contusions and abrasions to count. The gash on my cheek required stitches, and the doctor said it would probably leave a scar. There were no signs of internal bleeding, but he decided to keep me in the hospital for a day or two "for observation."

Naturally, the hospital people wanted to contact my mother, and I was forced to admit I didn't know how to reach her. I gave them all the information I had. Her name was Misty Dawson. She was a server at some swanky nightclub. She lived in a five-bedroom house with a guy named Arthur who owned apartment buildings.

Who takes care of you when your mother's not around? they wanted to know. We'll call that person.

I just stared at them.

Don't you have a father? How about grandparents? An aunt or uncle? A trusted neighbor?

I kept shaking my head. No, no, no, no.

Eventually a name came to me—Mrs. Moore. She needed to come pick Mason up, anyway. He'd ridden to the hospital with me in the ambulance.

Mrs. Moore and the police arrived simultaneously, just after the doctor had finished setting my wrist in a cast. Mrs. Moore rushed to my side and kissed me on the forehead, looking harried to the point of exhaustion. I figured she'd had just about enough of teenage girls and their shenanigans. I insisted she stay while I told the police about the evening's events. I wanted her to know what a hero her son had been.

The story I told did not include a haunted purse. I simply said I'd been worried about my classmate Emma Randall, who seemed to be troubled in some way. I'd followed her to Tim Tuttle's studio a couple of times and noticed that she was always upset when she left. Last night, I'd broken in to get to the bottom of things. I'd stumbled upon the hidden room and had also found Crystal's purse. When Tuttle had come after me, I'd been saved by Mason, who had a crush on me and had been following me for weeks.

I knew that my story sounded as pat and implausible as a lowbrow mystery novel, but the police seemed to buy it. For now, anyway.

Mason was lauded by the police for overpowering Tim Tuttle. He was grounded by his mother for leaving the apartment without permission.

Once I got situated in my hospital room, I called Toni. She listened to my story in shocked silence until I got to the part where Mason charged in to save me. Then she burst into incredulous peals of laughter.

"I can't wait to see the newspaper headline: " 'Girl saved by four-and-a-half-foot superhero'! Oh, Mason. Who knew?"

Her laughter tapered off, and when she spoke again, her tone was somber. "Maybe now you'll admit that you really do need people."

"What do you mean?"

"Earlier, on the phone, you said you don't need anybody. But you sure needed Mason tonight."

I stared out the window, at the blank black sky, which was all I could see because I was on an upper floor—seven or eight, I couldn't remember which. I said, "I guess sometimes I feel like I don't need anybody because I've been taking care of myself for so long." My words came slow and heavy because of the pain medication. "Mr. Owens calls me the girl who raised herself."

Toni grunted. "Well, you're not raised yet. And even when you are, you'll still need people. Everybody does."

She was silent for a moment, and I could feel something weighty coming, something she didn't want to bring up but was going to anyway. "Look, Libby, about this foster care thing—I know you're worried, but everything's going to be okay. Your mom's not going to let them put you in a foster home. Once she finds out about all this, she'll probably move you to that Arthur guy's house. Child Protective Services might make her take some parenting classes, but that'll be it."

Of course she wanted to believe I'd have a happy ending. If I didn't, it was partly her fault.

After we hung up, I called Lauren and gave her a condensed version of the story I'd told the police. Mainly I wanted her to know I'd found Crystal's purse, but she already knew. In fact, she was on her way to the police station. The police had contacted her parents after going through the purse and confirming that it was Crystal's.

"I'll come see you just as soon as I can," she promised. "We have lots to talk about."

The pain meds helped me fall asleep before I could dwell on the fact that I'd almost died tonight.

THE HAUNTED PURSE

The news about Tim Tuttle, and my role in his capture, traveled swiftly. Toni called Louie and Charlie, who proceeded to tell everyone in their neighborhood and probably half the population of the school district. The story was in the newspaper the next day. But because Mason and I were minors, our names weren't mentioned. Only our ages and genders were revealed. The focus of the story was Tim Tuttle's involvement in a child pornography ring. The police provided only scant details, saying that an investigation was underway. Readers were encouraged to stay tuned for further developments.

My morning bustled with visitors. First Alyssa and her mom stopped by, and while they were there, Louie and Charlie showed up. Then, to my surprise, Mr. Abrams came. Everybody brought gifts—flowers and candy and a crossword puzzle book and a zucchini from Mr. Abrams' garden, which I regifted to my day nurse. I'd had no idea people got presents just for being in the hospital.

Around ten-thirty, I was lying in bed half-dozing when I heard feet approaching, too clumping and tentative to belong to a nurse. I opened my eyes to see Tommy Sturgis holding a bouquet of Get Well balloons.

"Well. You've been having an exciting summer," he said, tying the balloons to the metal rail at the foot of my bed. "Getting chased by guys in cars. Almost getting murdered by our school photographer."

"Yeah, I'm kind of hoping for a boring fall."

"Aw, come on. You deserve better than boring. How about interesting, but in a good way?" He eased himself into the chair next to my bed. "I hear there's going to be a back-to-school dance. Maybe you'll be Dance Queen again."

"No thanks," I said, grimacing to show I meant it.

He nodded. "I get it. You're not into that superficial shit. Neither am I. You did look really nice, though. And I'm glad I got to dance with you, even if it was only for half a song."

I felt myself flush with shame, with regret. "I wish it had been the whole song. I shouldn't have let Connor cut in."

He let out a short laugh that had some wistfulness in it. "No, you really shouldn't have."

"You know," I went on, feeling strangely emboldened, "out of all the guys at the dance, you and Connor were the only ones who asked me to slow-dance."

He leaned forward. "You know why? Everybody was scared to death of you! You looked so gorgeous, like a movie star. Fast dancing was one thing. But slow dancing? To actually be touching you, to have to move you around the dance floor without stepping on your toes? Whole different story. Nobody could work up the nerve to ask you."

"But you did," I said.

"Yeah, I did. Because even though you looked amazing, I knew that underneath it all you were still Libby. My same old Libby."

My same old Libby. I liked the sound of that.

He said to let him know when I was back home. Maybe we could go see a movie or something.

I was still smiling when my next visitor arrived.

"Are you up to having company?" asked Peter Wittmeyer.

Chapter 58

Peter Wittmeyer came bearing gifts—a vase of pink roses, a small stack of teen magazines, and a teddy bear wearing a denim dress.

I eyed the bear dubiously. How old did the man think I was? Then again, I'd never owned a teddy bear—or any stuffed animal—before. I took it from him and nestled it in the crook of my arm.

"How are you feeling?" He dropped into the chair by my bed, which was probably still warm from Tommy's butt.

"Not bad." I became aware that I was kneading my bed covers in a way that conveyed anxiousness. I forced myself to stop. "They have me on pain meds. I should be back to normal in six weeks." I raised my cast-encased arm. "That's how long I have to keep this thing on."

He nodded heavily. "Look, I know I'm probably the last person you want to see. Well, aside from the guy who tried to murder you." He managed a crooked smile.

I shuddered. "I'm just glad they caught him. I was afraid he'd get away somehow."

"He tried to. The police found him upstairs, stuck in one of those tight passages like a giant worm. Apparently, he was trying to get to a window, though what he would have done when he got there is anybody's guess. He was bound up good."

"My friend Mason did that," I said proudly.

"Your friend Mason should consider a career in law enforcement." Peter rubbed his eyes, and I noticed how tired he looked. "I was down at the site all night. Tuttle's place. The police have the property roped off, and they brought in the FBI. You want to hear the latest?"

"Yes. Please."

"The cellar has a dirt floor, which is common in turn-of-the century houses. The police found signs of digging and decided to investigate. Turns out there are human remains buried down there."

He said it matter-of-factly, but I felt the hurt slicing his insides like shards of glass.

"Crystal," I said softly.

He bowed his head. "Probably. And others."

"Others?"

"So far, they've found three bodies. And they're still digging."

"Oh God," I said. The cellar was where I'd have ended up, too, if Mason hadn't come along.

"How did you know?" Peter asked abruptly. "How did you know about Tuttle? Why did you come to my house? And don't tell me you were returning old photos."

I fingered the white lace trim at the hem of my bear's dress. It really was a cute dress. I would have worn it myself if it came in my size.

"All I'm asking for is an explanation," Peter Wittmeyer said. "I just want to know how a teenager managed to solve a case that stumped an entire police department two decades ago."

I let a thick silence build up between us while I pondered the situation. Mae and Lauren would probably ask the same question, and Lauren, in particular, wasn't likely to back down until she got some answers.

"Okay," I said, with a sigh of surrender. "I'll tell you. I came to your house because I was investigating Crystal's disappearance. Because that's what she wanted me to do."

And then I told him everything. About buying the purse, about the items that had gone missing and, more important, the items that had appeared. I told him how I'd eventually realized Crystal was haunting the purse. How the clues she'd provided had helped me identify her killer and find her missing purse.

He listened impassively, his breathing deep and rhythmic like someone under hypnosis. As I wrapped up my story, he broke off eye contact and stared at his hands. I could tell he was trying to think of a polite way to tell me I was crazy.

"I know how wild it sounds," I said, rushing to put the thought into words before he could. "But tell me this—how else could I have known Tuttle had anything to do with Crystal's disappearance? How could I have found her purse in a house filled with junk?"

He ran a hand through his thinning hair. "Look, Libby, I don't doubt some of what you just told me. I believe you found things in the purse. But I think they were there all along. I just thank God you were smart enough to use them as clues to solve Crystal's case."

"She didn't just leave me clues," I said.

"Pardon?"

"She also used the purse to show her feelings. See, every time the purse got close to someone she loved—you or Mae or Lauren—it got warm. Like she was happy to be near you. When I was in Tim Tuttle's studio, it got cold. So cold." I shivered at the memory. "Like it was stuffed full of ice cubes."

He still looked skeptical, so I jerked my head toward the nightstand. "It's in the bottom drawer. I honestly don't know if she's still in there. She might have moved on now that Tuttle's been arrested. But you should check."

He hesitated, then bent toward the nightstand. I knew he was indulging me because I was a sad, battered girl lying in a hospital bed. He opened the drawer and hooked one finger under the strap. He lifted the purse out and set it on his lap, his hands resting on top. I watched his eyes widen in bewilderment as the heat sank into his legs.

"What the—?" He unzipped the purse and peered inside.

"Go ahead and look," I said. "Take stuff out if you want. You won't find anything. The heat is coming from her."

He stared at me in astonishment. I watched his disbelief dissolve into wonder. And then Peter Wittmeyer cried.

He pressed the purse to his face, his shoulders heaving. "Crystal? Are you really there? Oh, honey, I'm so sorry. What happened to you—it was all my fault. I should never, never have..." The rest of his words were unintelligible, woven in among his sobs.

I'd never seen a grown man cry before. I'd never seen anyone so heartbroken. I turned my head away, trying to give him some privacy. And I vowed then and there never to tell this man that I'd suspected him of murdering his stepdaughter.

When his sobs finally subsided, I said, "But it wasn't your fault she died, Mr. Wittmeyer."

Peter lowered the purse to his lap. His face was haggard and tear-streaked.

"I didn't protect her. Mae didn't want her going outside when she was at the dealership. She didn't think the neighborhood was safe—and clearly she was right. But Crystal didn't want to be cooped up inside. She wanted to explore the world. So I'd let her go out for an hour or so at a time. It was our little secret. To this day, Mae doesn't know."

"You should tell her," I said.

"I can't." He drew in a deep, hitching breath, and I could see that he was on the verge of breaking down again. "She would despise me. I ignored her wishes and got her daughter killed. That's something I have to live with. I don't want Mae to have to live with it, too."

"She's stronger than you think," I said. "She knows how much you loved Crystal. She knows you never, ever would have done anything to put her in danger."

A noise from the purse startled us—the click of a camera.

"Hey," I said. "I think Crystal just left you something. Look inside."

What Crystal had left was a homemade Father's Day card. Peter let out a surprised laugh, his eyes brimming with fresh tears.

"I remember this card!" he said.

He slid his chair closer to my bed so we could look together. On the outside was the standard child's drawing of two stick figures, a small one and a taller one, their bony four-fingered hands entwined. Printed above them in crude capital letters was *HAPPY FATHERS DAY YOU ARE MY BEST DAD*. Inside, on the left, a snapshot was pasted crookedly, a close-up of Peter, with startlingly thick hair and a young man's face, and Crystal when she'd been about five. Both were smiling at the camera, their cheeks pressed together.

The right side of the card was covered with Crystal's wobbly printing. *DADDY I LOVE LOVE LOVE LOVE LOVE LOVE LOVE YOU. LOVE CRYSTAL*

"I don't think she could be much clearer," I said, smiling through my own tears. "She loves you. She never blamed you. Mae won't either."

Peter Wittmeyer bowed his head, too choked up to speak.

Chapter 59

I knew that at some point I'd be getting visitors I didn't want. Visitors who wouldn't be bringing flowers and candy.

Ashley Henderson, a case worker from Child Protective Services, showed up Wednesday afternoon wielding a clipboard. She was youngish—twenty-seven or twenty-eight—but already had a vertical crease between her brows that suggested she spent a lot of time fretting over her cases.

"Well, we tracked down your mother," she said cheerily, as though this was good news. "Has she been to see you?"

I glanced up from the magazine I was reading. "No."

The furrow between her brows deepened. "Okay, Liberty, here's the thing. Your mother says she's not in a position to take care of you. Did you know she's expecting a baby?"

"Yeah."

"So we're going to have to place you in foster care."

"Surprise," I muttered.

"You can't be living on your own anymore. It shouldn't have gone on as long as it did."

I shrugged in a *whatever* sort of way and turned a page in my magazine.

"We've found a family who can take you," said Ms. Henderson. "They live in Fairmont."

That got my attention. I slapped my magazine shut and sat up very straight. "Fairmont! That's, like, twenty miles away!"

She scrunched an eye. "More like thirty. It's a nice little town, safe and quiet. You'll be staying with Noel and Marlene Pruitt. They have two children of their own and two fosters. They're coming to pick you up tomorrow morning."

"Isn't there anybody closer? Like in my school district?"

"Not at the present time." She flipped through some pages on her clipboard. "We do have a young lady currently fostering in the Halfway area. She'll be leaving the system in early January, when she turns eighteen. There might be a spot for you then."

I managed to suppress a gasp of dismay. "You think I'll still be in foster care in January?"

Her eyes met mine. Something heavy hung in the air between us. I felt my anxiety level rise.

Ashley said, "Your mother has decided to terminate her parental rights. She doesn't feel she can care for you properly now or at any time in the future. I'm sorry, Liberty."

I was so stunned, I could only stare at her. Then I began to laugh. *Oh, Misty Dawson, you got me good this time!* If our relationship had been a chess game, she'd have just checkmated me. If it had been a sword fight, she'd have stabbed me through the heart. This was brilliant, I thought. Why inconvenience herself with repeated small visits to berate and reject me when she could do it forever with this one sweeping gesture?

"Of course, we'll start looking immediately for a family to adopt you."

My mirth evaporated. I gathered my denim-clad bear into my arms and pressed my cheek against the soft fur at the back of its head. Who did Ashley Henderson think she was kidding? Babies got adopted. Nobody wanted an older kid. I'd be in foster care till I turned eighteen, like the Halfway girl she'd just mentioned. And if things didn't work out with the Pruitts, I might even end up in a group home.

"Mr. and Mrs. Pruitt will be here tomorrow morning at nine," said Ashley Henderson. "Be dressed and ready to go."

Chapter 60

The whole Wittmeyer clan trooped in around seven that evening—Peter, Mae, Lauren, and Lauren's husband, Mike. Mike was a study in brown. Chestnut hair, chocolate eyes, skin the color of river sand. He was even wearing khaki pants with a beige shirt and coffee-colored loafers. His crinkly eyes suggested he had a loose, generous smile, though he wasn't smiling tonight. No one was.

Mae and Lauren approached from opposite sides of my bed and hugged me—first Mae, then Lauren. They wore matching red noses. Mike dragged a chair from the other side of the room so both ladies could sit down. Then he and Peter left the room to find two more chairs.

"Oh, Libby, she's really gone," Mae moaned, dabbing at her eyes with a tissue. "I knew she had to be dead, but this is hitting me harder than I expected."

"I'm so sorry," I said in genuine dismay. "I never meant to hurt you."

"No, no. Don't be sorry." She reached out to clasp my hand. "Knowing what happened to her, finally—it means the world to us. You've brought my family closure, and that's all we ever wanted."

"Dad told us everything," Lauren said somberly. "We had no idea he felt responsible for what happened to Crystal."

I looked at Mae. "He was afraid you'd blame him if you knew the truth."

"Of course I don't blame him," Mae said stoutly. "Peter couldn't have loved Crystal more if she was his own flesh and blood. He just wanted her to be happy. Anyway, I always figured she was running around downtown. Crystal was an outdoor girl. No way was she going to stay cooped up in that building, regardless of what I wanted."

"So Cryssy's been haunting that old denim purse," Lauren said. She gave a small smile. "Saying that out loud, it sounds so crazy. And it was crazy to hear Dad say it. He's never believed in things like ghosts."

"Would you like to see for yourself?" I jerked a thumb toward the nightstand. "Bottom drawer."

Lauren pulled out the purse and set it on her lap. I watched her mouth spread into a wide grin. "This is incredible! It feels like there's a heater in there! Mom, here, you have to feel this."

Mae took the purse from Lauren and let out an incredulous sob as she felt its warmth. She hugged it to her chest. Tears dripped from her eyes and sank into the deep blue fabric where Crystal lived.

Peter and Mike came back carrying chairs and sat next to their wives.

"The funeral's in three days," Peter told me. "We'd love to have you there."

"I'd love to be there," I said. "But I don't think I can make it."

I told them I was moving to Fairmont to live with a foster family. I explained my situation in matter-of-fact terms, without weaving in any emotion. The Wittmeyers had enough troubles of their own. They didn't need me getting all blubbery over mine.

"Libby, I'm so sorry. We had no idea," Lauren said, giving my hand a sympathetic squeeze.

"It'll be fine," I said. "The lady from Child Protective Services says the Pruitts are a really nice family."

"I'll call CPS," Peter said. "I know the director. I'll tell him you're a close family friend and we need you to be at our daughter's funeral. I'm sure your foster parents won't have a problem with that."

Close family friend. Though I wasn't holding the purse, a flush of warmth spread through me.

"I can pick you up in Fairmont and drive you back afterward," Mike offered. "Peter, make sure you get the Pruitts' address."

And with that, our plans were laid.

Chapter 61

Peter gave us the latest on the police investigation. Quite a lot had transpired since early afternoon.

Five bodies had been unearthed in Tim Tuttle's cellar. One had been positively identified as Crystal.

The police had stitched together a pretty complete story, based on Tuttle's confession, the accounts Mason and I had given, items they'd found in Crystal's brown purse, the police file from twenty years ago, and interviews with people who knew Tuttle, including a few of his victims.

Tim Tuttle had been involved in a child pornography ring for nearly twenty-five years. Struggling to launch his photography business, he'd been lured into this seedier activity by his own innate perversion as well as the chance to make some extra money.

There were people in the world—sick, sick people—who got their kicks looking at sexualized pictures of children. And they were willing to pay good money to get those pictures.

Once Tuttle became a school photographer, he had access to thousands of potential victims. He targeted downtrodden kids, mostly girls. Kids whose parents were absent emotionally if not physically. Kids whose self-esteem was so low that abuse and degradation were all they knew, all they expected.

When Tuttle's older victims were asked by the police why they'd never gone to the authorities, especially once they'd grown up, they told one of two stories. Either they'd put their sordid past behind them and didn't want anyone dredging it up, or they'd made a career of seamy activity—prostitution, adult videos, modeling for porn magazines—and considered Tim Tuttle no worse than they were. Plus, they didn't think they'd be taken seriously if they did speak up. Who would believe that a highly respected, award-winning photographer like Tim Tuttle could be a child pornographer?

Some victims convinced themselves that Tuttle's work was art, not pornography. Unlike most child pornographers, Tuttle was a professional photographer. He knew how to make each picture a masterpiece of light, composition, color, and balance. He posed his victims against the same backdrops he used for his legitimate photo shoots. Sometimes he took them into the first-floor bedroom for shots on the crushed-velvet bedspread. His underworld colleagues called him the Classy Pornographer, and his work sold at a premium.

Emma Randall was one of Tuttle's most recent victims. The police had assured Peter that she would get counseling to help her overcome the trauma of her ordeal. She was also being moved to a different foster home, since the victimization by Tuttle had happened under the Fetzers' watch. CPS had already blacklisted the Fetzers. They would never be foster parents again.

Another victim, fourteen-year-old Jessica Wayfield, had been a friend of Crystal's. The police had learned about her from Crystal's journal. Crystal had made detailed entries about the "Tuttle case" she was investigating, including notes from conversations with Jessica. Tragically, Jessica, like Crystal, had ended up dead at the hands of Tim Tuttle.

Jessica was the pretty brunette whose photo had turned up in my purse, the one neither Lauren nor Mae could identify.

THE HAUNTED PURSE

It was probably inevitable that Jessica's path would cross Tim Tuttle's. She was a Downtowner, an inner-city kid from a large, broken family. Like me, she had a mother who saw her only as an inconvenience. To escape her miserable home life, Jessica spent most of her free time roaming the downtown streets. When Tuttle approached her about a modeling career, she wasn't hard to persuade. She quickly became his star pornography subject.

At some point, Crystal met Jessica, and the two became friends. Jessica eventually told Crystal she'd been modeling nude for Tim Tuttle. Crystal was horrified. In an effort to steer her new friend toward a more wholesome life, she got the girl involved with a youth group at a downtown church.

Jessica quickly latched onto religion as the governing influence in her life, and she decided to cut her ties to Tim Tuttle. When she told him she was quitting, he threatened to send nude photos of her to all the important institutions in her life—church, school, and family. Of course, he was bluffing, but Jessica didn't know that. Even so, she refused to back down. Having the world learn about her shameful activities was a price she was willing to pay, her due penance for sinning.

Tuttle, fearing that the girl's story would make its way to the police, lured her to the cellar of his studio. That was where he kept his sledgehammer. All it took to solve his problem was a blow to the girl's head. Jessica Wayfield was Tim Tuttle's first murder victim.

Jessica's mother did not report her missing. With six other kids at home, she barely noticed the absence of her fourth-born child. When Crystal went to Jessica's apartment asking about her, the mother said she'd probably run away to live with her dad. The dad moved around a lot, and since he didn't keep in touch with Jessica's mother, there was no way to know whether Jessica had ever arrived.

Crystal didn't believe that Jessica had run away, not when she was in the process of turning her life around. She suspected that Tim Tuttle had murdered the girl. Determined to expose his criminal activities, she made plans to break into his studio and search for evidence that would incriminate him.

Those were the last notes she'd made in her reporter's journal.

At this point in the story, Peter's voice faltered. He was very pale. Mae laid a hand on his arm. Peter cleared his throat, took a deep breath, and continued.

The journal wasn't the only piece of evidence in Crystal's purse. Her camera was there, too. Even after all those years the police were able to develop the film. The last picture on the roll showed Tim Tuttle photographing a nude preteen girl. The click of the camera had given Crystal away.

Tuttle had chased her through the house. When he blocked her path to the front door, she ran upstairs and tried to hide amidst the piles of junk. She must have known Tuttle would find her. But before he did, she stashed the purse in the pink bathrobe in a desperate attempt to protect her evidence.

I shuddered as I thought back on Tim Tuttle's proposition to me. "Have you ever considered going into modeling?" That was how it had started for so many others, including poor, doomed Jessica. If I hadn't already been making a little money, I might have taken him up on it.

THE HAUNTED PURSE

I supposed that going into foster care wasn't as bad as being a child pornography victim. It wasn't as bad as getting murdered. Whatever my future held, I would get through it.

Chapter 62

"They're late," said Ellie, the day nurse, telling me what I already knew. "Just sit tight, hon. I'm sure they're on their way."

I was sitting in the chair by my bed, my purse next to me. It was nearly nine-thirty. The Pruitts were supposed to have arrived at nine.

Were they backing out? The notion both thrilled and dismayed me.

Ellie brought a newspaper to help me pass the time. The front page offered the latest details of the Tuttle case.

All five bodies had been identified. Tuttle had confessed that, except for Crystal, all were child pornography victims who he sensed were about to divulge his secret. Once he'd started confessing, he couldn't stop. He gave the police the names of a dozen other child pornographers and sex traffickers. The case was going to have huge implications in terms of getting rid of scum who preyed on children.

And it was all because of Crystal.

I'd dreamed about her in the night. It had been a short, simple dream. There was no talk, no background scenery, just the two of us hugging. But, oh, what a hug! Our souls blazed with emotion—her gratitude, my grief, our mutual triumph. I could feel her love washing over me, warm and bright as heaven. I awoke to the unmistakable scent of her perfume, and this time it lingered in the air for several minutes.

And when I looked in my purse, I saw that the little bottle of perfume was back.

At ten-fifteen, Ellie popped into my room with a wheelchair. "They're here. Have a seat, hon; I'll wheel you down to reception."

"I can walk," I said.

"Sorry, hospital policy."

So I climbed into the wheelchair, my purse on my lap, the denim-clad teddy peeking apprehensively out of the top.

I wasn't feeling so brave today. A line of hypothetical foster parents kept dancing across my imagination. The ultra-strict religious fanatics. The illiterate, gap-toothed hillbillies. The secretly smirking child molesters. I was trying to hope for the best, but my optimism kept flickering, like a string of failing Christmas lights.

I wondered if the Pruitts would let me stop at my apartment to pack up my possessions. Or would they insist I leave every trace of my old life behind and start over?

The ground-floor reception area was filled with people milling around or sitting in the chairs that lined the walls of the huge space. I tried to pick out the Pruitts. Were they the overweight fortyish couple standing at the reception desk? The gray-haired twosome slouched wearily in side-by-side chairs? The well-dressed pair arguing near the door?

"Libby!" I turned around and saw Lauren hurrying toward me. Coming to say goodbye. Mike loped along behind her, smiling.

I struggled up out of the wheelchair. "Hey," I said, hugging her. "I'm just about to leave with my foster parents."

"So I hear," said Lauren.

"Take care, Libby," said Ellie, pushing the wheelchair back toward the elevator.

"Wait," I called to her. "Where are the Pruitts?"

"The Pruitts? Your foster parents are these folks right here. The Appelbaums. Mike and Lauren Appelbaum."

"What?" The word was little more than a puff of breath. I looked from Lauren to Mike and back again.

I wouldn't have expected Lauren to have any tears left, but she was crying again. "I know," she said, emotion rippling the words. "I know this is unexpected—it is for us, too—but it just feels right. We want you to come live with us, Libby. Not just as our foster child, but as our daughter. We want to adopt you."

"Adopt me?" The words grazed my brain but wouldn't sink in. "Adopt me? You want to adopt me?"

"We've been trying to have a baby for years," Mike put in. "It just hasn't happened. We think—we think you're meant to be our child. We think Crystal brought us together."

"Oh my God!" I said, as the reality of what he was saying sank in. I staggered a little. Mike caught me and held me against him, his arms warm and strong.

"Is this okay with you?" Lauren asked anxiously.

"Oh, yes. It's okay." I was crying so hard, I wasn't sure my words were intelligible. But Lauren and Mike got my drift.

We drove to my apartment in Lauren's compact car, orange-red like fire, to fetch my things. We were strangely quiet, the three of us. I supposed we were dazed by what was happening, by all the events of the past few days. By our suddenly altered futures. I took advantage of the silence to let my thoughts chug along inside my head. There was something I thought of saying, something that maybe needed to be brought to the forefront and discussed. Three times I opened my mouth to say it. Three times I backed down.

THE HAUNTED PURSE

The thing I wanted to say was, *I'm not her.*

Of course, they knew that, Lauren knew it, at least on some surface level. But deeper down, I wasn't so sure. I was the same age Crystal had been when she'd died. I was like Crystal in many ways, according to Mae. And I had a mystical bond with Crystal that no one else shared—we were like twins with our own secret language. I could see how Lauren might imagine that by adopting me she could get her sister back.

In the end, I decided it didn't matter. If Lauren—and Mae and Peter, for that matter—wanted to pretend I was Crystal, I would be Crystal. Because the truth was, I needed this family as much as they needed me.

Lauren and Mike described their house as modest, but to me it was a palace. The biggest bedroom, the master, was occupied by Lauren and Mike. The smallest had been converted into a combination office and sewing room. That left the in-between room for me.

The room had been decorated like a nursery in anticipation of the baby Lauren and Mike had never managed to produce. I loved the soothing pastels—the pale yellow walls, the peach gingham curtains, the mint-green pads that softened the back and seat of the white wooden rocking chair. Framed prints of big-eyed baby jungle animals dotted the walls—lion, monkey, elephant, giraffe.

The only baby-type thing missing was a crib. In its place was a queen-sized bed. This was where Mike's parents, who lived in Arizona, had slept when they came to visit. But not anymore. From now on, overnight guests would sleep in the family room. Mike and Lauren had already ordered a sofa bed.

"This is your room and nobody else's," Lauren told me firmly. "Don't worry—we'll redecorate. We can paint the walls any color you like. We'll go shopping tomorrow for curtains and wall art."

I walked around, letting the loveliness of the room engulf me like a quilt. Even the air seemed beautiful. Sparkly somehow. "You know what?" I said. "It's perfect the way it is."

"Really? Well, at least let me get the rocking chair out of here."

"No, no," I said. "I love that too."

The first night in my new home, I sat in that rocking chair and rocked my wounded soul. And I cried. I cried long and hard.

I cried in anguish for the mother who'd never wanted me, and in gratitude for the one who did. I cried in grief for Crystal, who'd never had the chance to grow up. I cried for the family who still mourned her. I cried in sympathy for Toni and Mason, who suffered every day because of their torn family. I cried in anger for the people who hadn't been able to see past my shabby clothing and dilapidated neighborhood to the person I really was.

I cried enough tears for the whole world.

Then I slept.

Chapter 63

My first weekend with Lauren and Mike, we had a cookout and pool party at Mae and Peter's place. Everybody was telling stories, talking about crazy, quirky things that had happened to them, trying to outdo each other. When it was my turn, I told them I'd been with Toni the evening she'd been caught at the Wittmeyers' garage window. I told how I'd hidden under their deck for hours and watched Peter clean the pool. I even confessed to peeing in the yard. Peter laughed so hard, iced tea came out his nose. I knew my family would tease me about that for years.

In the early evening, I went for a walk while the grown-ups drank wine on the deck. I liked knowing I could leave and return anytime I wanted. Mae and Peter's house was now one of the places where I belonged.

I walked down some streets I'd never visited before, admiring all the big, elegant houses. I'd always had contempt for the residents of the Hilltop, thinking all rich people were jerks. But Peter and Mae were good people, and they surely weren't the only ones. I supposed the ratio of good people to bad was the same among the upper class as anywhere else.

Faint voices wafted from the large red-brick house to my right. One, a female voice, stirred an unpleasant visceral response in me before I could work out why it sounded so familiar. I turned to see a man in the yard, hosing down shrubbery. A woman was leaning over the porch banister, talking to him.

The woman was my mother.

I scuttled to the edge of the property and peered around a tall shrub. That slender, dark-haired man must be Arthur. He looked like a nice, ordinary guy, not the evil slum lord I'd envisioned. And he didn't strike me as someone who would hate kids. He glanced up at my mother. She said something in a teasing tone, and he laughed.

A seed of hope sprouted within me. Like so many other guys, Arthur was weak enough to have had his head turned by my mother's beauty. But that didn't make him a bad person. I wanted to believe that aside from that one flaw, he was a decent man, one who would be a good father to my soon-to-be little brother or sister. I wanted to believe he would neutralize my mother's negative influence.

My gaze strayed to my mother. She'd let her hair go back to its natural shade, the same as mine. It was shorter, too—shoulder-length—and nicely styled. And her clothes were different—less whorish, more matronly. Her pregnancy was starting to show, her belly rounding slightly as if a new planet was forming inside her. Obviously, Arthur hadn't kicked her out.

How about that, I thought. My mother had built a respectable new life for herself. She'd created a new persona—matron in a high-class neighborhood. She probably had elegant neighbor ladies over for tea. Maybe she'd joined the local garden club.

The funny thing was, I was doing better, too, and in a similar way. Like my mother, I'd escaped the inner city. I had pretty clothes and a nice house and people who cared about me. Misty Dawson and I, we were two high-speed trains running on parallel tracks a hundred miles apart, both heading into futures far brighter than our shared past.

The thing about parallel tracks was that they would never intersect.

They would never intersect, and that was fine with me.

Chapter 64

Toni was crying. "I have something to tell you."

"Oh God. What now?" I took the phone into my bedroom and shut the door.

"I need to tell you in person." She sniffled. "I'm coming over."

Now that I lived in Rosedale, I wasn't far from Mr. Moore's house. Toni was back to living with her mom, but she and Mason spent every other weekend with their dad and Jan.

When Toni arrived, I got us situated in the family room. I loved this room, with its accents in sherbet shades so delicious they made your mouth water—lemon and lime and orange. Lauren brought us sodas and a bowl of tortilla chips with guacamole dip and then faded away to give us privacy.

"We're moving!" Toni howled, covering her face with her hands. "Really far away. Like, three hundred miles. My mom got a job in the town where my grandparents live. We're going to live with them while Mom saves up enough money to buy us a house."

"Oh, Toni!" I said, tears springing to my own eyes. "I'm going to miss you so much!"

"I'll miss you, too. But, hey, we're juniors. Before you know it, we'll be done with high school. Maybe we can go to the same college. Then we'll graduate and get jobs. And husbands. You can marry Tommy Sturgis—"

"Toni!" I laugh-sobbed in exasperation. "We've only been going out for a few weeks."

THE HAUNTED PURSE

Things were going really well with my first boyfriend. Unlike Connor, Tommy was a true gentleman. He spent a lot of time at my house, and we often played board games with my parents. Lauren and Mike said he was one of the good guys.

"I know, I know," Toni said. "Just let me have my fantasy. You'll marry Tommy, and I'll marry—I don't know. Somebody."

"Jared Berzansky?" I suggested.

She gasped dramatically. "Jared? Why would you say that?"

"Because of all the flirting you guys used to do on the school bus."

She started to protest but quickly gave up. "Okay, maybe I do like him, just a little. But that's never gonna go anywhere, since I'm moving. Anyway, I'll find somebody to marry. And you and me, we'll tell our husbands we have to live next door to each other. Our kids will be best friends, just like us."

"That sounds great," I whispered.

In my heart, I knew this was the end. Toni and I had never really been on the same wavelength. Proximity had drawn us together; distance would drive us apart. We'd stay in touch on social media, at least for a while, but our lives would no longer be entwined.

Toni's gaze kept drifting to my cheek. "I guess that scar's always going to be there, huh? God, your face used to be so perfect. Now it's not. Seriously, you could have been a model."

"It's okay," I said. "I never wanted to be a model."

The truth was, I kind of liked my scar. I liked how it marred my beauty, made me less appealing to the wrong kinds of people. Gave me a look that was different from my birth mother's. Plus, it was a reminder of the things I'd endured, the crises I'd survived. That scar, staring at me from the mirror each day, would never let me forget the fact of my own resilience.

I was, after all, the girl who raised herself.

"Life," Toni said philosophically. "You just never know how it's going to turn out,"

"You never do," I agreed.

Chapter 65

It might seem like getting adopted by Lauren and Mike was my happily ever after, but it wasn't. The change in my circumstances was simply a new chapter in my life, one with its own ups and downs.

The first few weeks were magical, a short season of domestic bliss worthy of some sappy TV movie. Then the fairy dust settled and Lauren and I started butting heads. The problem was, she wanted me home most of the time, whereas I was used to coming and going as I pleased, like a feral cat. I kept getting grounded for slipping out of the house at odd hours or violating my curfew. She wanted me in by dark every day, even on weekends, which I found totally unreasonable. Especially considering that dark was coming earlier and earlier as the days got shorter.

Mike recognized the trouble we were in and set us up with a highly rated family counselor, Dr. Sheila Wright.

Our first session didn't feel like counseling. Instead, it seemed like a friendly visit with a distant relative. We even had tea. We told Sheila a mostly accurate version of how Lauren and I had met, being careful to leave out the ghost part. Our visit consisted largely of mundane chit-chat, but every so often Sheila would throw out a question about how our life as a family was unfolding and then sit back to watch the three of us interact.

The second session was very different. Sheila zeroed in on Lauren like a guided missile.

"Lauren, you are smothering this girl," she said, though she said it without pronouncing her R's. Sheila had a heavy Brooklyn accent and big round glasses and long, dark, unstyled hair.

Lauren's head flew up. "Wh-what?"

"You have her on such a short leash, she can barely move."

"What are you saying? Are you accusing me of being a helicopter parent?" Lauren's head pivoted in short, jerking movements, like a bird's. She did this when she was stunned or agitated, and in this case she was both. She looked at me, then at Mike. "Is that what you guys think? That I'm overprotective?"

I stared resolutely at my lap. No way was I going to answer that. Mike cleared his throat and said bravely, "Maybe a little."

Lauren made an "uhhh!" noise of outrage. "How can you think that? I'm just trying to keep Libby safe. Nobody knows better than I do that bad things can happen to teenagers."

"Lauren. Dearest," Sheila said. "Bad things can happen to anybody."

"Hey. My sister was *murdered*," Lauren shouted, her eyes filling with tears. "And the same thing almost happened to Libby."

"That," Sheila said, poking a forefinger into the air, "was a very unusual set of circumstances. One begat the other. But the fact is, very few teenagers get murdered. Think about it. Of all the teenagers you've ever known—your students, your relatives, family friends—how many have gotten murdered?"

Lauren opened her mouth to argue further, but Sheila pressed on. "It's perfectly natural for you to be haunted by what happened to your sister. That was a terrible, terrible thing. But you are projecting your grief and anxiety onto Libby, and that has got to stop. Trust her to take care of herself. She's been doing it for years."

Lauren cried so much during that session, I wondered if Sheila was going to charge us extra for all the tissues. In the end, Lauren conceded that, okay, maybe her maternal grip on me was a little tight. My curfew got adjusted to nine o'clock on school nights and eleven on weekends.

I was mentally celebrating this victory when Sheila turned her machine-gun eyes on me and said I would have to make some sacrifices, too. For starters, I had to stop slipping out of the house like an escaping prisoner. I needed to announce where I was going, who I would be with, and when I would be back. And in some cases, I would have to ask permission to go in the first place. Sheila told Mike and Lauren to buy me a cell phone so we could keep in touch when I was out.

The following week's session was all about me. Sheila said we were going to do a fun exercise. She would ask rapid-fire questions, and I had to respond with the first thing that popped into my mind. Half a dozen questions in, she asked, "What's your biggest fear?" And I replied, "That Lauren and Mike will give me back."

As soon as the words were out, my eyes opened wide in astonishment. Then I burst into tears.

That was news to me! Amazingly, I'd been oblivious to my own worry. But there it was. In the deepest corner of my heart, I feared that Mike and Lauren would eventually have their own baby, and they would love it in a way they could never love me. Or I would do something so terrible, they would decide

I was too much trouble. Or they would simply get tired of being parents and would take the necessary steps to undo the adoption.

As I sobbed into my hands, Mike and Lauren flanked me on the couch, stroking my arms, patting my back, murmuring assurances. I was their daughter, now and forevermore. Our arrangement went far beyond legalities. They'd already grown to love me, and they would never give me up. They'd decided they didn't want any more children. We'd been through so much, the three of us. They wanted to devote all their time and attention to me.

Sheila said it might take me a while to feel truly secure. I was scarred by my mother's rejection of me just like Lauren was scarred by her sister's murder. She urged me to keep reminding myself that Misty Dawson was an anomaly among the human race. The vast majority of parents, both natural and adoptive, did not cast their children off like unwanted goods.

Chapter 66

One snowbound day in mid-January, I got to thinking about the purse and its impact on my life. Both good and bad things had happened to me because of it—but how did they stack up against each other? I wanted to know. So I got a piece of notebook paper and wrote across the top, "Bad things that happened because of the purse."

Then I made a list.

— *I got kicked off Ms. Eckhart's favorites list and didn't get the social studies award.*

— *I made my mother mad when I lost her prescription.*

— *Toni got arrested and had to go live with her dad.*

— *I was trapped under the Wittmeyers' deck and had to pee in their yard.*

— *I got stalked by that carload of boys.*

— *Child Protective Services found out about me.*

— *I hurt myself falling down Tim Tuttle's stairs.*

— *I almost got murdered.*

— *I have a forever-sadness inside me because of what happened to Crystal.*

— My mother ripped my heart out of my chest.

None of those things would have happened if the purse hadn't come into my life—well, except for maybe the last one. Knowing my mother, I had a feeling she would have ripped my heart out one way or the other.

Then again...

The notion of parallel universes popped into my head. One day in eighth-grade science class, we'd had a lively debate about them. I still wasn't sure I believed there were multiverses where countless alternate realities played out for each and every person. But if they did exist, that meant there were places where my life story was unfolding very differently...

I'm standing in the doorway of my mother's hospital room, nervously clutching the strap of my one and only purse, an old black safety-pinned thing that I should have replaced years ago. My mother lies in bed, gazing down at a big pale-blue burrito in her arms.

She called last night as I was heading off to bed. "Hey, Libby, you got yourself a new baby brother. I'd love for you to come see us in the hospital."

Against my better judgment, I've come.

She looks up and spots me. Her face seems to be lit from within, like a paper lantern. "Libby! Come meet your new brother."

I trudge over and slip into a chair next to the bed.

"This is Liam," she tells me, tilting the burrito so I can see the round little head nestled in the crook of her arm. "Liam Arthur. Here, you want to hold him?"

"No, that's okay."

THE HAUNTED PURSE

"Don't be scared. You won't drop him."

Reluctantly, I half-stand long enough to take the blanketed bundle from her and then sink back into the reassuring sturdiness of the chair. Liam weighs practically nothing. He's making rhythmic grunting noises in his sleep.

"He's so tiny," I marvel. "I didn't know he'd be this small."

"Seven pounds, five ounces," my mother declares. "You were even tinier—six pounds, ten ounces."

"Wow. You remember that?"

"I remember everything about your birth." Her voice quavers. I look at her sharply.

"Oh, Libby," she says. "I've been such a terrible mother. I've done the worst possible thing. I've treated you the same way my mother treated me."

Her eyes glisten. She wipes them with the palms of her hands. "Going through this pregnancy, giving birth again, it's been a wake-up call. It's made me realize how horrible I've been to you."

Something hopeful rises within me, but I quash it. "Really," I say flatly.

"I'm thirty-one years old. It's time I grew up. Time I stopped being so damned self-centered. Better late than never, right?" She tries to smile. Instead, her mouth twists into a grimace of woe.

I study her face. It looks changed somehow, as if the bones have shifted beneath her skin, molding her into someone different. Someone noble and dignified and maybe even capable of love. I think she loves her infant son. But what about me?

She stares back at me. There's a softness in her gaze I've never seen before.

"I know," she says, squeezing her eyes shut for a moment. "I know that 'sorry' can't begin to make up for the way I've treated you. But I'll say it anyway. I'm sorry. Sorry for not being the mother you needed, the mother you deserved. I just hope—" She chokes on that last word. "—I hope I didn't screw you up too bad."

I wrench my eyes away and murmur, "It's okay. I'm turning out okay."

I don't tell her about my patchwork parent. That's what I call the conglomeration of adults who've helped me in my growing-up journey—Mrs. Garcia, Mrs. Moore, Mr. Owens, Mr. Abrams, Selena, certain teachers at school, and random strangers who've parented me in vague and minor ways.

I drank their kindness like mother's milk, and it nurtured me. It kept me grounded.

"Things will be different from now on," my mother says fiercely. "You're coming to live with Arthur and me."

"What? I thought Arthur hated kids."

She shakes her head. "That was all in my imagination. Arthur's a wonderful man, Libby. He's excited about becoming your dad. You know why he isn't here right now? He's back home, getting your new bedroom ready for you. You wanted the one with the bathroom, right?"

I nod dazedly.

"Arthur's repainting the walls and replacing the carpeting. He's doing the work himself, because he wants to make sure everything is perfect for our girl. Oh, and your new furniture should arrive tomorrow." She shoots me a brave smile. "It's a start, baby. A new beginning for us. If you can find it in your heart to forgive me."

Liam squirms in my arms and opens his eyes, and I'm stunned to see that they're her eyes; they're mine. The three of us, we belong to something ready-made. We're an exclusive unit tied together by the silken strands of our DNA.

Suddenly I'm sobbing.

"Oh, Mom, of course I forgive you! I don't blame you for not knowing how to be a parent. You were just a kid when you had me. But you're figuring it out now, and that's the important thing."

She's crying, too—loudly, forcefully, her whole body heaving, her face a wet, blotchy, contorted mess. "Oh, my sweet girl! You don't know what that means to me. I love you so much! I'm going to make things up to you, I swear. We'll go shopping every weekend. We'll have chick-flick nights with popcorn and soda. We'll get manicures and bake cookies together and—"

"Oh!" she says, interrupting herself with a little giggle. "I almost forgot. Arthur and I are getting married next month. Will you be my maid of honor?"

As the scene dissolved in my head, I was dismayed to find my real self crying. Savagely, I rubbed my eyes with my shirt, trying to wipe away every trace of misplaced sentiment.

If that hospital visit happened anywhere, it happened in a parallel universe far, far, *far* away.

In a nearer universe, this was probably how it went down.

The purse never comes into my life. Nobody ever finds out I live alone. My mother lets me stay in the apartment while I finish high school, and I continually pick up tutoring gigs to fund my shopping excursions. I'm valedictorian of my high school graduating class. I get that free ride to college the guidance counselor tantalized me with. I graduate from college with honors, and maybe I even go on to earn a graduate degree. I get an amazing job and make more money than I can spend. Maybe I get married and maybe I don't, but my life is rich and meaningful. It's filled with people I love, people who love me back. Misty Dawson isn't one of them. We never see each other again.

Of course, in my universe, neither of those scenarios played out. What happened was, my mother got charged with child abandonment and had to pay a thousand-dollar fine. Humiliated and furious, she pinned the blame on me and decided she was justified in washing her hands of me.

And, yes, she had a baby boy, but she never called to tell me. Mae heard about it from an acquaintance on Arthur's street.

When I was done exploring universes, I went back to my list, focusing now on the good things that had come about because of the purse.

— *I got my Dance Queen gift card back.*
— *Connor Tipton didn't do anything worse than kiss me.*
— *Crystal's family finally got closure.*
— *Tim Tuttle and those other criminals got sent to jail.*
— *A girl named Libby Appelbaum was loved into existence.*

The second list was shorter, but it was the one that counted.

Chapter 67

By springtime, I had three new purses that I swapped out regularly, depending on my outfit. The denim purse sat on the top shelf of my closet, soulless as a deflated balloon. My eyes were drawn to it every time I opened my closet door. I took it down from time to time to check for a message from Crystal, but nothing ever materialized.

The wondering was driving me crazy. I wanted to believe she'd moved on, but at the same time I longed to hear from her. Would the torment ever end?

One day I woke up knowing it was time. Dad drove me to the thrift store and pulled alongside the curb.

"I'll be just a minute," I said.

Selena was at the front of the store, arranging a bunch of wallets on a table.

"Libby, hey! I haven't seen you for ages."

"Hi, Selena," I said. "I have a donation."

She took the purse from me and held it up. "Nice! This'll go quick. You sure you want to get rid of it?"

"I'm sure." I reached out and fingered the soft denim one last time. Then I turned and walked out the door.

The ghost was gone, but there was plenty of life left in that old purse.

A Note From the Author

Did you enjoy *The Haunted Purse*? If so, I hope you'll consider leaving a review on Amazon, Goodreads, Bookbub, or another book site of your choice.

Reviews help authors develop credibility and gain a readership. They guide readers to books they might be interested in. They enable you, the reviewer, to share your opinions with the world. Leaving a review is a win-win-win situation!

A review doesn't have to be long, though it certainly can be. It's sufficient to simply state a few things you liked about the book. Did the characters resonate with you? Did the plot keep you turning pages? Would you recommend the book to others? These are some of the things you might comment on.

Thank you for reading my book.

Kimberly Baer

About the Author

Kimberly Baer is an author and professional editor who wrote her first story at age six. It was about a baby chick that hatched out of a little girl's Easter egg after somehow surviving the hard-boiling process. Nowadays she writes in a variety of genres, including young adult, middle-grade, and adult romantic suspense. She lives in Virginia, where she likes to go power-walking on days when it's not too hot, too cold, too rainy, too snowy, or too windy.

Visit her at **www.kimberlybaer.com.**

Follow Kim on social media:

Instagram: @kimberlybaer_author
BookBub: @authorkimberlybaer
Goodreads: @Kimberly Baer
BlueSky: @KimberlyBaer_Author
X [formerly Twitter]: @kimberlybaer14
Facebook: @AuthorKimberlyBaer